ABOUT THE AUTHOR

Because **Charlie Cochrane** (
jobs of choice—like manag
mystery novels include the
series, and the contempor
published, she has titles with Carina, Riptide, Endeavour and Bold Strokes, among others.

A member of the Romantic Novelists' Association, Mystery People and International Thriller Writers Inc, Charlie regularly appears at literary festivals and at reader and author conferences with The Deadly Dames.

This edition published in 2018 by Williams & Whiting

ISBN 9781912582310

Williams & Whiting (Publishers)

15 Chestnut Grove, Hurstpierpoint,

West Sussex, BN6 9SS

AN ACT OF DETECTION

CHARLIE COCHRANE

WILLIAMS & WHITING

The Case of the Overprotective Ass

London 1950

Chapter One

"Not so haughty, milady. You're on the *Swift Apollo* now and the captain's word is law." Toby Bowe was a handsome man, but the innate cruelty in his voice was reflected in his expression, coarsening his naturally good looks. His slim mouth was curled in a leer and his blue eyes shone dark.

"Captain? You're not fit to bear the title. You're a black-hearted pirate and I won't bow to your commands."

"You won't? What if you were made to?" Toby loomed over his prisoner. "Your fine Commodore Neville can't come to your aid here. Look at the ocean, milady—there's not a sail to be seen."

"You're not worthy to sup at the commodore's feet, you scurvy knave..."

"Scurvy, am I? Just wait, you saucy wench...oh, I can't go on with this, Alasdair. How can anyone talk such twaddle? Even Fiona can't believe in any of it."

Toby laid down his script with a sigh and ran his hands through the sort of unruly hair that even a pirate would have been ashamed of. His dark blond locks—usually slicked back with Brylcreem for the better depiction of fighter pilots or His Majesty's soldiers—were hanging rakishly loose. "Why do we get given such rotten scripts?"

"I don't think the studio's bothered about the quality of dialogue so long as the cinema goers suspend disbelief." Alasdair Hamilton, 'The Man with the Golden Frown', employed his trademark expression. The trio of Bowe, Hamilton and Fiona Marsden were the darlings of post-war British cinema, a touch of glamour and excitement in a world where austerity still hadn't been shaken off. And when they weren't lighting up the screen, they lit up the gossip columns, story after story and photo after photo of their latest exploits. Toby (hair carefully controlled on these occasions) was generally depicted with some heiress to a retail empire on his arm while Alasdair squired one of the minor European royals, usually chosen because the olive shades of her skin brought out the dark auburn of his hair.

Landseer wasn't bothered if people said they went for formula over art, Alasdair always getting the girl, Fiona, and Toby suffering nobly as second fiddle. Toby didn't complain, not given the off-screen perks; Fiona always got Alasdair by the time the credits rolled, but Toby kept him to go home with. Somehow or other the newspapers never seemed to get wind of that juicy little tidbit.

"Anyway," Alasdair got up from the chair where he'd been taking Fiona's part and ran an elegant finger along his friend's sleeve, "you'll be a wonderful pirate king."

Toby snorted. "Judging by the costume sketches, I'm more Prince Rupert of the Rhine than Long John Silver. Perhaps if La Marsden's dress shows enough cleavage, the people who've paid good money to see this tripe won't notice how the plot's been stolen and the dialogue resembles..." He struggled for an adequate metaphor. "Something you'd scrape off the ship's head. It's worse than your costume."

Alasdair swiped the side of his lover's head with the script they were supposed to be learning. It was a lovely day, the sun streaming through the drawing room windows, and no amount of either hard work or insults were going to spoil his mood. "The wardrobe girls think I'll look very authentic." He raised his left eyebrow—the one newly ensured with Lloyd's and said to be worth fifty thousand pounds in box office takings. “Do you suppose that any officer in King George’s navy wore quite so much braid or so many flounces?”

“I think you’ll look like the Queen of the May. Not unattractive, though.” Toby stroked his friend’s chin. “Better than La Marsden.”

“At least you get to kiss her in this film—that makes a change.”

“And is that any sort of a consolation? Especially when she blacks my eye straight afterwards. I’d rather,” Toby’s fingers started to insinuate themselves under Alasdair’s collar, “be kissing the commodore.”

“Have you ever come across these modern acting theories? About inhabiting the role?” Alasdair, rather unsportingly, broke the clinch and the romantic mood.

“They’re worse tripe than this bloody script. Why on earth do you ask?” Toby was tetchy. It wasn’t fair, really. Under the constant scrutiny of the gossip columns, they had to be jolly careful to wangle any time together and rehearsing was a perfect excuse to be alone. They had to make the most of it—they should be making the most of it right now—and someone was insisting on ruining the mood.

“Because I thought we could employ it here, see if we can make this wretched script come alive.” If there was a bit of a spark in Alasdair’s eye, Toby didn’t notice it.

“Thinking myself into the role of Pirate King, you mean?” Toby shut his eyes and imagined a little frigate, all elegant lines and a Jolly Roger at the masthead. “It might work…”

“Ah. I had more in mind that I’d be the pirate for this particular exercise. You, my love,” Alasdair gently withdrew himself from smacking range, “need to find some empathy with Lady Jennifer.” He suddenly pounced, grabbing Toby and pushing him towards the Chesterfield. "Now, milady, you'll find out what life aboard a pirate ship is really like."

Toby shrieked. An impressive, feminine shriek, a good octave above his normal register. "Scurvy knave, unhand me." He tried to swat Alasdair's arm away, half-heartedly; the settee was big and comfy.

"Sheathe your claws, ma'am. I'm tired of grog and I mean to drink from your lips tonight."

"Ooooooooh." Toby gave a marvellous impression of Fiona's standard on-screen response to anything frightening or annoying or surprising. Ex-public schoolboys were said to find it particularly stimulating, because it reminded them of sick bay and Matron. "Touch me not, my name's...actually temptation won't really work, will it, Alasdair, cut that line...touch me not in the name of Saint Hyacinth!"

"Don't call on yer saints to 'elp 'ee now, missy." They were at the edge of the Chesterfield now and one slight tip was going to send Lady Jennifer into grave peril and Toby into delight.

"Elp 'ee now, missy? You've gone awfully common all of a sudden—distinct shades of Mummerset, as well. I thought Black-Hearted Fitzroy the pirate king was supposed to be rather posh, wrong side of the noble blanket and all that? Gone to the bad when the love of his life died of smallpox? That's how I've been trying to play him."

"Oh for goodness sake, are you going to allow me to try to ravish you or not?" Alasdair, giving up on the script entirely, grabbed his lover's face between his hands and kissed him heartily. "Anyone would think you didn't want to be snogged."

"Lady Jennifer doesn't." Toby grabbed the script, fanning himself with it demurely as he went back into role. "Prithee, sir, do not divest me of my maidenhead."

"That's never in the script—the censor wouldn't allow it." Alasdair grinned. "If you're going to improvise, at least do it realistically."

"Spoilsport. Oh prithee, sir, do not molest me." Toby looked coyly over the top of the thick wodge of paper. Lady Jennifer might be saying no but Toby was a different kettle of fish. That settee was calling and it was singing a dirty song. "Actually, Alasdair, if you were Fitzroy, I'd be inclined to say to hell with the Commodore, cast aside my corset, put on breeches and join your pirate band." Toby threw down the script and threw himself onto the Chesterfield.

Alasdair sat down next to his lover, worming his arm around Toby's waist, squeezing the succulent flesh lurking just underneath his silk shirt. "I'd say there's nothing like it, milady. Especially if you get to share the captain's hammock."

"There's an idea. That could be modern acting at its very best." Toby reached up and ran his fingers through his Alasdair's hair. "Come on, the script can wait." He pulled his friend's face towards him. "And if you're a good boy, while we're about it, you can talk to me like a pirate."

"Ah, milady. Then I'll be a-takin' these here breeches of yourn and..."

Unfortunately, all pirate talk, real or feigned, had to be put on hold as Morgan, Alasdair's incredibly discreet manservant, knocked loudly, gave enough time for those present to make themselves decent, then entered the room to announce that a Mr. Fisher was on the phone and seemed to be in an agitated state.

***

"The Old George theatre, please." Toby settled himself into the cab, wondering how Morgan had managed to conjure one up so quickly and from almost nowhere.

"Actually, drop us in Trafalgar Square, if you would." Alasdair settled down beside his friend. "I wouldn't mind a few minutes' walking and talking time before we face Johnny and whatever so-called crisis he's dreamed up this time."

"I suspect there won't be any crisis at all. He'll just be after money for charity. He usually is." Toby watched the pedestrians struggling with umbrellas in the drizzle. London wasn't at her best-behaved today, despite it being June. "We'll be soaked through, in spite of our overcoats, but I'll take the risk. I've always had a soft spot for St. Martin's Lane, ever since Wings of Love débuted there."

"Ah yes, of course." Alasdair turned his gaze out onto the streets, too, thoughts turned inwards to a flood of memories.

Wings of Love had been the first production for the threesome, five years previously. Alasdair remembered reading the in-production press releases for the film with an ironic smile. The words that he was quoted as saying—I look forward very much to beginning filming, especially with so lovely a co-star—had been used as evidence of the likely blossoming of a classic on-screen partnership with Fiona Marsden, something that Landseer pictures would have loved. Worth pounds at the tills.

He'd never said the words, but they couldn't have been more fitting.

Whichever bright spark in the press office had actually written his comments, they'd inadvertently hit on the entire truth, but it wasn't La Marsden, as she was beginning to be called even then—though never to her face—who'd been the object of his anticipation. Right from the first meeting when they'd taken the pre-publicity stills, it had been Toby Bowe who'd got his leading man all of an internal flutter, on set and off.

Alasdair had heard of the term love at first sight, of course, although he'd pooh-poohed it as being fit only for a fairy tale. It had never happened to him, and therefore it couldn't exist. But when Toby strolled into the room, a hint of swagger in his gait and a huge grin on his face, Alasdair had realised that such a thing not only could but did happen, and it had just come around the corner and thumped him one.

"Penny for your thoughts?"

"Not in public," Alasdair whispered. Aloud, he said, "I was just thinking about Fiona's dress, the one she wore for the opening night."

"Dress? Is that what it was? I've seen more material in a handkerchief. Ah, we're here." From Trafalgar Square, they took to a series of small roads and back alleys to get to the theatre.

"I was worried the cabby was going to ask about Fiona. As usual." Toby pulled up his collar.

"Tell me about it. Questions concerning Fiona always seem to end up with enquiries about whether we're knocking around together." Alasdair sounded cross, not just at the weather.

"I heard a rumour she's got some sprig of the nobility on the hook. Maybe she's given up on you at last." Fiona would never catch Alasdair...but it was fun watching her try.

"Maybe. And maybe Johnny has given up on you, as well." Alasdair gazed straight ahead, never giving Toby even a sideways glance. It was always the same when the topic of Johnny Fisher got broached. His attempted seduction of Toby in Brighton—and the various passes which he'd made before and after—were perennially held up and used in evidence against him. Alasdair couldn't stand the man.

"I should jolly well hope so. He's not even my type." Toby drew his collar up even further. "I know what you're up to, trying to delay our arrival at the theatre so you can work yourself up sufficiently for whatever scene you anticipate playing out. Well, I'm not prepared to dilly-dally about, not in this weather." He broke into something like a trot and scooted along the street, bounding through the door of the theatre shaking the water off himself like a dog. Alasdair sighed and followed, at a more leisurely pace.

The Old George theatre sat back from St Martin's Lane, trying to look both classy and brassy at the same time. It dated back to the Naughty Nineties and, inside, the opulence of the era hadn't faded—neither bomb nor death watch beetle had got to it, nor had the damp risen in its walls or dripped into its timbers. It was currently riding a wave of popularity, giving theatre goers the sort of entertainment they craved. You could sail a damn sight closer to the wind than in the cinema, if you were canny enough.

Johnny Fisher had been left the place in his great uncle's will, and a better legacy a man couldn't have had. The theatre was in his blood—while he hadn't been born in a trunk it had been a damn close run thing—and his family had expected him and his brother to enter what had been the Fisher profession these last four generations. Johnny had taken up his expected role quite willingly and trod the boards from Fleance through Ernest onwards and upwards. Now he picked and chose his stage roles, preferring to manage his little nest egg and to direct productions.

Johnny's secretary, a lad with the biggest Adam's apple Toby had ever seen, ushered them into his office—his splendidly opulent office—and Johnny produced a bottle of whisky. "Thank you for coming so promptly. I wasn't interrupting anything vital, was I?"

"Just going through a script, that's all." Alasdair's voice seemed convincing, although a touch too airy and light to suggest complete candour. "Practicing our lines."

"Ah, the glamorous life of the actor." Johnny took an elegantly tooled silver case from his pocket and offered both men a cigarette. Both refused, although they encouraged their host to carry on in spite of them. "I have a favour to ask the two of you."

"Which set of waifs and strays has caught your eye this time? Shall I get the cheque book out straight away?" Toby made an elaborate mime of reaching into his inside pocket.

Johnny laughed. "Not on this occasion, although keep me in mind next time I organise a war widows' treat and want you to act in it."

"I think I'd rather pay the protection racket money and just give you fifty quid straight up." Alasdair rolled his eyes.

"As you wish. It's only a theoretical question, at the moment." Johnny lit his cigarette; it looked like an actor's gesture, aimed at ladies in the front row of the circle. "What I do have in mind is all too real and all too puzzling." He paused, his wrist and hand forming a stylish angle, clearly all for effect.

"Out with it, then." Alasdair didn't want Toby getting impressed with the grace of the actor-manager's movements.

"My secretary has disappeared. He didn't turn up for work just over a week ago and I've not seen hide nor hair of him since." Johnny looked genuinely concerned, although he was such a natural actor that any appearances had to be taken with a whole cellar of salt, let alone a pinch.

"Then who was that lad who let us in? The one with the Adam's apple?" Toby tipped his head towards the door.

"Haven't we all got Adam's apples?" Alasdair raised the uninsured eyebrow.

"Not ones the size of a melon, we haven't. Not a bad looking lad apart from that." Toby held up his hands in a gesture of innocence. "I can't help noticing these things."

"His Adam's apple or the fact that he's pretty?" Johnny said, grinning. "That's Hampson. I got him from an agency the day after Robin disappeared, just to tide me over. There's something about him I can't quite pin down—he lacks a sense of humour and that unnerves me, I suppose. With Robin I could have a laugh."

"A bit of friendly banter?" Toby nodded. "Makes for a good working relationship."

"Exactly, but with Hampson, it's different. There's no point in teasing the unteasable. It's like," he reached over and tapped Toby's hand, "trying to seduce the unseducable." A glint in his eye suggested he was doing it in part because Alasdair would be miffed.

"That would be me, then." Toby whacked the hand that was molesting him. "Any complaints about his work?"

"No, nothing on the business side of things. He's doing fine, but he's not the same." Johnny tapped the ash from his cigarette into a marble ashtray. "And he's not that way inclined, in case anyone's got a roving eye. He's far too interested in the chorus girls."

"But he's not Robin?" Toby's question implied that Robin might just have been that way inclined.

"It's not what you're thinking." Johnny had evidently caught the drift. "There was no 'interest' between us. He was just the best assistant I'd ever had. One hundred per cent reliable, too."

"Until he went walkabout." Alasdair sat back, enjoying his erstwhile rival's discomfort. "Hardly counts as reliable, does it?"

"That's my whole point." Johnny sounded exasperated, although whether at his secretary or at Alasdair wasn't clear. "If he'd been habitually late or tended to go off for a day or two, then I wouldn't be so worried. I want to know if he's in trouble of some sort and whether I can help."

"I would have thought the police would be better suited to finding that out—why haven't you contacted them?" Alasdair was finding this whole interview more and more perplexing.

"I did contact them. I'm not an idiot, whatever else you think of me. Don't answer that." Johnny stubbed out his cigarette forcefully. "I held fire that first day, just in case word came through. The second day I rang the police, after I'd checked his lodgings and had been told he'd left for work as usual the previous morning."

"And the police said?" Toby was clearly trying to sound the sympathetic one of the pair.

"They said they had better things to do with their time than go hunting grown men."

"Did they, by Jove? I'll have a word with my father about how his officers are addressing the populace." Toby grinned; when your father was the Chief Constable of the Metropolitan Police, you could make sure your friends were treated with a bit of common decency. However, embarrassing his father by being caught cottaging wasn't something Toby was ever going to risk.

"Well, they didn't use those exact words, but that's what they meant. Unless there was evidence of a real crime—a ransom note or some other indication that Robin hadn't just got fed up and gone—then they weren't that interested." Johnny opened his cigarette case, looked like he was about to have another, then slapped it shut and put it away. "If I'd found he'd had his fingers in the till, it might have been different, I suppose."

"And had he?" Alasdair's ears pricked up. "Been dipping his fingers in the till?"

"No evidence of anything like that. Straight as a die and everyone liked him." Johnny shrugged.

"You've contacted his family?" Alasdair asked with a sniff. "That seems the obvious thing to do. Maybe his mother was taken ill and..."

"No mother," Johnny interrupted the flow. "Nothing closer than a grandmother and she's slightly gaga."

Alasdair was beginning to be interested in the case. "I can't deny I love an intellectual puzzle."

"Oh yes," Toby said, "to see him with The Times crossword is to observe poetry in motion. Cinema acting hardly stretches anyone's mental resources, does it?"

Alasdair nodded. "To take on a real investigation would be a challenge, and we could always say we were conducting research for *The Hound of the Baskervilles*." If only it had been someone other than Johnny Fisher asking. "So why is it so important for you to find Robin? There's every chance he's just fallen into the Thames or run away to be a sailor or lost his memory. Whatever's happened, he either doesn't want to be found or has no choice in the matter."

"Because it bothers me. Why should any decent, respectable man vanish into thin air unless something untoward has happened? And if nothing untoward has occurred, you tell me where he went. I want to make sure he's safe and not in trouble. If he's got himself in a hole, I'd like to help dig him out."

"You can't dig someone out of a hole, Johnny." Alasdair looked smug at the muddled metaphor.

"I wish we could help, but I think you're overestimating our capabilities. We may play Holmes and Watson on the screen, but we've no experience in real life." Toby spoke softly, clearly afraid of treading on his friend's dreams. "That's assuming I've got the right end of the stick and you're actually asking us to do some sleuthing on your behalf. *The Case of the Disappearing Secretary*."

"Couldn't you call it research or something?" Johnny smiled sweetly; he wasn't daft, he knew he'd get further pleading with Toby than he ever would with his partner. "Getting prepared for *The Hound of the Baskervilles*?"

"So we're to take to Dartmoor in search of your erstwhile employee, are we?" Toby's eyes were bright—worryingly bright, as far as Alasdair was concerned.

"I hoped you wouldn't have to go as far as that. I guess I just had London in mind...I hadn't really considered what might be involved." Johnny was suddenly serious, his normally happy-go-lucky outlook submerging under his genuine concern. "Look, don't take this up if you don't have the time or the inclination. It was a stupid whim anyway, thinking that you might succeed on a wild goose chase."

"Stupid?" Whether he'd intended it or not—and whatever else he was, Johnny was a brilliant actor—he'd hit on just the right form of words, and approach, to get Alasdair to change his mind. If Johnny Fisher didn't think Alasdair capable of something, then Alasdair was definitely going to prove him wrong. “If the police are disinclined to pay attention, then I don’t see why we couldn’t take an interest in the case, as we won’t be treading on their toes. It’s a couple of weeks before work starts on our pirate film, with just the premiere of *A Scandal in Bohemia* in between. I’d like to see how much headway we could make in that time.” He glanced at Toby. “Give us all the information you have and we’ll see where we get to.”

The huge smile Johnny broke into suggested he’d manipulated the whole situation to get the outcome he wanted, but Alasdair did his best to ignore the fact. “Wherever you can get has got to be better than total ignorance, which is where I am now. I’ll pay all your expenses, of course.”

“You will not.” Toby at last got the chance to speak. “Have this as a present from us, in honour of your new production. In return we want a couple of tickets for the best seats in the house, as soon as it’s bedded in. If you think it’s worth seeing, of course,” he added.

“Worth seeing? It’ll be the hit of the season.” Johnny slapped his hands on the desk. “Only shouldn’t that be four tickets—two for you and two for your alleged girlfriends of the moment?”

Toby groaned. “I suppose you’re right. Unless you get us a box, of course, and we can take my mother and sister along. People will assume that Alasdair’s got a thing for her and no young fillies will end up disappointed.”

“Won’t she be disappointed? Your sister, I mean?”

“Oh, no. She’s got her eye on a sailor boy and he quite likes it when he’s on a tour of duty and one of us squires her around town. Keeps the bees away from the honey. Now…” Toby tapped the arm of his chair, “information. We can’t start finding out anything if we’ve just got this chap’s first name.”

"I've kept a file." It was right at hand, suggesting that the man had been well-prepared for this whole exercise, and confident—rightly—of seeing it through to the desired outcome. "Take it. And good luck."

Alasdair rose, picking up the file and flicking through it. The first impression was favourable, at least in terms of legibility and organisation. Not a lot in the way of information, though. Maybe this wasn't going to be easy as his offended audacity had hoped. "We'd best be amongst it, then. We'll keep you up to date with what we find." Still, he felt rooted to the spot, unwilling to take the first step on an uncharted road.

"Come on, we've got work to do, Sherlock." Toby took his friend's arm and guided him towards the door. "Although I'm lucky my Holmes thinks his Watson has a degree of intelligence. Quite a different set-up from the original."

"You can say that again. Don't remember Sherlock leaping into the sack with his beloved doctor." Johnny held out his hand for his friends to shake. "Let me know as soon as you turn anything up. I know it's an imposition, but I suspect you're my only hope."

Chapter Two

They'd left Johnny's office and were down some stairs and along a corridor before Alasdair could trust himself to speak."Why us?" He might have accepted the commission but that didn't mean he was happy about it.

"The police weren't interested, and..."

Alasdair cut across his friend; there was no time to waste. "I understand that, but why us? Why not a private investigator or someone else with the relevant experience?" He had a horrible thought. "He's not still after you, is he?"

Toby snorted. "I should bloody well hope not. Surely he's got the message by now? No, I don't think this is all some cunning strategy to somehow get me alone and wheedle his way into my boudoir. Even if it was, give me some credit for being able to resist him."

"I'm sorry." Alasdair bit his lip.

"I'll accept your apology if you look more contrite. Better. Now, are you sure, absolutely sure, that you want to take this case up?" Toby looked genuinely troubled.

"Of course I do, if only to see the smile wiped off his face when we succeed." Another horrible thought. "Are you saying that you'd rather not be involved? You seemed so keen in there that I assumed..."

"You assumed quite right. I'd like to find anything to keep my mind off this bloody awful fiasco of a pirate film." Toby grinned. "I quite fancy a diversion."

"Then that's a perfect motivation for both of us. You to stave off ennui and me to put one over on our smug friend."

"Then, as your Commodore Neville has such a habit of saying, 'There's not a moment to lose.'" Toby bounded down a little run of five stairs and strode off along another corridor,

Alasdair scurrying to catch up. They walked down to the foyer, the time for decision-making getting ever closer. Toby stood by the desk where they sold programmes and gave a huge, appropriately theatrical sigh. "Any idea where we should start, then?"

"Mr. Bowe?" A sandy haired young man, very earnest behind metal-rimmed spectacles but not bad-looking—apart from the knobbly Adam's apple—came hurtling through a door and leaped across the foyer. "Mr Fisher said he's terribly sorry, but he forgot to give you this." He held out a small black-covered book.

Toby took it, perusing the pages and nodding his head. An address book. "Thank you, Mr...?"

"Hampson."

"Hampson. I'll try to remember the name. I suppose this book belonged to Robin Pierce?"

Hampson nodded. "That's why Mr. Fisher wanted you to have it. That he should come to you for help, though..." He shook his head and turned on his heels, mission accomplished.

"What on earth did he mean by that?" Alasdair frowned.

"Probably thinks the same as us—that we're actors, not detectives, and that this is probably all going to turn out for the worst." Toby pocketed the address book safely against the rain which was still pitching down outside. "We should show him. Show the both of them. Where would Sherlock begin?"

"Bugger Sherlock. I'd begin with finding a decent pub, having a pint of beer and giving that book—which I note was sent down to you but I'll try to ignore the fact—a dose of reasoning. There's not a lot of time and we don't want to be chasing wild geese."

Toby hid his grin behind the collar of his coat. He knew Alasdair liked playing the great detective best of all the roles he'd had at Landseer, not least because it meant the on-screen romances were kept to a minimum in order to please the purists. Even Toby got more of a look in with the ladies, Watson being the one with an eye for the fair sex as far as Conan Doyle was concerned. "Righty-ho, Sherlock," Toby risked as they took to the street, ignoring what sounded like a ribald but whispered reply.

They walked in the direction of a decent hostelry, found themselves a table and got outside of a couple of pints. Soup and rolls were ordered, raincoats hung up and the address book given the once over. The names might have been copied straight from the pages of the telephone directory for all the information they provided; once they'd eliminated Johnny Fisher and some other contacts from within "the business," the rest were a meaningless jumble. There were only two Pierces listed, a woman—presumably the granny who'd gone gaga—and another who'd been scratched out. Deceased?

"What next in *The Case of the Secretary's Address Book*?" Toby had consumed the first restorative mouthful of beer, but it didn't seem to be making the way forward any clearer. At the moment he felt like taking a pin and choosing where to start at random. Surely investigating couldn't be that hard for a pair of intelligent men? They just had to find their feet.

"I suggest we pick half a dozen names each and try to visit them all over the next two days, separating to cover more of the ground." The beer seemed to be making Alasdair particularly decisive.

"Selecting names at random doesn't seem entirely logical, Sherlock." Toby shrugged. "Just have to hope we strike lucky sooner rather than later." Over the soup, they split the list, choosing their six names simply on a geographical basis, people listed in London or close by. Enough of the day was left for them to make a bit of progress, if they got going quickly and enticed fortune into favouring them.

"I'll start by tackling the distaff side of the equation." Alasdair tapped the list he'd copied from the book. "There's plenty of meat to get my teeth into here."

"I'm not sure I appreciate your choice of phrase, especially if you do have only female names on your list, but I'll assume it's poetic licence." Toby cuffed his lover's arm. "The game's afoot."

"One more Holmes quote and I may have to smack you, public place or not."

"Save it for tonight. I assume we're still on for a bit of supper?"

"Absolutely. Got to get our strength up for the big opening night." Alasdair grimaced.

"I'd almost forgotten about that." Toby lowered his voice. "Better leave it at supper, then, and not extend matters to a taxi home and an overnight stay. If there's anyone from the press milling about, I don't fancy having to nip out of the back door and down the alleyway again. It's not just undignified—I almost ripped my trousers last time. I'm starting to get the feeling of prying eyes on my back."

***

Alasdair's cab sped—as much as any cab could speed in London—up the road, leaving Toby to set off for the exotic environs of Kensal Rise, where Pierce had his lodgings.

Toby got his cab to stop at the end of Pierce's road. A gentle saunter along the street would cause less of a kerfuffle than a stranger pulling up to the door and discharging himself dramatically onto the pavement in front of the area steps. The properties here were in pretty good nick—if the bombs of the Blitz had touched this particular road, then the repairs had been done quickly and with good taste. It was what his mother would have called "still a nice area," even if some of the houses had become sets of lodgings.

The one he sought had a London plane tree outside. Now that the rain had blown through and the sun had deigned to make an appearance again, the tree's shadow danced across the front steps. Toby took a deep breath, just like he did before the cameras rolled. So what if he really was going into someone's house to ask all sorts of intrusive questions? It was just another role. He knocked at the door.

"Mrs. Chivers?" Toby smiled at the bright-eyed, grey-haired woman who answered the door.

"That's right, sir." Mrs. Chivers peered at him and then gave a gasp of surprise. Toby knew the look well—the shock of seeing on her own doorstep the man she'd last viewed from the "one and nines" in the local cinema. "I'm sorry to be knocking on your door out of the blue, but I'm trying to locate Robin Pierce on behalf of his employer, who's an old friend of mine."

"Mr. Pierce? Oh yes, of course." Mrs. Chivers ushered Toby in, listening attentively to his story about helping out this old friend, although he was sure she didn't believe a word of what he said. He wondered whether she'd made up her own theory about him practicing his Dr. Watson persona. Still, at least she was endeavouring to be helpful; he'd honestly thought he'd be chucked out on his ear, so perhaps having a well-known face was going to be an asset. Toby was offered a chair in the parlour and a cup of tea, neither of which he felt he could politely refuse.

"I believe that about a week ago Robin Pierce just didn't turn up for work. Have you seen him since?" Toby asked, settling into his chair.

"I haven't, sir. Neither hide nor hair." However, as the landlady then pointed out rather ashamedly, a woman had to live and she'd let the rooms already. "I've put all Mr. Pierce's belongings, such as they are, into a cupboard in the cellar in case he should return. They'll be nice and safe there. I told the police that, but they didn't seem particularly bothered."

Police? So the constabulary had taken an interest in the disappearance, however cursory a one. "I think you did the right thing on both counts, Mrs. Chivers. If Pierce comes back here and finds he's got nowhere to stay, he'll have no right to complain. Had he left much behind?"

"Just about everything, as far as I can see, sir." Mrs. Chivers shook her head. "He must have left with the clothes he was standing up in and whatever he'd stuffed into his pockets. Not even, as far as I could see, a change of smalls."

Toby remembered his mother's insistence that he always wear clean underwear in case of an accident; the logic of the stipulation still defeated him. Still, it was odd for Pierce not to have taken at least a bagful of things if he was deliberately going off and, say, working his passage somewhere. "Most odd about him leaving his stuff."

"It is, very odd. And I don't know of any relative I could pass the bits and pieces on to." The kettle must have been already on the boil when Toby arrived; a girl knocked the door and came in with a handsome brown pot. Toby was delighted to see the colour of the brew—dark and strong—so he had high hopes of the quality.

"Thank you." He took his cup and waited for the maid to leave the room. "So you haven't the remotest idea where he might have taken himself off to? Not the daftest little theory of your own that you couldn't tell the police?" Toby smiled the devastating smile that made the fans swoon and inevitably got him anything he wanted with whoever it was tried upon.

"Now it's funny you should say that, Mr. Bowe." Mrs. Chivers quickly glanced out of the parlour window as though she expected to see one of the men from Scotland Yard lurking on the pavement. "There was a thing or two I wouldn't have minded saying, but..."

"But you didn't like the attitude of the officers involved?" Toby grinned and sipped the tea he'd been given. It was a smashing brew. "I've heard that said before, especially where the lady concerned has discernment and common sense." He could take to this investigating lark; it was much better than talking like a pirate.

"I don't want you to think I'm tarring all the police with the same brush. Our local bobby's a real gentleman and as honest as the day is long, but those detectives chaps! I wouldn't have trusted them to find the baby's rattle, let alone my poor Mr. Pierce. I'm glad that nice Mr. Fisher has sent you along to solve things." Mrs. Chivers beamed her confidence that this equally nice young gentleman was going to produce her former lodger like a rabbit from a hat. "Trust him to try to help out."

"You know Johnny Fisher, then?"

"Oh yes. Well, I wouldn't say that I know him, but I was once up west doing some shopping when I saw Mr. Pierce coming out of a restaurant alongside this lovely-looking chap. Just like a film star." Mrs. Chivers suddenly blushed, evidently remembering that she was at present talking to a real-life film star. She hurried on. "My lodger introduced him as his boss—so charming."

"And what can you tell me that you wanted to tell the police before they blotted their copybooks?" Toby brought the conversation away from the potentially dangerous area of Johnny's looks and considerable allure.

"It's about a visitor he had a day or two before he disappeared. They had a bit of a row and Mr. Pierce was shaking like a leaf afterwards, he was so wound up. I told the police all about that, but it was like talking to my garden wall." Mrs. Chivers leaned forward, conspiratorially. "So I never let on about the fact that same bloke has been hanging about here on and off ever since Mr. Pierce left, watching the place like a hawk. He can't have done away with him or he'd not be lurking, would he?"

That sounded like a real stroke of luck, a potential lead this early on in the proceedings; one up for Dr. Watson. "Aren't you worried enough to tell your local bobby and get this chap moved on?"

"I have done." Mrs. Chivers leaned even further forward, as if imparting a great secret. "And I've told him I'm more intrigued than worried, so he's to let it be for the present."

"Maybe we can do better than that." Toby copied the conspiratorial movement, narrowing the gap between them. "Perhaps I might be lucky enough to catch this chap and ask him what he's about. He's not out there now, is he, by any wonderful chance?"

"Bit early for him, if he sticks to his usual routine. He usually gets here around three o'clock, but I'll just check. In case he's made an exception for you." Mrs. Chivers twitched the curtains as if she was just straightening them. "No, it's all clear. Although if you wait a while, he might turn up."

So Toby waited— twenty minutes of twiddling his thumbs, drinking tea and wondering if this really was better than learning lines. He kept one eye out of the window and one on *The Times*. After ten minutes or so, a figure appeared from up the street, a man who didn't seem to be progressing in a typical manner. Toby called his hostess and convened a conference by the bay window.

"Suspect in sight at ten o'clock, or whatever they say." Toby grinned. "Is that our man?"

"Oh, yes. I've seen him going up the street like that before, all shifty, so I've kept an eye out." It was a very beady eye if the landlady's present expression was anything to go by. "There's no need to hurry out straight away—you might frighten him off. You finish your tea first and let him get settled. He always hangs around for a while."

"Watching out for our mysterious Mr. Pierce?" Toby wasn't sure he wanted any more tea; he was in need of what Black-Hearted Fitzroy would call "the head," as it was.

"There's nothing mysterious about my Mr. Pierce." The landlady sounded put out. "I'm sure something's cropped up, that's all."

Toby wasn't so sure about that —if anything had cropped up, it probably wasn't above board. He had a feeling for those sorts of things, what his mother would have called "a feeling in the waterworks." Talking of which..."May I just use your toilet? I'm terribly sorry."

"No need to apologise. It's all that tea." Mrs. Chivers seemed delighted at the thought of a film star using her lavvy—Toby just hoped it was inside and not at the bottom of the garden. "Just up the first flight of stairs and it's across the landing. I'll keep an eye on our friend here." She took up a watchman's post at the curtain's edge while Toby found much needed relief. He returned much more able to concentrate.

"Nothing to report," Mrs. Chivers said, beaming.

“Is there any way I can reach the street from the back of the house?” Toby didn’t want to frighten his quarry by coming out of the house he was observing and making straight for him. It was difficult enough to do anything by subterfuge, given his well-known face.

“If you go through the kitchen door and down the path, there’s a little alley that runs along the back of all the gardens, coming out halfway down. Our friend over there would have no idea which property you’d actually come from.” Mrs Chivers considered her visitor. “Do you mean to confront him out in the street or will you simply follow him?”

“That I’ve yet to decide. I suspect it’ll depend on what he does when approached.” Toby grinned with boyish enthusiasm. “It might even end up with a chase!”

“If it does, you’ll regret having that second biscuit,” the landlady replied, grinning in return. She showed her guest into the garden.

Toby made his way down the path, let himself out by the wicket gate and wandered along the narrow weed-strewn alley until he found the street. The man across the road eyed him suspiciously as he emerged onto the pavement, clearly realised this wasn’t the man he was looking for and then took no further notice.

Toby, deciding that a head-on assault would be best, crossed the road, smiled in what he hoped was his most winning manner and doffed his hat. “Excuse me. Are you waiting for Robin Pierce, by any chance?”

His quarry was a well-built lad, although the sort who’d seemed to have stopped taking exercise when he’d left school, for the muscle was already running to portliness. His clothes were well-cut enough for Toby to pitch him as outside Pierce’s class...although, since he didn’t know much about the missing man, that was an awfully big—and perhaps unjustified—assumption.

"As a matter of fact I am. How on earth did you know?" The stranger seemed a bit suspicious, although Toby could hardly blame him. It would put the wind up anyone to be suddenly accosted in the street, especially by a film star.

"I didn't know, I just guessed. You see, I've been trying to catch up with him myself." Toby was ready to spin a tale about how he'd been keeping the back of the house under observation, but the stranger didn't seem to want to ask. Instead, he sighed, appearing to wilt a bit. "Don't tell me that you have a sister, too? Or is it a cousin this time?"

"Not quite." Toby didn't want to lie—too much—so he decided a mixture of half-truths would be the best strategy. As Alasdair had found in the pirate scene they'd played out in the drawing room, his forte didn't lie in improvisation, "I'd rather not be too specific, but the lady in question actually had a very near miss and I just wanted to get a few things clarified."

"Is that what you call it, clarified? I'd call it delivering a bloody great trouncing." The stranger's face was turning purple with suppressed rage. "That swine Pierce deserves it all in my sister's case. Only I can't lay hands on the bounder. He's never here when I try to catch him and I don't know where he works." He ran his fingers through his hair. "I spend every moment I can spare watching his door."

"It's no use trying to find him at his work, believe me." Whatever the trouble was, Toby had enough loyalty to Johnny to want to keep him clear of it. "His employer is after him, too. Robin Pierce seems to have disappeared into thin air."

The stranger snorted. "Gone to ground with some woman, no doubt. Yet another poor dupe. I should have given up by now, but I'm determined to do something." He banged his left fist into the palm of his right hand. Toby wouldn't have liked to be on the wrong end of that impact.

"Your sister has no idea where he can have got to?"

"My sister?" The stranger rolled his eyes, more and more like the hero in an overacted melodrama. "She refuses to talk about him. I think if she hadn't made such an error of judgement, she'd have something to say, although at least she won't have to regret her foolishness for the rest of her life." He stopped abruptly, having said far more than he should have to an outsider. "Let's just say something...unfortunate...has happened and she's rather unwell at present."

"Ah." Toby wasn't sure what he was expected to say in response.

"I think ultimately it'll all be for the best." The man got out a handkerchief, mopping his crimson brow. "All she's given me is the address she had for him before he became persona non grata. Oh, and the name of his tailor, but a fat lot of good that'll do either of us."

"His tailor?" Toby felt he'd turned over two pages of script and had missed some key part of the plot. "Am I missing the significance of that?"

The stranger shrugged. "Beats me. I've never understood how the female mind works." He scratched his head.

Toby couldn't help grinning; if this chap had been working as an extra for Landseer, he'd have been chucked off the set for being too obvious.

"You never know what you can learn from a tailor's mark." Toby counted members of the profession as a highly reliable source of tittle-tattle, if you could get on their good sides. "It's always possible they might have another contact address for him, somewhere they sent the bill. Which establishment are we talking about?"

"Waites."

"Waites?" Toby whistled in surprise. "Robin Pierce does move in elevated circles. Old Mr. Waite doesn't even let you look in the window unless you're connected to the House of Lords." Which, luckily enough for the cause of the investigation, Toby was, via his paternal grandfather. Lords spiritual as opposed to temporal, but they both counted in the mind of whichever Mr. Waite now counted as the "old" one.

"That's what I'd heard, so I haven't even attempted to follow it up. They'd probably have the police move me on if I loitered opposite their hallowed portals." The man sighed. "Another dead end."

"Not necessarily. Look, have you got a card or something telling me where I can contact you?"

"I'm not sure if I should. I mean, my sister might not like me bandying the family name about." All the bravado seemed to be ebbing away.

"Oh, I'd be very discreet. I was just thinking I'd go along to Waites—don't worry, I can wangle not being thrown out on my beam end—and see what I can sniff out." Toby put on his appealing face. "If I have your address or telephone number, I can share anything I manage to ascertain."

The man thought for a moment, then reached in his pocket and produced one of his cards. "Thank you, I'd appreciate that very much. Only make sure you don't let anything on if you ring and my sister answers, will you?" He produced a pen and scribbled the exchange and number on the back of his card. "Much safer." Toby wondered if he was starting to see clues in everything and, like Watson, missing what really counted.

James Paddick, 14 Dunedin Avenue, SW10. It sounded like a decent address.

"If you don't hear from me, I've drawn a blank. Otherwise…" he waggled the card.

"Grand. But if you do find Pierce, you will let me have first thump at the cad, won't you?"

***

Alasdair sat down on a bench, wiped his brow and swore to himself. In all the stories that he'd read for research, he'd never known Sherlock Holmes to have such a run of bad luck. He never seemed to call on young ladies and find that they'd died after a routine operation went wrong, just two weeks previously. He didn't then visit the next address on the list and find that the chap he wanted had gone abroad on business and was likely to be away for the next month. He'd have considered the address book and made all sorts of Smart Alec deductions about what had happened. All in all, Sherlock Holmes was a bit of a bloody pain. Alasdair felt like kicking him in the seat of the pants.

He decided to have one last try, despite the only address left to him in London being the other end of the Piccadilly line. He had to have something to show for his endeavours; Toby would only crow over him otherwise.

He felt frustrated as he knocked on the door of his destination and his mood didn't improve with the sudden appearance of a great slobbering dog in the bay window to his right. As a double for *The Hound of the Baskervilles* it would have been perfect—huge paws and a great maw accompanied by a fierce, deep bark that made the glass shake.

The door was opened by a young chap who seemed to show no sign of recognising Alasdair or his name, although he was happy to invite him in, as if discussing a friend's disappearance with a total stranger was as everyday an occurrence as paying the milkman.

"I'm glad to be able to discuss the matter with someone, Mr. Hamilton, because it really is out of character for Robin to do such a thing." They'd hardly got over the threshold into the hallway when Freddie McDermott started gabbling.

Alasdair wished he'd been quicker getting his notepad out and starting to make notes. "So his employer, Mr. Fisher, said. He's the one who's asked us to get to the bottom of things. You can imagine how worried he is."

"So am I. Robin's a gregarious type—we've met up once a week for the last two years. Then all of a sudden, he didn't appear in the pub for our usual Tuesday pint or two, and I can't get hold of him in any of his normal haunts." McDermott opened the door to the front parlour, where the great hound still perched on a chair, looking out of the window. Clearly whatever was going on out there was much more interesting than the man who'd just come in.

"That seems to be the general pattern," said Alasdair, who hadn't got enough information to know if that was true but felt it was the thing to say. "Not being where he's supposed to be."

McDermott offered his guest a chair. Alasdair took it, awkwardly perching at the edge, the covers being awash with dog hairs. "I've asked around and not even his lady friends seem to have an inkling of where he's got to. Which is rather peculiar, as I would have thought if he needed to go to ground he'd have taken off to one of them."

"You're not aware of anything that was bothering him? No worries or thr...Oof!" Alasdair was winded as a mass of canine flesh suddenly leapt into his lap, rather like Toby at his more adventurous, but not as sweet-smelling. About as slobbery, though.

"Voyce! Get down." McDermott attempted to drag the hound off his guest. "I do apologise, Mr. Hamilton. He just likes dribbling over people and getting them to pet him."

That sounded a bit like Toby as well. Alasdair hid his feelings of distaste and made a mental note not to get too near whichever dog they had playing *The Hound of the Baskervilles* itself. He tentatively scratched the thing behind its ear.

"He'll like that," McDermott said, grinning. "I had to lock him in the kitchen when Robin came around. Used to make him sneeze. Robin, not Voyce. He won't set you off?"

"No, not at all. Just leave him be, Mr. McDermott—he can sit by my feet if he wants." Alasdair knew nothing about dogs, but the thing's resemblance to his lover, in habits if not in looks, made him think it might like what Toby liked. The theory seemed to work; Voyce soon settled down, and the question about Robin Pierce's worries could be asked again.

"He always played his cards very close to his chest." McDermott scratched his head. "He told me about his latest flings and gossip about the theatre, like the scandalous stuff he thought his boss was getting up to."

Alasdair considered pressing the point but, as he could guess what the scandal was—probably the incident in the Turkish bath—he passed over it.

"Although when it came to things that really mattered, Robin always used to clam up. He would usually tell me in his own good time and long after the event if something had got to him or he'd been going through a rough patch. Liked to tackle problems on his own and not talk about them until they were behind him. *Come to think of it…*"

Alasdair pricked up his ears; he liked the sound of Come to think of it. In a script, that often preceded a key line. This investigating lark was proving easier than anticipated, after all.

"I think there must have been some matter playing on his mind. The last two times we've met he's been ridiculously lively, almost fey if that makes any sense." McDermott waved his hands airily, as if casting about for the right word. "In the past, that's usually been a sign he's had things to work through."

"But you have no idea what things they were this time?"

"Not a sausage." A light seemed to go on in McDermott's brain. "You could try asking a girl called Millie Stamford."

"Was she one of Robin's girlfriends?" Alasdair recognised the name off his list; it was one of the contacts he'd tried to make earlier that day.

"Depends what you mean by girlfriend. Not one of the usual flash pieces he liked to go dancing with—Millie's a sweet, old-fashioned sort of a girl. They'd known each other for years, her and Robin. More like brother and sister or close cousins than sweethearts." McDermott stroked his ear thoughtfully. "She'll be the one to know."

"Now that's a shame. Millie Stamford died a fortnight ago." Alasdair delivered his bombshell and watched carefully to see what reaction it caused.

"She's dead? I had no idea." McDermott appeared genuinely shocked and upset; he called the dog over, as if comforting it. "That's a shame, eh, Voycey? Do you know how it happened?"

"She was in Bart's for an operation and had a bad reaction to the anaesthetic. I spoke to a friend of hers just a few hours ago. She said Millie never regained consciousness. I'm sorry. If

I'd have realised, I wouldn't have broken the news so insensitively."

"Poor little thing." McDermott shook his head. "I didn't know Millie that well, but Robin often mentioned her, to the point I felt I knew her better than I did. Sorry I can't help you any further."

"You've been as helpful as anyone's been today. Thank you." Alasdair shook McDermott's hand and was let out. He was halfway back, getting ready to meet Toby and talk over their discoveries, when he realised that on more than one occasion, the man with the ghastly dog had referred to Robin Pierce in the past tense.

Chapter Three

"Hello, Sherlock!" Toby waved a menu at his friend and indicated the chair next to his. Langan's was a pretty exclusive place—you couldn't get a table unless you were extremely well in with the restaurant manager, so it was just as well the man concerned was smitten with Toby's younger sister. It was a fitting setting to relax in after a hard afternoon of investigating, especially when they were given the benefit of an alcove table, where they could talk without being overheard but still look out over Hyde Park and London at its bustling best.

Alasdair grinned. "I've always hated you calling me that, up until now." He settled into his seat, took a cursory look at the menu, then laid it down. "I never realised how much fun Holmes must have had. Watson, too, when he wasn't being belittled. You don't mind the films weren't cast the other way round?"

"Not at all. You may not quite resemble the Paget sketches, but you're a sight nearer to them than I am." Toby attempted a Sherlock-style pose, failing miserably. "Sleuthing going well?" He scrunched up his nose. "And pardon me for saying so, but don't you whiff a bit of dog? Isn't that taking research a bit too far—pursuing the Hound of the Baskervilles?"

"Bloody thing." Alasdair quickly looked around to make sure he hadn't offended some little old lady or passing bishop. "It was Freddie McDermott's dog and it's lucky to still be alive, I can tell you."

The waiter shimmied over and took their orders; food supplies were still not back to what they should have been and rationing made acquiring several items tricky, but Langan's always managed, somehow, to have plenty of good stuff to offer its customers.

"Did you learn anything from the mutt's owner? The Mysterious Case of the Slobbery Dog?"

"Slobbery Dog that needed a boot up the backside." Alasdair employed "The Golden Frown." "I found out Robin Pierce had been a bit overexcited the last few weeks, as if he was worried about something and needed to work it through. And apparently an old friend of his had died, although I knew that already, as I'd tried to visit her earlier." Alasdair explained the interview in further detail, then rubbed his temples, taking care to avoid the precious eyebrows. "How did you fare?"

"Fair to middling." Toby related the events of the afternoon. "So we can confirm the impression he was a real ladies' man and that he'd got at least one of them into trouble. That wouldn't be the case with the girl who died, would it? Some delicate operation that went wrong?" They'd got away with "bloody", but you couldn't dare say 'illegal abortion' in Langan's.

"It was an operation but not, I think, the sort you have in mind. It was at Bart's, for goodness sake, or at least that's what I was told." He stopped, unsure. "I don't suppose the girl was lying, to protect her friend's memory?"

"I have no idea, not being there at the time. I think we have to go into this with the basic assumption that someone or other's likely not to be telling the whole truth." Toby tipped his head towards the waiter and the talk of investigating was put on hold until they'd started to satisfy the inner man.

"What else did you learn?" Alasdair finished his soup. It was good—maybe not back to pre-war quality but getting there.

"That Pierce shopped at Waites, which is a bit of a shock in itself. How he could afford it, I'm not sure, and why they even let him in through the door amazes me. He didn't appear to be that well-off, you know. I've seen his digs, and unless he was slumming it for some reason, I'd put him at the lower end of middle-class." Toby shrugged. "Perhaps his godfather is a bishop or something."

"Maybe he's a disgraced scion of some noble family, having to make his way under a false name and all that stuff about being orphaned is eyewash. Did you by any chance drop into Waites on your way here?" Alasdair had already guessed the answer from the smug grin of his friend.

"Of course, I did. They were just on the verge of closing, but the lure of fitting me out for a new dinner suit—and you do keep telling me the existing one's a bit of a disgrace—made them keep open and take my requirements. They wielded the tape measure and I asked innocent-sounding questions."

"What did you find out from the land of the inside leg measurement?" Alasdair hoped it would be a damn sight more than Watson usually managed.

"Just that Pierce had ordered a suit about a month ago and a very nice one, at that. Young Mr. Waite showed me it."

"So he hadn't been back to pick it up?"

"Well, clearly, Sherlock." Toby rolled his eyes. "Don't state the bleeding obvious." The waiter arrived with the chicken chasseur, luckily not in time to hear the "bleeding." "Still, that's another thing to suggest he left in a hurry and had more important things on his mind than new suits."

"I think all the evidence points that way. Now, what would make a man go off in what seems to be just the clothes he was standing up in? Fear?" Alasdair eyed his chicken with relish; he hadn't realised how hungry he'd grown. No wonder

Holmes was always depicted as being skinny if investigating burned off so much food.

"Fear. Hm." Toby took a mouthful of chicken and chewed it thoughtfully. "Fear for his life—that's possible. Fear for his reputation? Less so, I think, if his string of affairs is so well-known among his friends."

Alasdair lowered his voice. "Do you think he was being blackmailed about another matter, one we've yet to turn up? We're not the only people with something to hide."

"The old, 'All is known. Fly!' trick? He got the message and he flew?" Toby shrugged. "It doesn't really accord with what his landlady said—you'd have taken a suitcase with you if you were escaping abroad, surely? So what else could trigger such a sudden upping of sticks? How about if he had been made a once in a lifetime offer and had no time to turn back to put his hand on the plough, as it were."

"That's a point." Alasdair stabbed the air with his fork. "Perhaps we're looking at this the wrong way up, assuming it had to be the thought of some disaster looming that made the man vanish in a puff of smoke. Maybe some rich American said "Come and be my secretary, only make it snappy as the liner leaves from Southampton today." And off he trotted with just a new toothbrush from Timothy Whites and the sock full of money which he always carried in his briefcase."

"Sounds like the plot for one of those American comedies. I can see Jimmy Stewart in the lead," Toby said, pushing a piece of chicken through his sauce like a ship cleaving the ocean. "I suppose we need to find out about liners and the like. Of course, we're making an enormous assumption here."

"What's that?"

"The assumption that Pierce hasn't just been bumped on the head and tipped over a cliff or met some other gruesome end."

Alasdair couldn't be bothered with worrying about making assumptions. You had to go with your instinct. "Fisher says the police checked hospitals and things. And we know from what the landlady said that they did make some sort of serious enquiry. Seeing as they didn't come back to Mrs. Chivers with bad news, we can assume he's still alive and well." He tucked away the last bit of chicken and felt smug.

"Not so fast. Pierce's body would only have come to light if some hiker or Boy Scout or equally unfortunate individual had actually found it. If he's hidden away in dense undergrowth or been tipped down a disused mineshaft, then he might not come to light for ages. Whether Pierce chose to vanish or was made to disappear against his will, we have to keep looking. I think I'm going to follow this lead." Toby waved the calling card belonging to the man he'd met in the street.

"I thought you said this Paddick chap couldn't help you?"

"He couldn't, but I bet his sister might. I'll try the Dr. Watson charm on her and see what she has to say. It'll have to wait a few days, though." Toby said with a glint in his eye, "there's the opening night for A Scandal in Bohemia to negotiate tomorrow."

"Oh, joy. I'd almost forgotten. We'd better have pudding to keep our strength up." A necessary evil, opening nights. The Lord alone—or, more specifically, Landseer's publicity department—knew which poor unsuspecting starlets had been drafted in to hang off their arms, looking lovely in dresses which would have to go back to the couturier the next day. Alasdair suspected he and Toby put a damn sight more into their acting in the stalls and foyer than they did in the finished product up on the screen.

"Just smile, look aloof and, if the newspaper reporters are female, try your frown on them." Toby gestured for the waiter to come and tempt them with suet-laden delights.

They enjoyed the pudding but didn't bother with coffee or linger chatting. Opening nights meant getting plenty of beauty sleep the day before. Stepping out onto a pavement that had at last dried, they asked the doorman to call them two cabs, and waited.

"There's Mr. Adam's Apple." Toby pointed across the street to where Johnny's new secretary was standing.

"Looks like he's waiting for someone."

"If it's one of Johnny's showgirls and he's thinking of taking her to Langan's, I hope he's booked a table. Very embarrassing on a date, to be told there's no room at the inn. Especially when it's obvious there is." The first cab arrived and Toby piled into it, leaving Alasdair, before his own taxi pulled up, to wonder what Hampson was doing here and why he was looking quite so surreptitious. Had they been making another huge assumption—that the clue to Pierce's disappearance had to lie outside the Old George? Was there a possibility that Hampson could have had something to do with his predecessor's disappearance?

Alasdair shook himself, trying to shake any illogicality away. Could anyone be so desperate for a job that they'd commit murder?

***

The next day, any further investigation had to take a back seat to studio business. A BBC Home Service radio team was visiting Landseer Studios and Toby had to be on hand for them to interview him. Landseer paid him and they called the tune.

He and Alasdair always made a point of meeting up, though, prior to an opening night, to bolster each other's nerves against the ordeal to come. So Toby had arranged for his valet to drop him off at Alasdair's house half an hour before the official studio cars were due to come to whisk them away. Such customs had to be observed, or who knew what sort of bad luck would follow?

"I'll be looking at tomorrow's reviews with particular interest." Toby picked a piece of fluff, one that matched Alasdair's waistcoat, from his own stiffly starched shirt. They'd just managed a furtive, highly pleasurable snog.

"You never read the reviews at all. Why make an exception now?" Alasdair eyed his lover from top to tail; Toby was stunning in evening dress, the tightness of his waistband accentuating naturally wonderful posture. He wished they didn't have to go to any first night and could just go to the grand opening of the drapes on his four-poster bed, instead.

"I won't be reading my reviews, silly bugger. What I want to know is what the purists are going to make of it." Toby picked up his copy of The Adventures of Sherlock Holmes. "And will Sir Arthur Conan Doyle be turning in his grave afterwards?"

"I don't see why. Last time, that Holmes expert seemed to think we'd given one of the best portrayals of the pair he'd had the pleasure to see or hear." Alasdair couldn't help beaming with pride, especially as it had been Toby's Watson which had come in for special praise. Even the most conservative of fans couldn't find fault with his interpretation.

"But he's not seen the script for this latest one, has he? This time Fiona's not Mary Morstan—she's Irene Adler and she doesn't keep her affections just for the King of Bohemia or Godfrey Norton." Toby poked his lover's chest. "It may only be a very short and terribly tame romantic scene in the general Hamilton-Marsden scheme of things, but the Conan Doyle fans are going to be baying for blood at the kiss."

"But she's *the woman*. That kiss could almost be counted as canon." Alasdair didn't sound convinced or in the least convincing, not even to himself. Anyway, Holmes has girlfriends in the books. Doesn't he get engaged at some point?"

Toby snorted contemptuously. "That would hardly count. It was in the cause of investigation and meant nothing more than patting a horse would have done if Holmes had been playing a cabby. I might have been more convinced if Fiona—Irene—had still been in her trousers for your romantic scene."

"Like when she pretends to be a boy?" Alasdair had a feeling about where the conversation was going.

"I must say you looked convincingly put out when you realised who'd duped us. Prematurely, if you go strictly by the chronology of the books, but..."

"And your point was? Your chauffeured car is going to be here in five minutes." Alasdair tapped his watch.

"Don't use that gesture. I remember it from The Roaming Heart and, while it was dramatic onscreen, it butters no parsnips with me." Toby grinned, grabbing his lover's wrist and stroking it. "That's a nicer gesture. Deposit down on payment to come, once all tonight's shenanigans are over. Anyway, the point I was making was that Sherlock Holmes might have been romantically interested if he thought he really did have a young man in his arms, rather than a King's mistress."

"I suspect you're right but think of what the purists would have made of that, let alone the Lord Chancellor. We'd be hanged at dawn." Alasdair reluctantly let go of his friend's hand—he could hear the car pulling up outside.

"On with the motley." Toby risked a small kiss to Alasdair's cheek. "I suppose this isn't a bad life, even if so much of it is behind drawn curtains and locked doors. Don't forget I love you."

"And I love you, too. You alone."

Toby made his way to the front door; the chauffeur was one of Landseer's men, employed for his discretion and safer to use than a taxi driver who might wonder why Toby Bowe often had to be picked up from his co-star's house or vice versa.

Alasdair watched his lover go, twitching back the curtains to get a glimpse of Toby looking gorgeous as he slid elegantly into the Bentley. It seemed silly—irrational—to be talking such a lot of soppy nonsense almost every time they met, but you never knew what might happen. The war had taught them that; you couldn't assume that you'd meet your lover again any time you were parted.

Maybe some glorious day they'd be able to travel together to an opening night or another equally swanky 'do'—travel together to anything other than a rugby international or with a 'chaperone' of sorts in tow. Or maybe things would never get better and they'd be wearing masks all their lives, always playing a part for the public as they played a part on the screen.

Chapter Four

The next morning dawned grey, not that Alasdair saw much of it. They'd waited around for the first papers to come off the presses. Then he'd pleaded a headache and returned home—alone. After an opening night, there was always the risk of fans keeping a beady eye on proceedings or lurking around the streets, trying to spy where they lived. So Alasdair slept late, waiting until morning had almost slid into afternoon before being driven to his lover's house, where Toby's valet North settled him at the dining table over a late breakfast and piles of newspapers.

"Seen the reviews?" Toby bounded through the dining room door like a great puppy, eyes shining and—if he'd had a tail—tail a-wagging. All the analogies with Voyce the slobbery dog seemed justified.

"Some of the early ones, last night." Alasdair took a swig of strong tea, hoping it might speed the process of getting his brain awake.

"Well, they're not lining up outside to lynch us. Yet," Toby added, helping himself to a slice of toast and purloining a nice crispy piece of bacon off his friend's plate.

"Hey, I was keeping that rasher. It's the best bit." Alasdair swatted at Toby's hand but was too slow to catch it.

"Then you won't mind sharing it with me, will you, oh love of my life?" Toby broke the rasher in half and gave the nicer part to Alasdair, evidently extremely pleased to have purloined any at all. "I've not eaten yet. Been out like a light until about half an hour ago."

"Did you stay long after I went?" Alasdair poured his lover a cup of tea, hot and strong just as Toby liked it.

"No. There was nothing really to keep me after you'd gone, but I thought it would have looked a bit obvious, following hard on your heels, even if we weren't, for once, going in the same direction." Toby sipped his cup of tea distractedly; something was troubling him, for the stream of prattle to become sluggish. "I stayed about another half an hour. Saw Fiona to her cab. Thought that was a nice touch."

"And?"

"And what?"

"And what's bothering you? There's something you're not telling me." Alasdair waited; patience usually worked where badgering rarely did.

"Not sure it's anything at all, really. I just had the feeling I was under observation while I was bundling Fiona into the car and avoiding her kissing me." Toby frowned. "Like when you're reading and you know somebody's looking over your shoulder. Still, at least the reviews look good." He added a couple of newspapers to the number already spread over the table. "You've not lost the old magic."

"Neither have you. 'The Watson of his generation,' one of these said." Alasdair scrabbled to find the article among the pile of newsprint.

"That would have been *The Times*." Toby produced it from his own collection. "Not sure how happy Fiona will be, though." He pursed his lips. "Hardly a definitive Irene Adler was one of the kinder descriptions. Poor girl's not going to find a lot here to paste into her scrapbook."

"Maybe the gilt's worn off a bit?" Alasdair ate the last of his toast before his lover could steal that, too. "She's hardly a great actress and it's starting to show. Suffering nobly and falling in love with the hero she can get away with, and her looks have made up for any deficiencies so far. She suffers beautifully."

"You're right, of course." Toby poured himself another cup of tea. "Maybe it's just as well, given all the talk from Landseer about doing *Hamlet* after *The Hound*, with Fiona as Ophelia. These," he indicated the papers, "should put the tin lid on that mad idea."

"Oh, yes." Alasdair smiled. "We should be extremely grateful for small mercies."

"Maybe we should make a case for continuing to work with Fiona. She's just ever so slightly..." Toby cast about for the right word, one not too insulting. "...dim. We could end up with some other girl, one who takes a sight too much interest in the private lives of her co-stars."

Alasdair shivered, just a touch overdramatically. "I can't even bear to think about it. You know, there have been plenty of times I've hoped Fiona would go off and marry herself a foreign prince or something, but hearing you put it like that, I quite like the way our bread's buttered. Safe."

"Safe as it might be, given the circumstances," Toby sighed. "Let's just hope she doesn't take umbrage with these."

Alasdair put aside the papers. "What did you make of that man from *Reveille*?"

"The one with the face like a weasel? I didn't make anything of him. Mind you, he seemed a bit disappointed you'd gone. He'd got a picture of all three of us together, but he said he wanted the pair of us to pose for his photographer. Holmes and Watson." Toby stopped, dubious. "Lucky escape, I think."

"Maybe it was just as well I'd taken an early leave. I'm never happy when anyone other than the Landseer photographers takes pictures of just you and me.

Interpretation is everything. Look at those photographs of Edward and Mrs. Simpson on the yacht." Alasdair shivered. "Did he say anything, this reporter?"

"He didn't say anything peculiar, although there was a definite insinuation in his voice when he spoke about how we gelled together on screen."

Alasdair ran his hand over his heavily insured eyebrow, fingering it into perfect shape. "I hope that's all he meant. Our working relationship."

"Please God." Toby sighed. "I've always dreaded anyone wondering why none of our arm-decorating ladies have ever become arm-decorating brides. Am I being paranoid about it? His questions, and having this feeling at times I'm being watched?"

"Perhaps it wouldn't hurt for us to have a period of being more careful."

"More careful? How could we be, without giving up seeing each other at all?" Toby swept the papers from the table in frustration. "I'm sick of having to hide."

"We have no choice." Alasdair reached across, taking his friend's hand to caress it. "We'll have to explore all the nuances of our public performances as well as those on screen. Subtlety."

Toby smiled. "If there's a quality you possess in spades, it's subtlety."

Alasdair couldn't help laughing. "My agent always said it held me back in my stage career. 'Alasdair, my boy, the fine nuances of expression or posture are largely lost on the back row of the dress circle. Besides, they'll never see that eyebrow of yours twitch at that distance. In films, subtle gestures come into their own. That's where we'll pitch you, laddie.' I guess he was right."

Toby tried to wrest another cup of tea from the pot, spirits—at least temporarily—lifted. The knock on the door from his valet was so subtle that Toby's hand didn't even shake the pot. "Yes, North? We're quite interruptible." That wasn't always the case; the 'knock and wait' procedure had spared many blushes on both sides.

North shimmered into the room. "I found this on the mat. Looks like it was hand-delivered." He handed Toby an envelope—good, pre-war quality—marked *Mr. T. Bowe* in an elegant flowing script.

"You didn't see who left this?" Toby turned it over in his hands, obviously reluctant to open the thing just yet.

"I'm afraid not, sir. I did take a look up and down the street, but the culprit seemed long gone." North eyed the table. "Would you like more tea?"

"Coffee, I think. Does that suit you, Alasdair?" There was an almost artificial lightness in Toby's voice.

The temperature in the room seemed to have fallen five degrees. "Yes. Thank you, North, your ministrations have brought me back to life this morning." Culprit—such an odd choice of word.

Toby picked up a spare table knife and slid it along the back of the envelope. "I bet it's a request for an autographed picture. I only hope they've put in a stamped addressed envelope—I can't subsidise all of my fans." He didn't sound as if he believed it for a moment, and still he didn't take the letter out.

"Are you hiding something from me?" Alasdair had an awful, sick, leaden feeling in his gut that he knew exactly what might lie within its lines.

"I've had one of these before." Toby at last drew the letter from its paper prison.

"Hate mail?" No. "Blackmail?"

"Not that, either. At least, I don't think so." Toby wrinkled his nose in thought. "Something much odder." Odder but no less disturbing, given the pallor of Toby's face. "Read it for yourself." He passed the letter across the table, hand shaking.

Dr. Watson? I don't think so. Give it up now, before it's too late. Not what Alasdair had expected, by any means. Certainly not the usual, "If you don't want all the world to know about your dirty little habits, then leave fifty pounds in used notes in an envelope in the gent's toilets at King's Cross Station". He'd known people to get those. And to pay up, too.

"What did the previous letter say?" Alasdair struggled to make sense of what was going on.

"You can read that, alongside it." Toby left the table and went over to the sideboard, rummaging in a drawer. "I was going to chuck the thing but...well, it almost amused me."

Conan Doyle would turn in his grave. Sherlock and the Doctor? No, no, no.

"See, the handwriting's identical and it's on exactly the same sort of good quality paper." Toby frowned. "Hand delivered, like today's offering was."

"It's the same signature, too, if you can call this a signature," Alasdair added, running his finger along the last line. *An admirer of the real Holmes and Watson*.

"I just thought it was sent by a nutcase, at first. I've known people have letters from rabid fans of other actors complaining that their favourite didn't get the role they should have and ridiculing the performance of the man who got the part. But after last night and that awful unsettling feeling that we're being watched, I'm beginning to wonder if there's more to it." Toby sighed.

North arrived with the coffee, so promptly that he must have had it almost ready the first time he'd come in. Toby thanked his valet and politely dismissed him back to the kitchen, insisting they could look after themselves. He poured out two cups and ran his fingers through his hair. "Please tell me it's nothing more than a disgruntled John Gielgud fan who wants to see him as Watson."

"I sincerely hope they'd never thrust that casting on me. I mean, he's a good actor but he's not my Watson, is he?" Alasdair played the dialogue lightly; Toby was clearly getting upset over this.

"Be serious."

"If you want me to be serious, then I can't tell you what you want to hear. If it's about our roles, then why didn't I get one of these? Or Fiona?" Alasdair sipped his coffee without his usual appreciation of the fine brew North produced. His mind and senses were all occupied elsewhere.

"Maybe he or she—the writer—finds Fiona's performance acceptable. Or maybe they don't have either of your addresses." Toby shrugged. "You never know. Fiona could well have had some of these and has been too upset or embarrassed to tell anyone."

Alasdair couldn't help smiling. "You're turning into a proper little detective, aren't you?" He reached across and stroked Toby's hand. "A second mystery to get our brains around. We should give it some serious consideration."

"What do you think I've been doing since the first one came?" Toby snorted, although he returned the caress with more affection than his sharp words suggested. "I think the fact that I'm the only one to have received one of these kind little notes probably rules out any connection with the films."

"When did you get the previous letter?"

"Two days ago." Toby returned the caress. "Why?"

"I had a thought, one that could have gone out the window if you'd said it came last week. If it's barking up the wrong tree to link these letters with our roles on screen, I wondered if they might be related to Robin Pierce's disappearance, instead."

"Now, that's good thinking. The dates would certainly work." Toby produced the puppy dog smile that broke a million hearts up on the silver screen. "Now, why would someone want us to give up investigating?"

Alasdair put his brains into action. "Let's say person or persons unknown have done away with Pierce, for profit yet to be established."

"There are an awful lot of unknowns in this. Sherlock wouldn't approve, let alone Conan Doyle."

"Oh, hush." Alasdair slapped his friend's arm. "Look at it the other way, then. If someone's trying to put us off, then that proves they need to divert attention."

"I'm not sure the logic's completely sound, although it feels a bit better." Toby took a teaspoon and started to doodle on the tablecloth with it, marking out his thoughts as he spoke. "Who knows we're involved? Apart from Johnny."

"The people we interviewed that first day. And Hampson." Alasdair rapped the table. "Of course. That would explain why he was outside Langan's—he was keeping a watch on us."

"Maybe. There's definitely something odd about him—I can feel it in my waterworks." Toby laid down the spoon with an emphatic clatter. "Right. These letters become part of our investigation. There's no point in taking them to the police as there's not actually been a threat made. We have to handle this ourselves."

"Well, let's take one thing at a time, my dear Doctor." Alasdair got up, rounding the table and taking his friend's face in his hands, all the better to plant a huge kiss on his lips. "I wonder if Sherlock ever got to do that. Off screen."

"You mean off-book." Toby returned the kiss, with interest. "Hmmm. Very nice," he purred. "I could dally here with you all day, but it won't get Johnny's mystery solved."

"Is that all you can think of?" Alasdair went into La Marsden mode, when she'd played a wronged and slightly shrewish wife. "Playing second fiddle to a missing person case. Has it come to this?" He fell back onto a chair, dramatically if a little over-elegantly.

"If you're not careful, the wind will change and you'll be left looking like Fiona for the rest of your life." Toby leaned down, planted another smacking kiss on his lover's lips. "I'm going to go and play at sleuths." He grabbed Alasdair's hands and pulled him up. "Off to see James Paddick's sister, I think, although we should drop into the theatre, first, and let Johnny know what we've discovered."

"Must we? Really? Back to *The Case of the Flirtatious Theatre Owner*?"

"Yes, we must, if only because it's good manners. Get your jacket on." Toby slapped his friend's backside and pushed him towards the door, grabbing a last swig of coffee en route.

***

"So they set the hound of the Baskervilles on you, Mr. Holmes?" Johnny had listened to his friends' stories with evident appreciation. He'd proved surprisingly astute, asking questions at all the right places and about all the right things. "At least it doesn't seem as deadly as Conan Doyle's beast."

"I've never seen such a slobbering brute. I'm not sure it would take a man's throat out, but a victim might drown in its dribble." Alasdair wouldn't have gone so far as to put money on it, but Johnny seemed to give Toby a sideways glance at the mention of slobbering, as if he'd made the same mental connection between the man and over-affectionate dogs. Alasdair's unease had started when Toby had walked through the door of Johnny's office without so much as a '*by your leave*,' as if he owned the place.

"Well, you've got further than I could have hoped." Johnny beamed briefly at Alasdair, then turned the full force of his smile on Toby. "See, I knew you had it in you."

"It's been quite fun, really." Toby suddenly seemed inhibited. He smiled nervously at Alasdair, as if imploring him to wrestle away the conversation and have that bright gaze taken away from him. "Hasn't it, Alasdair?"

"I suppose it's been better than I expected." Alasdair didn't want to admit any such thing to Johnny, even if he was having a great time, but he was putty under the power of such a beseeching look. "We want to see this through to finding a solution."

"Quite right, too." Johnny was interrupted by a knock on the door. "Sorry about this. Yes, come in." Hampson's scrawny face appeared around the door, his Adam's apple bobbing with excitement.

"Excuse me." The secretary nodded both his head and his Adam's apple towards the visitors. "Mr. Fisher, there's a chap from *Tit-Bits* here—he wants to do an article about your new play. What shall I tell him?"

"Say I'll be available in ten minutes and delighted to oblige. Thank you." Johnny waited until the door had closed before sighing. “Robin Pierce wouldn’t have even needed to ask.”

“You said that Hampson came to you from an agency?” Toby fiddled with his tie-pin, a habit which came into play when he was thinking things through. When the tie-pin was wobbling, the grey cells were in action.

“Yes. One I’ve used before to find staff. Why?” Johnny leaned forwards, evidently perplexed. Alasdair hid a grin; wasn’t the man smart enough to have thought of the possible connection?

“We did wonder if he’d been so desperate for a job that he’d found a novel way of engineering himself one.” Toby reached across the desk and punched Johnny’s arm, slightly more vigorously than playfully. “It’s not so daft a theory as you seem to think. You say you’ve used the agency before—was it recommended to you?”

“Come to think of it, no. I stumbled across it one day while I was just wandering around trying to fill some vacancies.”

Alasdair refrained from asking, “How did you know where to go wandering?” Johnny probably knew all about where to go wandering in London in search of all sorts of things, most of them unmentionable in polite company.

“Anyway, the agency’s respectable.” Johnny tipped his head towards the office door. “And he seems a cut above the average temporary clerk.”

“It’s possible he’s been following us.” Alasdair leapt to the defence of Toby’s theory. “He was lurking about outside Langan’s when we were at dinner, that day we were here and got our commission. We have to explore whether there’s a connection.”

“I suppose it’s possible, but it seems an awfully long shot. How would he have known I’d have approached his agency to find Pierce's replacement and that they'd have assigned him the place?" Johnny looked defiantly at Alasdair, even though it had been Toby's suggestion.

"He might have planned to turn up here." Alasdair waved his hands at the office door. "You know, ostensibly on the off-chance that there might be a vacancy. Lo and behold, he finds you have one. Being offered it legitimately would just have been a bonus and taken away some of the leg work."

"I hope you're not just clutching at straws." Johnny said, shrugging.

Alasdair stopped himself replying, afraid that he'd turn the air blue if he gave immediate vent to his feelings.

Luckily, Toby stepped in. "That's hardly being fair, you great noodle. We're just exploring all the avenues."

"I'm sorry." Johnny addressed his apologies mainly to Toby, Alasdair only getting a sixteenth of a second's worth of a glance.

"I think we should get on with the exploring, then." Alasdair rose, deliberately not extending his hand for Johnny to shake, nor making any other effort at good manners. "Great noodle" was one of Toby's pet names for him and it didn't seem right to be spreading it about, applying it to all and sundry. Especially someone so all and sundry as Johnny Fisher.

He almost dragged Toby from the office.

"Okay, Sherlock. I guess there's not a moment to lose," Toby said, grinning at Hampson, who immediately leapt up, reaching for the items on the coat stand.

"Your hat and boots?" The secretary smiled disingenuously as he presented them with the former if not the latter.

"Not quite. The Hound isn't our quarry today." Alasdair slipped into his overcoat, nodded briefly to what he assumed was the man from *Tit-Bits*, and then opened the door for them to make their escape.

Halfway down the stairs, Toby suddenly stopped, almost in mid-stride, nearly making the pair of them go arse over tip. "Hold on a minute. I may be getting even more paranoid, but I could swear the man in the office is the same one as last night, the one who wanted the picture. The one who said he was representing *Reveille*."

"Maybe he's not with a particular paper." Alasdair narrowed his eyes. "Some of these chaps do syndicated stuff that pops up everywhere."

"Yes, but then they usually don't align themselves with a particular rag." Toby looked up the stairs again, as if trying to penetrate through the wall and see what was going on. "What if he isn't with either paper?"

"If he isn't, what the hell is he up to?" The penny dropped. "You're thinking he's something to do with those letters?"

"I don't know what I'm thinking, apart from the fact that there's something wrong and I can't put my finger on it." Toby rubbed his forehead. "I feel there's definitely something off-kilter—nebulous, maybe, but real enough. Does that sound daft?"

"Actually, it doesn't." Alasdair cuffed his lover's arm. "Look, you go off and see Paddick. I'm going back to the office and see what I can find out. If we're going to help Johnny Fisher, then he can stump up some help in return."

Chapter Five

Toby alighted at West Brompton tube station and headed east, the road layout he'd studied in the A to Z laid out in his brain like an image off the silver screen. He'd always had an excellent visual memory, much to Alasdair's annoyance as he usually struggled with maps. Toby could navigate the shoals and channels of London like an experienced pilot rounding the Goodwin Sands. The address on James Paddick's card had brought him to the depths of west London; it made an immediate favourable impression.

The Paddicks' house was the sort of traditional four storey Georgian residence that used to occupy whole swathes of London, but that was before the blitz had levelled a number of them and changing social patterns had seen more of these properties end up split into flats. This house—by the lack of the telltale plethora of doorbells and the single house number on the card—appeared to have survived intact one way or the other and was a possible indication that, in a time of post-war austerity, the Paddick finances were still healthy.

The maid who answered the door did a theatrical double take when she saw who was standing on her step; before she had time to re-gather her befuddled thoughts, Toby raised his hat, gave his name and asked to see James Paddick. He was shown in and asked to wait, or at least that's what he thought he was asked, the girl's voice having become so weak and timid that she might have said anything. He hoped he hadn't inadvertently agreed to some sordid proposition.

"Mr. Bowe!" James Paddick came into the hall and shook his visitor's hand. He looked a lot more at ease on home turf than the nervous figure who'd been standing outside Pierce's lodgings "I thought it was you when we first met, but I couldn't be sure. Have you run the fox to ground?"

"I'm afraid not. We're—Mr. Fisher and I—fairly certain he's just upped sticks. Even his best friend has no idea where he's got to." Toby inwardly kicked himself for having said *we*, even though he'd made a smart recovery. He was here to ask questions on behalf of his imaginary female relative and didn't want Paddick to turn the tables and find out what he was really up to. "I called at Waites, where they told me Pierce had ordered a rather nice suit but hasn't collected the thing. It suggests he's either cleared off, leaving most of his worldly goods behind him, or he's been bumped off and hidden away by some enterprising murderer and has no longer need of earthly goods and chattels. I really don't think there's any point your hanging around his digs trying to find him there."

"Is that all you came to tell me?" James seemed disappointed.

"Actually, I came to ask an enormous favour. Would you let me talk to your sister? I know it's a terrible imposition, but I think she'd be able to help me make a bit more sense of the whole affair. She might even mention something that she'd be reluctant to tell you." Toby tried to appear at his most fraternal and trustworthy, the friend of the hero.

"Are you implying my sister keeps secrets from me?" Paddick bridled.

"Not at all. But I have a sister myself and she can be a perfect ass at times. There are all sorts of things she doesn't mention for one reason or another that turn out to be crucial. Little facts which mean nothing to the feminine mind but are of immense value when sifted by the masculine powers of logic." Toby smiled, praying that Augusta would forgive him for making light of her deductive powers. Having got a double first in Physical Sciences at Cambridge, she was by far the cleverest member of the entire Bowe family.

The ploy seemed to work, judging by the change of expression on James's face. "That's right, you know! Beats me what goes on in their brains half the time. Why Charlotte should have seen fit to take up with that little toe-rag Pierce in the first place..." He broke off, shaking his head. "Come on, she's in the drawing room."

Charlotte Paddick was not at all what Toby anticipated. He'd expected an easily-led, timid little wallflower, but Charlotte was a big, sporty-looking girl—the type who would be captain of the lacrosse or hockey team. Definitely not the sort who seemed like she'd end up getting pregnant by some gadabout.

"Charlotte," her brother introduced his sister with enormous care, as if she were some aged invalid who needed constant nursing, "this is Mr. Bowe. The actor. Only he's not here to act, he's doing some investigation on behalf of a cousin—was it a cousin or was it your sister?—and wonders if you would be up to helping him?"

"If I can." Charlotte indicated a chair for Toby to plonk himself in. "Could you rustle up some tea for us, James? I'm absolutely parched."

Paddick nodded, plainly registering the request for what it was—a dismissal, and none too subtle a one—and sauntered off.

"Is this by any chance about Robin?" Charlotte didn't waste any time in getting to the point, something for which Toby was enormously grateful. "If there's a woman involved, I guess it has to be."

"It is, indeed. I'd like to start by thanking you for helping me out, and also by coming clean." Toby grinned. "I do have a female cousin, but, as far as I know, she's never had anything to do with Robin Pierce. I'm afraid I had to invent her involvement in the case."

"For James, of course." Charlotte smiled, nodding her understanding. "He's a good sort, but really not very bright. We won't complicate things for him, although I hope you'd be candid with me."

"I will, especially as I'd like to ask you some intimate questions. I'm simply doing this on behalf of a good friend who's extremely worried. Mr. Pierce was his secretary—and a damned good one—and he wants to make sure the man's not in any sort of trouble." Toby tried to spread his big speech out and not gabble it like some nervous starlet. "The police could only help up to a point, so he's called in some favours from his friends."

"Is that Johnny Fisher? Robin always spoke well of him." Charlotte brightened, as any red-blooded girl might have at the thought of Johnny.

"Miss Paddick, have you any idea at all what's happened to Robin? Or where he might have gone? I promise I won't tell your brother a thing about it if you wish to speak in absolute confidence. Don't want any bloodied noses on my conscience." Toby changed expressions to the earnest and appealing persona, the one he'd used when playing Orlando in *As You Like It*.

"If I could, I would. I might not tell James if I knew where the swine was lying low, but I'd be happy for you to know. Except there's nothing to say." Charlotte didn't look angry or even rueful, which was surprising in itself, given what was supposed to have happened to her. "If I knew where he'd hidden himself away, I'd be over there like a shot. It isn't just

James who wants to have a word with him. Or bloody his nose."

"Your brother did sort of allude to what might have happened between you and Robin…" Toby felt at a loss for words, but he needn't have even bothered to feel self-conscious. Nothing seemed to embarrass Charlotte.

She laughed heartily, in the style Toby's mother would have called "jolly hockey sticks." "My poor silly ass of a brother." The arrival of said brother, needlessly accompanying the maid who bore the teapot, interrupted Charlotte's flow. Only when he'd been got rid of, less subtly this time than before, could she continue. "James is an idiot of the first water. I bet he told you I got pregnant and then lost the baby. Well, didn't he?"

"Um, as a matter of fact…" Toby felt heat running up his face and hoped he didn't look too much like a beetroot.

"I could brain him at times. He's built up this whole idea of me getting into trouble and Robin being the bounder responsible. It's all complete rubbish, of course." Charlotte poured the tea in the same no-nonsense way she appeared to apply to everything. Maybe Robin Pierce had taken up his metaphorical hockey stick and run away from being organised and umpired.

"What's the truth of the matter, then? I'm extremely confused about everything." Toby gave up on looking appealing; maybe if he'd been able to imitate a hockey stick or whatever vile implement of torture they used in lacrosse, he'd have more allure.

"I thought I might have been expecting, but I wasn't. It was just that I'd been off-colour and the normal way of things got upset." Charlotte smiled heartily again, clearly pretending not to notice that her guest remained scarlet at her casual allusions to the female plumbing system. “He thinks I fabricated that part of the story to cover potential disgrace, but I had nothing to hide. I’ll admit I got a bit mopey over Robin, more than I should have done. I knew he had a bit of a reputation, right from the start, although when I heard about all the other women he was supposed to be still knocking about with, I got rather silly and ...” She stopped, for once unsure of herself.

“And what?” Was there to be the time-old admission of, “I said I’d like to see him dead”?

“Threatened to throw myself off Westminster Bridge. It was a stupid thing to do, very soppy and melodramatic, and after a few days I snapped out of my mood.” Charlotte attacked a piece of cake with her fork; whether she thought it was a hockey ball or Robin Pierce’s backside, who could tell? “But poor old James took it all far too seriously. And the more I tried to laugh it off, the more he thought the lady protested too much, as it were.”

“So he’s been hanging around Robin’s digs every day hoping to catch the blighter and thrash him?”

“Has he?” Charlotte’s eyes opened wide. “I didn’t know that. James told me he goes to the British Museum after work to look at the cartouches. He’ll be the one getting the thrashing at this rate.” She flung her fork down, as if it were her brother she were slinging about. Toby was beginning to have some sympathy with Robin Pierce.

“Mr. Bowe, let me put you entirely straight about this mess. I was an idiot to fall so heavily for Robin. I knew he’d had a string of sweethearts before, because he made no secret of it. And I knew he could never love me—he told me on our very first date that he was just looking for a bit of fun. No commitments. It *was* fun for a while, I felt very modern.”

She snorted at her own stupidity. "But, like a silly schoolgirl, I decided I wanted to be committed to him. I even managed to persuade myself that if I threw myself into loving him, he'd change and there'd only be me for the rest of his life. Then I found out he had at least two other women on the go at the same time as having a fling with me."

"What did you do?" Toby remembered the fire in Charlotte's eyes when she'd slammed down the fork. Surely she hadn't been the one to do away with the obnoxious Robin Pierce?

"I confronted him about his behaviour. He just laughed and said if I wanted a serious relationship, then I was shopping at the wrong store. He said he'd only ever had one love, and it wasn't me or the two other tarts he was seeing. I thought about thumping him on the spot, but it's a bit awkward doing that in the street outside Selfridges. So I just came home and cried myself silly." Charlotte looked disdainful, as if it were another woman who'd got herself into such a pathetic situation. "And I haven't seen the swine since."

"Thank you." Toby realised there was little more to be said. It was the old, old story of a nice girl almost going to the bad over an absolute bounder. He'd better have a word with James before he left about laying off the whole Pierce business, or else the bloke might find himself with a hockey stick rammed up his backside. At least they were getting a clearer picture of Robin Pierce; maybe when they had that jigsaw completed, they'd pretty well have the solution.

***

Alasdair sat in the waiting room while the man from *Tit-Bits*—or *Reveille* or whatever it was—sweet-talked Johnny. If Hampson was surprised to see him back so soon, he hid it well, returning to his typing as soon as he'd buzzed the message through. With Toby's instinctive wariness buzzing in his brain, Alasdair was determined to make a little headway here, too. He sneaked a look at the type of paper Hampson had on his desk, but it didn't seem to match that of the mysterious letters.

"I believe we saw you outside Langan's, a couple of days back." Alasdair spoke in the sort of voice which would easily reach the back of the upper circle, making sure he couldn't be politely ignored.

Hampson looked up, with a belligerent expression that suggested he might reply with, "So what? It's a free country. Am I not allowed to stand where I want?" But he forced a smile and said, "We have our monthly meeting there. Nice establishment."

Alasdair had never heard Langan's hotel described with such an insipid word as 'nice,' nor was he aware that it hosted meetings; perhaps the war had made everyone reconsider their business practices? "Really? Yours must be an august institution to be allowed to meet on such hallowed ground."

"We have connections." The secretary's voice had slipped up a social rung or two. He sat looking smug.

"You sound like a league of master criminals." It should have sounded a stupid comparison, but Alasdair felt he'd delivered the spur of the moment line with aplomb.

"Not quite, although I'd like to think we all possess complex minds." The secretary looked even more self-satisfied; Alasdair added him to the list of people he'd like to thump, directly in line after Fisher.

"Complex minds?" Something in the line struck a chord in Alasdair's brain, something which also chimed with an expression the secretary had used earlier. What had that been?

"A complex mind—all great criminals have that. Didn't you know?"

Hampson's smug face only escaped having its nose bashed in by the opening of the internal office door and the emergence of the reporter, with Fisher in tow. Alasdair's belligerence had to find vent elsewhere. "Excuse me," he said, turning his most charming smile on, "did you say you were from Tit-Bits?"

"That's right." The man nodded.

"Then you must excuse me. Someone pointed you out at the opening night for *A Scandal in Bohemia* and I could have sworn they said you were from *Reveille* and were looking for a photo. Have you moved jobs in the last few days?" It was all spoken with a charming insouciance, but the barb struck home.

"I'm afraid you've been misled." The man then turned and smiled nervously at Johnny, "I suppose there are so many of us at that sort of a do it's easy to get mixed up."

"Mr. Chesney, I hope you haven't come here under false pretences." Johnny raised his hand to cut off the reporter's protest. "It happens, you know. I've even had someone pretending to be conducting interviews with bit part players—from the human-interest angle, of course—just so that they could get closer to their favourite chorus girls." Whether that was true or not, Alasdair couldn't tell—he'd forgotten what a good actor Johnny could be when he put his mind to it.

"You can check with my editor if you want." Chesney gestured towards Hampson, who produced a slip of paper and a pencil. "I'll write down the number. You'll see my story checks out, no matter what people say." He gave Alasdair a filthy look and left.

"What was that about?" Johnny tipped his head towards the door.

"I'll tell you in your office." Alasdair let himself get comfy on the big leather sofa and refused all offers of a drink, alcoholic or soft, before he spilled the beans. "Toby's been getting some odd letters." He explained what he knew about the strange communications, Toby's increasing feeling that they were under observation and whether it could all be linked to The Case of the Disappearing Lothario.

"If it's blackmail, they'll make their demands known sooner rather than later. But it doesn't sound spiteful enough for that." Johnny leaned back, sending smoke rings towards the ceiling. "I'm surprised you're entrusting me with this sort of confidence, though. I didn't think you either liked or trusted me."

Alasdair resisted the temptation to say, "I don't, on either count." Instead, he said, "We think you might be able to help us, as we're helping you. Knock for knock."

"I was worried you were going to say 'an eye for an eye.'" Johnny stubbed out his cigarette. "Right, what can I do?"

"Find out about Chesney, for a start. He was snooping around at the premiere—and he definitely wasn't representing *Tit-Bits* then—determined to get a picture of just me and Toby together. That's something we always avoid."

"And you think he's trying to get evidence to incriminate you?"

"Maybe. I wish we had more to go on, apart from Toby's feelings. He's not one to be skittish, so if he's got a nebulous sensation he's being watched, it's likely there's something at the bottom of it."

“I’ll get Hampson straight onto the case.” Johnny began to get up, but Alasdair motioned for him to sit again.

“I’d bypass him and ring yourself. And go through the operator—I wouldn’t be too sure that Chesney has actually given you the correct number for *Tit-bits*, rather than just that of a friend who’ll oblige by saying anything required.”

“I take the point about the telephone number, but Hampson could manage that for himself. Unless...” Johnny tipped his head towards the door and lowered his voice. “You really are suspicious of him—that wasn’t a joke?”

“It’s too important to joke about. His explanation for what he was doing hanging about outside Langan’s seemed thin.” No, not thin—odd. “Would you see what you can turn up?” Alasdair swallowed his pride. “If not for me, then for Toby, to put his mind at rest. Neither of us wants to see him unduly upset.”

“If you put it like that, how can I refuse? I’d do anything for Toby.”

Johnny’s nose was only saved from a collision with Alasdair’s fist by the timely arrival of Hampson, putting his head round the door after only the briefest of knocks. “This just came in the second post. It wasn’t marked ‘Confidential,’ so I opened it...” His words died away as he handed the letter over to his employer and then left the room.

“Well, well.” Johnny perused the letter, shook his head, read it again, and then passed it across to an increasingly impatient Alasdair. “Robin Pierce sends me his—highly belated—resignation. So he isn’t dead.”

“Are you sure he’s written this? It’s not some extremely adept forgery?” Alasdair held the paper to the light, as if the answer lay in the watermark. “At least I can say that the paper's not the same as the stuff that's been infecting Toby's letterbox."

"I've been looking at that writing for two years. As far as I'm concerned, it's unmistakable."

"Hm."

"There was a wealth of meaning in that 'Hm'. You used it in *The Roaming Heart* and it said more than six dialogue boards in a silent film."

"I was just thinking that, if it's genuine, the timing's interesting. There's no date on this," Alasdair held out the paper, "so has someone been hanging onto it? And if they have, what do they think they've gained?"

Johnny shrugged. "Time?"

"But that just begs more questions. Time for what? If you were trying to divert suspicion because you'd knocked Pierce on the head and hidden his body, finding the resignation letter in the process, you'd have sent it there and then. Pierce would have seemed to have left his job quite legitimately, if abruptly, and nobody would necessarily have gone looking for him." Alasdair was delighted with his chain of logic.

"I was right!" Johnny looked like he was about to give Alasdair a hug, then thought better of it. "Getting you two on this. I'd have never worked out half as much as you've done. I need to work out a better way of repaying you than just a box for the show."

Alasdair resisted saying, "All I want is for you to stop making eyes at my bloke." Instead, he smiled in a suitably dignified fashion and said, "In the interim, you can pay us back by running this Chesney to ground. While you do that, I'm off to investigate the contents of Hampson's waste paper bin."

"Waste paper bin?"

"Yes. I assume that's where he's put the envelope."

"The envelope?"

What fun to watch Johnny looking so mystified. "Of course. So I can see where and when that letter was posted. And compare the writing on that with Pierce's."

Chapter Six

Morgan gently rapped the door of Alasdair's drawing room and waited the requisite number of seconds before entering. Even though Toby wasn't there, the waiting after knocking was too ingrained a habit to break.

Morgan brought an offering of tea and little biscuits. Alasdair drank it sitting at the piano and tinkling a tune, eyes not on the keys but on the silver-framed photographs gracing the top of the instrument. He and Toby at a premiere. He and Toby laughing on holiday with the rest of the Hamiltons. He and Toby—and Fiona—in that first, fatal publicity still. Every day of filming *Wings of Love* had been both joy and torture. It had felt like being seventeen again and going through the agonising phases of a crush.

He'd thought he was long past that game, but he'd caught himself at it today, weighing and measuring Toby's interaction with Johnny, looking for little telltale signs of something or other. He picked up the photograph, tracing over the faces with his fingers. Maybe Toby had once had a crush on Johnny, even back at the time this picture had been taken—he'd come straight into the project from appearing in one of the man's drawing room comedies.

"What are you mooning about?" Toby strode into the room, as if desire and thought had conjured him up. Alasdair certainly hadn't heard the doorbell ring—maybe Morgan had been hovering in the hall, waiting for their guest. Or had Toby used the servants' entrance, as he was less likely to be seen coming in that way? Who knew whose eyes were watching the house, especially now?

"I was thinking about our first date. At the Savoy."

"Was that a date? Really? I thought it was just a few drinks to celebrate the end of filming." Toby leaned on the piano, admiring the photographs.

"I counted it as a date," Alasdair replied, as if that was definitive.

"Whatever it was, I remember it in vivid detail. You wore the most amazing coral striped shirt. Brought out the stunning colour of your eyes." Toby caressed his lover's face, but only in its photographic form. "We talked about those dreadful Ivor Novello auditions." He bent down, evidently aiming to give Alasdair a kiss, but the arrival of Morgan at the door to announce that supper was served—the man's timing was certainly unfortunate, at the moment—cut short the little love scene.

Morgan had laid the table in the dining room: plates with salad and fresh bread rolls, a bottle of hock already opened and two glasses half filled. They took their seats, Alasdair side on to his guest, and waited for the manservant to reappear bearing a small frying pan hot from the stove.

"Omelette." Toby smiled happily. "Those auditions—it gives me the collywobbles just to think of them. Ivor Novello told me he was trying to put together a musical version of *The Importance of Being Earnest*. Did anything ever come of it?"

"I don't think there ever was such a project. I suspect it was all a nifty ploy for him to get his hands on young men." Alasdair snorted and got stuck into his omelette. "Not that I think he fancied me. I failed miserably." He stopped suddenly, fork halfway en route to his mouth. "You never told me how you got on."

Toby smiled, looking up from his plate. "I failed as well, although on different grounds. Not that I minded, seeing as *Wings of Love* came along instead." Toby started to tuck in again, deliberately avoiding his lover's eye. "I've always suspected my not getting the part in that play was due to not succumbing when old Ivor made a pass at me."

Alasdair looked up sharply, almost dropping his fork. "You kept that quiet."

"Did I? Well, it's no great secret. He made a pass, I gave him the cold shoulder, consequently no Jack Worthing for Toby Bowe." Toby took a swig of hock, fortifying himself.

"What did he do to you? Was it a little off the cuff remark along the lines of spending a weekend in Brighton looking at the script?" There was a cold edge to Alasdair's voice.

"Nothing so subtle." Toby forced a smile, playing the scene light. "He—well, I believe the only appropriate term is 'goosed me.'"

"Like Johnny Fisher did?"

"So that's what this is all about. The perennial issue of how far Johnny got. Haven't we knocked that bloody nail on the head by now?" Toby looked down at the last piece of omelette as if wondering whether he had the heart to eat it. "I won't even grace that question with an answer. This is beneath you, Alasdair."

"I'm sorry."

"No, you're not." They were going to have it out now, one way or the other. "Will you just let this bloody thing rest? Johnny Fisher was nothing to me. Johnny Fisher is nothing to me. You are all the world to me. What more am I supposed to say?"

Alasdair fiddled with his cutlery. "I don't know."

"Do you think I'm lying?" Toby eyed the wine bottle and then the wall behind his lover's head, as if he was thinking of lobbing the thing. "Look me in the eye. That's better. Do you think I'm lying? Don't you trust me?"

"No. Yes." Alasdair sighed. "I don't think you're lying. I do trust you. I don't trust Johnny Fisher."

"I don't trust Johnny Fisher, either. But he was a good friend to me—and that's all it was, friendship—before I met you." Toby sighed. "I won't let that old camaraderie come between us. Tell you what, ring him up and tell him to shove this Pierce investigation lark up his arse."

"No, that's unreasonable." Alasdair took his friend's hand, gently squeezing it. "I'm being unreasonable. I won't mention it again."

"Bet you will. And I bet you'll think of it." Toby returned the caress. "Leave it be, please. It'll eat you up and it'll gnaw at our love like a ship's rat." He suddenly grinned. "Now there's classy dialogue for you. The Commodore should be saying it to La Marsden."

Alasdair laughed, not letting go of Toby's hand even when Morgan came in to get the plates and ensure that wine glasses were topped up before the arrival of some slivers of apple tart. "Do you remember any of the dialogue for *Wings of Love*?"

"Could I ever forget it? All that clever stuff about the question that, once asked, changes things forever. I used the same words to chat you up." He looked straight into Alasdair's eyes, just as he'd done before; and, just as before, he was clearly edging his way towards something momentous, but still taking care in case he'd misinterpreted everything. "I know that if I make this request, then we shall have turned a corner that can't be rounded again."

Alasdair sighed. "You spoke them very nicely. Better than I said them to Fiona in the film." Alasdair lifted Toby's hand to his lips and kissed it; he'd done that to Fiona, too, in a way that implied that if the cameras ran any longer, he'd be dragging her up to bed. "Then you asked me whether I'd rather kiss her or you."

"And you got so angry because your answer was 'You,' and you couldn't put it into action there and then." Toby grinned at the memory.

"I had to wait a whole three days to snog you. The longest of my life."

"How could I ever forget? You must have been desperate all that time. I certainly was. Remember Newton Stewart?"

How could Alasdair forget? They'd travelled up to the Bowe family hunting lodge, ostensibly to open it up and prepare for the hordes descending later the same week. May on the west coast of Scotland, as the sun beat down on a sea of almost Mediterranean blue; they'd lain out on the roof, roasting on blankets under the sun's rays, mother-naked and no shame between them.

They'd made love out there. A first time that had been mad, intemperate, from their very first kiss to bodily union in a matter of two minutes, or so it had seemed. Maybe it had been ten or fifteen. The second time had been slower, in a huge four-poster bed in the best guest bedroom; there'd been plenty of kisses—and sex—since then, all of it good.

"Are you really asking me the same question again now?" Alasdair asked, rousing himself from pleasant reminiscences to answer Toby. "About turning the corner?"

"No. I'm asking you to say good riddance to your groundless jealousy for Johnny Fisher, because I won't put up with it any longer." Toby might be smiling, but he was plainly in deadly earnest. "If you can't do that..." He shrugged.

"I promise." Alasdair swallowed hard and tried to sound convincing, even if it was only to persuade himself. This was clearly no idle threat. "I'm sorry. I don't mean to be so vexatious. And I take back the idea of telling Johnny to insert this case up his rectum, no matter how appealing the idea seems. I want to solve it, to metaphorically spit in his eye, prove I'm the better man. I'm your man."

"Hallelujah!" Toby threw up his arms as if he was at an old time revivalists' meeting. "At last you see sense. It's you and me against the rest of the world, and if we're divided, the shield wall will break and the bastards will sweep over us." Toby took a large mouthful of tart, chewed it with obvious relish, then attacked the next piece with his fork. "Now, if we're to get any further, we need to compare notes. Mother's reported back...or, rather, she hasn't, because there's nothing to report. Pierce doesn't appear to spark any of her early warning systems as far as gossip goes. Sherlock Holmes never seemed to have as many dead ends, did he?"

"I suspect he had loads of the bloody things but Watson didn't bother to report them." Alasdair snorted. "Nor all the cases he botched."

"You could be right. Anyway, I'll tell you Charlotte Paddick's revelations and you tell me where you got to with your witnesses."

"I didn't see get around to seeing any. I've been chasing another hare."

"A hare and not a wild goose?"

"The only connection with a goose is Johnny Fisher. No," Alasdair raised his hand, clearly afraid he'd overstepped the mark again. "I take that pun back. Let me explain." He guided Toby through the tale of his return to Johnny's office, presenting his deductions as neatly as Holmes might have. "And, of course, it turns out the man at *Tit-Bits* hadn't sent a reporter at all. I listened while Johnny rang him."

"I knew it. Did you ring anyone at Reveille?"

"Of course, and we drew a blank there, too. Nobody had heard of Chesney." Alasdair finished his tart, elegantly scooping the last morsels up.

"So not one of their usual syndicated contributors?" Toby looked worried. "I don't know whether to feel pleased at being vindicated or worried that my fears are proving accurate. Did you try the number Chesney gave?"

"Oh yes. I was allowed the privilege of that, as it was my idea. Got through to someone who said he was the entertainments editor, but I suspect he'd have said he was the Queen of Sheba if I'd asked him." Alasdair smoothed his uninsured eyebrow, thoughtfully. "I tried it out, ringing back later, from a telephone box. I asked if that was the Spencer Hotel and could I speak to the manager. He sounded a bit taken aback, but he soon confirmed I'd got the right number. It was impressive improvisation."

"And what about the envelope?" Toby's question was interrupted by the arrival of Morgan, who relocated them into the drawing room for coffee. Once they were settled, the detective talk resumed. "Did you winkle out all sorts of things you could rub Johnny's nose in the dirt with? I bet he didn't like having to admit that you're smarter than he is."

"Unfortunately, it told me very little, as the date part of the postmark was smudged and the envelope had been typed. It was posted in Palmers Green, though."

"I wish I'd brought that address book with me. We could have seen whether that links up with any of the entries."

"That can keep until tomorrow. If Pierce is in Palmers Green, he can wait there and if he was just passing through, taking a random stop off a bus, then he's long gone." Alasdair sipped his coffee contentedly. "You'll be pleased to know I made sure Hampson saw me poring over the envelope and looking like it contained clues of great significance."

"Good thinking. Did he react at all?"

"Unfortunately not. Although I'm sure he looked uncomfortable over the Chesney business. His Adam's apple was up and down like a tart's knickers."

"Like your pants when you're in the mood." Toby drained his coffee in one gulp, laying down the cup then drawing his hand along his friend's leg. "So where next with that business?"

"Onwards and upwards, of course. I think we're getting the hang of this. Johnny's going to ask around to see if anyone else has run up against Chesney and I've asked him to keep an eye on Hampson, too, just in case all of this links up into one great big tangled web."

"Thank you for swallowing your pride and taking such a step." The finger inched higher.

"It was in the interest of the case." Alasdair swallowed again, but this time in the service of keeping his composure. "If the resignation's genuine, then the 'threatening letters to put you off the scent' horse doesn't run."

"Unless it's Pierce himself who doesn't want us running him to ground. Charlotte Paddick seems the sort of girl to get a bit overbearing. Any man might have run for the hills screaming."

"At her bossiness?"

"Not quite." Toby shut his eyes to better rack his brains for the right word, as he'd done to great effect in *A Scandal in Bohemia* when Watson had been trying to pick his way through the problem. "Too hearty. I felt quite exhausted after less than half an hour with her."

"Do you really think it possible he's gone to ground just so she can't find him? It would explain the sudden disappearance, but not, I think, his failing to take a change of clothes."

"Excellent point." Toby's wandering fingers wandered some more, making it difficult for his friend to concentrate entirely on missing secretaries. "If there are girls wherever he's gone, he'll have taken a spare outfit to impress them. I suspect you'll sneer at me for jumping to conclusions, but there's a woman, or women, at the centre of this case. Didn't the man with the dog say something about a girl?"

"Millie Stamford? Trouble is she's dead, so that lead died with her. Unless he's repining on her grave, weeping." Alasdair shut his eyes, trying to have one or two more lucid thoughts before they both gave in to the inevitable and wended their way up the wooden hill. "Maybe I should go back and question McDermott again, especially now that we know that Pierce is alive. Or was alive when he wrote his resignation."

"You do that, and I'll see what the address book has to deliver. And do you think I should get Father onto Chesney's tail?" Toby added. "I don't like getting the old man involved in my private affairs."

"This has gone beyond private. It's a case of impersonation, so surely the police could be legitimately involved?"

"I'm not sure he's committed any crime yet." Toby shrugged. "I'll sleep on it and see what the morning brings. I usually think better then."

"A good night's sleep and a soft bed are the cure to many ills." Alasdair tapped his friend's knee. He favoured his companion with a meaningful look which managed to convey the need to skip the rest of the coffee, turn off the light, get up the stairs and forget about the wretched Robin Pierce and the equally dreadful Chesney until morning. All that acting experience had to come in useful off-screen as well as on.

"Doctor Bed's certainly calling me. I could sleep for weeks."

"Oh." Alasdair wondered if he'd misinterpreted the wandering hands.

"Oh, so you don't have sleep in mind, at least at the moment? Were you thinking we might do the crossword together?" Toby was leaning close now, body hard—literally—against Alasdair. It was plain that if he had crosswords on his mind, then other parts of his body possessed more active ideas.

"Do the crossword? If that's a new euphemism for sex, then yes." Alasdair's mind raced with smut. "Will you be the one inserting the answers or is it my turn?"

"You choose." Toby's cool cultured tones were hoarse, his breathing becoming a bit ragged. Black-Hearted Fitzroy the pirate had better not be quite so lifelike when he was attempting to seduce Lady Jennifer onscreen or the Lord Chancellor would whip his cutting scissors out and then have them all up in front of the beak. "Are you down or across or is there a totally new position on the cards?"

"Whatever you want. It's been far too long—days and days. It feels like months. I think I'm getting desperate." Alasdair snuggled tighter against his friend, as close as the settee—and the setting—would allow.

"I can tell. I think I'll have a bruise on my leg tomorrow, you're digging in so much."

"That won't be the only place that's bruised, if you play your cards right. At least none of them are likely to show up on screen." Alasdair got up, reaching out, pulling up Toby with him. “Come on, before we shock Morgan. He may be tolerant, but there’s a limit to what servants should be made to endure.”

***

The bed was large and inviting, a small fire in the grate keeping off the edge of a chilly evening and newly laundered sheets smelling faintly of lavender. The setting would add to the pleasure of lovemaking, although the act itself—the familiarity with each other’s bodies, the practised giving and taking of pleasure—was the important thing. They’d had sex in large beds in luxurious bedrooms, in small beds in country inns, and, on one notable occasion, in a long-abandoned but dry and spacious air-raid shelter. It had all been good.

Toby unbuttoned his shirt, easing it from his waistband. Often, they stripped each other, but this time, both recognised the urgency of the occasion—too much dallying or premature excitement and those crossword answers would come out in all the wrong places. They were both naked before they even risked a kiss, although it was worth waiting for—hot, passionate, desperate, just like the people who shared it. Since that first, reckless bout of enthusiastic sex, they’d usually taken things slowly, using all their knowledge—gleaned from each other and erstwhile lovers—to heighten the experience, to delay the moment of ecstasy until they were frantic beyond measure. This time they wouldn’t indulge; it would be a replay of that first crazy union.

“Come on, now.” Toby dragged Alasdair onto the bed, and on top of him. “Now.”

“I need to get ready…” Alasdair wasn’t sure he’d be allowed time to, not at the rate Toby was pulling him closer. “It’ll never work, otherwise.”

Toby let him go, urgency taking second place to practicality. “Don’t make me wait too long. Please.”

Alasdair didn’t need to see the desperate look in Toby’s eye; the rest of Toby’s body was speaking volumes.

“I’m going as fast as I can.” Alasdair rummaged in the drawer for the Vaseline. “Things are very delicate at the moment, and if I don’t take it carefully, I’m going to make a mess of our big love scene.” Found the bloody thing. “And I’m not sure I’m in any fit state for a quick-fire reshoot.”

“I wish you hadn’t said that. How can I face my next romantic encounter as Watson with a straight face when all the instructions will sound like double entendres?” Toby lay back, smiling. “The *Man with the Golden Frown*? You’re the *Man with the Smuttiest Mind in Christendom*. Oh.” A sharp intake of breath as the Man with the Smutty Mind made some smutty moves. “You keep doing that and it’ll be me making a mess of things. Literally.”

“I’ll do this instead, then.” Alasdair mounted the bed and then mounted his lover, slowly and expertly bringing them into union and then to rapture. Nothing mattered now—Johnny’s advances, Alasdair’s jealousy, threatening letters or disappearing secretaries—nothing except two people, deeply in love and showing it in one of the best ways they knew. Maybe they used words, a fervent “I love you” whispered into the air or spoken, muffled into a lover’s shoulder, but neither man needed to protest his love for the other. Afterwards they lay quietly, drifting in and out of satiated sleep. “I’m glad you chose me.” Alasdair snuggled his head on Toby’s shoulder, the most comfortable—and comforting—pillow he knew. “You could have had anyone.”

“Same applies to you. You didn’t have to cast your lot in with me, but you did.” Toby kissed his friend’s head. “Now, sleep. Or you’ll be good for nothing come morning.”

“I will. Goodnight, sweet prince.” Alasdair settled down, full of happy feelings which not even any lingering thoughts of Johnny Fisher could dispel.

Chapter Seven

"Just look at this story." Alasdair flung down the newspaper on the breakfast table, scattering toast crumbs everywhere. "I've never even met the girl." What a pleasant thing to wake up to, the morning after the sort of blissful night he'd had, to find the papers interviewing some idiot who reckoned you were about to announce your engagement.

Toby picked up the offending rag, perusing the gossip column. "Dancing with her last night in celebration of the release of *A Scandal in Bohemia*—and till all hours? You dog, Hamilton. I wonder where I was supposed to be?"

"No doubt if you read enough of these," said Alasdair, stabbing the newspaper with his finger, "you'll find out. It's an outrage."

Toby reached over and tapped his arm. "Really? It provides a very nice smokescreen, which is just what we could do with at the moment, if we're under observation. Would you like the world to know where you really were and what you were really doing?"

"Maybe they'd put it on the crossword page." Alasdair shook his head, although he was smiling. "The studio bosses would have kittens—at least the ones who don't already know. What would your mother say?"

"She'd go and horsewhip them. My mother could have ridden roughshod through the Mongol horde. Woe betide anyone who gets in the way of her children's happiness." Toby drew his fingers along his lover's hands. "Like a mother hen with her brood under her wings, that's the old girl. I'll warn her that this latest story is all stuff and nonsense, but, if I were you, I'd smile furtively and look knowing if anyone else questions you about your imminent engagement."

"You're right. You always are." Alasdair drained his cup and held it out to be refilled. "So where next? Where's the key to unlock our Gordian knot?"

"Mixed metaphors there, Alasdair. Sherlock would not be amused. Pierce or Chesney?"

"Either or both. Not fussy. I'm sure I can cope with two mysteries in tandem."

"After last night's performance in bed, I'd have thought very little was outside your capabilities." Toby reached for another slice of toast; he needed to restore his energy. "I have this hunch that the answer to Pierce's disappearance will turn out to be as simple as good old Alexander getting out his sword and cutting the eponymous knot apart. Talking of which, did you hear a rumour that project might be on the go again? You as Alexander and me as Hephaistion?"

"I did hear something along those lines, although they've got the types wrong. I suppose it could be fun, even with La Marsden as that awful Roxanne woman. It'd certainly be a money spinner."

"Wouldn't it just? But dear Fiona wouldn't like us faffing about in chitons. She'd be upset that my bosoms are bigger than hers." Toby chuckled, which made Alasdair laugh; they couldn't stop until Morgan came bearing coffee and a stern look. "Seriously though, given censorship and all, Gainsborough could hardly portray the real relationship between those two, could they?"

"Ah, Toby, they might be able to edit the script, but the Board can't censor the way you and I look at each other, can they?"

"In which case, maybe it's as well it's still on hold." Toby, suddenly serious again, clearly couldn't shift the feeling of being watched from his mind.

"Right. We're going to solve everything before we have to hit the high seas. Or the lake at the studio, to be more accurate."

"I tell you what we'll do," Toby got up, putting on his coat preparatory to braving both the morning air and avoiding any autograph hunters who might have accumulated at the end of the road. "You go back to McDermott and his ghastly mutt and find out what he can tell you about that girl who was Robin's friend. I'll go and see what the address book—and, failing that, Charlotte Paddick—can yield in the matter of North London."

"And Messrs. Hampson and Chesney?"

"God knows." Toby swiped a last piece of toast and left.

***

Toby returned home just in time to pick up the post from the mat, much to North's annoyance. A shame to spoil the man's fun and usurp his rightful job, but the master of the house wanted to see if there were any more anonymous missives—hand delivered or otherwise—among the legitimate deliveries. He was right; the usual sort of envelope lay at the bottom of the pile, presumably dropped in just before the mid-morning delivery, or else the eagle-eyed and -eared North would have picked it up already.

That was the last straw. Desist now, for all our sakes.

"I'll have a coffee, please, North. In the morning room." Toby took all the post, most of it getting short shrift as he sat by the window, trying to enjoy the welcome sunshine. None of it was as urgent or important as the single little sheet.

What was the last straw? Toby wished he knew when the letter had been written; had it been written this very morning, and did it refer to his sharing Alasdair's bed? No, that still felt the wrong hare to be coursing. Something in the Pierce case, then, the real developments concerning Charlotte Paddick or the resignation letter? Unless it was related to the phone calls they'd made about the mysterious Chesney.

Toby slapped his leg in frustration just as North came in with the coffee. "Thank you. I hope it's up to its usual strength—I need all the help I can get."

"Is there anything I can do to assist you?"

"Not at present, unless you can find a missing man and figure out what these are about." Toby showed his valet the latest letter, fetching the other two while he was at it. "See? No demands, so unlikely to be blackmail. We think they're related to this business with Johnny Fisher's secretary."

North read the letters, then cocked his head to one side like a bird. "You have eliminated entirely any connection to your performances in the Sherlock Holmes films? That love scene in A Scandal in Bohemia might just have been the last straw. They can be very fanatical, the supporters of Sherlock Holmes. Apparently, they send letters to Baker Street hoping he can help them solve their problems."

"Oh." Toby had an awful thought. What if they'd misled themselves, too wrapped up in the business of Pierce to see beyond it? What if their first instincts had been correct, and this was just an irate Conan Doyle enthusiast? Worse still, what if this angry aficionado knew about him and Alasdair and thought there were some subtle message being put into the films about Holmes and Watson having some sort of romantic relationship behind the scenes? That would certainly make Conan Doyle revolve in his grave like a top.

"Yes, sir?" North looked suitably concerned.

Toby dissembled. "I was just thinking that asking a fictional character to locate your aunt's long-lost will sounds as desperate as asking two actors to find your missing secretary. You didn't happen to see anyone lurking about in the street just before I arrived home, did you?"

"Only the postman. Oh, and the man collecting for soldiers' welfare."

"Soldiers' welfare?"

"Yes. I didn't like the look of him. He said he didn't want money, just something he could auction, something to do with your role as Doctor Watson, funnily enough. He knew you lived here." North drew himself up to his entire five-foot-six and mustered all his considerable dignity. "I sent him off with a flea in his ear. He can contact Landseer if he's legitimate, which I doubt he is. Nasty-looking chap, more weasel than man."

Toby had never had a moment where he could have fairly said that the scales had fallen from his eyes. Until now. "Could you just describe this man to me?" North's description, as it unfolded, matched Chesney perfectly. "I think I know him, although I have no idea what or who he actually is. His previous line has been impersonating reporters. He certainly wants to get close to me. And Alasdair. If he turns up again, invite him in and keep him here until you can get the local police to come and take him down to the station."

"On what grounds, sir?"

"Threatening letters, for a start. I'll get my father to sort out the rest."

When the coffee at last got consumed, it was almost as a toast to the breakthrough. If only Pierce's address book would turn up something equally noteworthy. But there was no mention of Palmers Green in the thing, nor of any contacts within a couple of miles of it. Toby decided that wandering around the place looking lost wasn't a realistic approach to take, although he wasn't sure he had a better option. He phoned Johnny, drew a blank there, then picked the receiver up to contact the Paddick residence. If Charlotte couldn't come up trumps, then he'd have to give up this particular lead.

The frosty toned butler initially answered. The length of time it took for between him laying the phone on the table and Charlotte appearing suggested he'd sought permission from his employers—or maybe her brother—before allowing her to pick the phone up.

"Hello?" The hearty female voice on the end of the telephone let Toby know he'd finally got through to the right person.

"Miss Paddick? It's Toby Bowe."

"I know that. Marriott informed me." Charlotte sounded like she was about to add some jovial endearment like "you clown," but seemed to think better of it. "I assume it's about Robin?" There was a wistful hint to her voice suggesting she'd have been happy for Toby to reply that it had nothing to do with that cheating bounder, and it was actually about dinner for two at the Savoy.

"Exactly," Toby relied, perhaps a bit too promptly. Better to make things absolutely clear from the start. "I was wondering if Palmers Green meant anything to you. In relation to Robin Pierce, I mean."

"Oh." Charlotte's tone implied that she was slightly deflated at the lack of direct interest from Toby, although still putting a brave face on things. "None of his painted Jezebels lived in the place, I'm fairly certain. Unless there were ones I didn't know about."

"I can't find any listed there in his address book." Toby sighed, getting ready for the "well, thank you, anyway" bit of the conversation.

"There's always his aunt, of course."

Toby's ears pricked up. "Aunt? I don't remember seeing one of those in the address book." Was this the "Pierce" scratched out of the address book?

"You wouldn't have done. She's been shunned by the family. Well, by his mad old grandmother, which is all that remains of the family," Charlotte laughed. "And Aunty Clarice wouldn't be Robin's sort of person at all."

Intriguing. "What on earth did she do to fall from grace?"

"Joined some sort of peculiar closed order or something along those lines. Like a nunnery, only not quite. Gave them all her money, which was the cause of the hoo-hah. Grandmother Pierce wasn't bothered about her taking up with religious nutcases but paying hard cash for the privilege was a different matter." Charlotte lowered her voice; maybe James was in the offing. "Robin's family is well-off, you know. Living where he lived and working where he did was just one of his many acts of rebellion."

"Sounds like a pretty mutinous crowd. And you say, despite that, your Robin didn't approve of what his aunt had done?"

"He's not my Robin anymore, Mr. Bowe, and I'll remind you to remember the fact." Charlotte Charlotte's tone had turned unnaturally huffy; surely, she was putting on an act for her brother's benefit? Or was he reading too much into everything? "From what you know of him, do you think that he'd have approved of giving up the pleasures of the flesh and devoting oneself to a life of service?"

It didn't seem likely he'd entertain such notions, but if it was someone else making the sacrifice, there seemed no reason to make a fuss. Unless Robin had expected a slice of

Aunty's cash? "Well, if you say he wouldn't, then I suppose not. Thank you."

Toby put the phone down, frustrated. Another lead come to nothing, all a coincidence of time and place. It was possible Pierce had been to beg his aunt for money, although if she'd given everything to this sect then that would have been a wild goose chase, surely? Unless he had gone, and then been captured by this strange mob, forced to write his resignation and...

No, that was too far-fetched, even for the wildest of Sherlock Holmes tales. The Case of the Kidnapped Secretary.

Right. If he couldn't get any further regarding Pierce, he could damn well follow up Chesney. Toby decided to go down to Landseer's publicity office and see if anyone there could tell him some more about the imposter. Surely, he must have had some form of invitation or official identification to have been allowed to mingle with the stars on the opening night? Telephoning would have been easier, but he felt badly let down by that apparatus, having drawn two blanks. Face-to-face might bring him more luck.

Toby was halfway down the street, en route to the main road and a better chance of hailing a cab, when he spotted a familiar figure on the corner. Chesney himself, if Chesney was actually the name he'd been born with. Toby got the impression the man was trying hard not to let on he had the house under observation, but Toby could see right through the charade. He sauntered along the road, deliberating ignoring the man on the other side until he came opposite, when he dashed across, taking advantage of Chesney having turned his back for a moment, probably in an attempt to hide his face.

"What the hell are you playing at?" Toby had his man, if not quite cornered than backed up against some railings. Chesney didn't look much of a physical specimen—Toby felt confident he could outpace him if he decided to run and could easily match him in a fist fight, should it come to that. Black-Hearted Fitzroy stood for no nonsense. "Out with it."

"Nothing. A man's allowed to stand where he wants, isn't he? It's a free country." These were the exact lines—said in the exact same way—that a bit player in *A Study in Scarlet* had used when spying on someone he intended to blackmail, Landseer having taken the usual liberties with the plot. The association of ideas made Toby even angrier.

"Yes, it is a free country. Several of my dearest friends died to keep it so." Toby's own line, for once. "I like to think they died to keep it the sort of place where a man's free from being spied on. Or from people harassing him."

"I wasn't aware I was harassing anyone."

"Then what were you doing trying to get hold of some of my things from my valet?" Toby held up his hand to prevent any reply. "And don't tell me you're collecting for charity. I believe that as little as I believe you're from either *Tit-Bits* or *Reveille*."

Chesney blanched; that barb had hit home. "I'm a fan. I wanted something to keep as a souvenir."

Toby didn't believe that, either. Maybe the man was looking for an old jacket, with a letter left carelessly stuffed in the pocket. Whatever the truth, Toby wasn't sure he'd hear it any time soon. "Fan?" He snorted. "So why the irate letters? And don't deny knowledge of them. My valet saw you drop today's offering through the letterbox." A stretching of the truth, if not a downright lie, but it had the desired effect.

"Oh." Chesney looked uncomfortable, frightened and about to confess all, but he suddenly rallied. "I could take this to the police, you know. It's not right, you making all sorts of allegations against me and defaming my character."

"If you want to go to the police, I'll take you there myself. I have nothing to hide." Toby prayed that his manner wouldn't give the lie to that statement and that Chesney wouldn't call his bluff. He could always fall back on his father's name and reputation to see him through, but he didn't want to risk it, given how ineffective a safety net that might prove.

"Look," Chesney's face appeared more weasel-like than usual, "it started with the films. You playing Holmes and Watson."

"What's the problem with that? And what's it got to do with you, anyway?" This was becoming more peculiar at every turn. "And who do you mean by 'we'?" Please God it wasn't some secret society, so beloved of Conan Doyle.

"Can't you work that out, Dr. Watson? Or do you need Sherlock with you?" Somehow Chesney managed to make the words "Watson" and "Sherlock" sound like the worst sort of insult. "Every clue seems to slip through your fingers, doesn't it?"

Toby wasn't so blind with rage that something in that line didn't ring a bell. Something that could be important if he could only pin it down. "I don't need to work it out. I'll thrash it out of you if need be."

"Like Mr. Hamilton looks like he's going to do?" Chesney cast a glance across the street. Toby turned, glad to see that he'd got backup, only to discover he'd fallen for the oldest trick in the book, one he'd played on his schoolmates when he was a boy. Alasdair wasn't there, and Chesney had taken advantage of Toby's split second of inattention to leg it, hurtling up the road like a prize sprinter.

Toby gave chase, almost got tangled up with a huge Silver Cross pram being wielded by a formidable-looking nanny, then spotted his quarry at the end of the street, about to get into a taxi which was pulling up. He almost made it, but near wasn't good enough. Chesney sped off, yelling something out of the window. Dive, devil, what was it? Oh. "Drive like the devil."

Of course. As Toby got his wind back things began to make sense, or as much sense as this business seemed to make at present. "Drive like the devil," was a line straight from *A Scandal in Bohemia*, both the short story and film. And he was prepared to put a fiver on the bit about clues slipping through their fingers coming from one of the Holmes stories. Coincidence? He doubted it.

***

Alasdair arrived outside McDermott's house convinced he was on the verge of finding out something crucial to the case. This was the point in films and books where the breakthrough usually came, wasn't it? He knocked on the door and smiled brightly when McDermott opened it.

"Oh, hello." The man didn't seem too surprised to find Alasdair on his doorstep. "Has Robin turned up?"

"I'm afraid not, although we seem to be getting warmer." Natty bit of dialogue—he was proud of that. "That's why I'm here, to clarify some points."

"Righty-ho, then. Come in. I've locked him up." McDermott indicated vaguely in the direction of what Alasdair guessed was the kitchen; the actor made a mental note to refuse all offers of refreshment and thereby risk the monster's release. "I said 'Voyce, you're a great lumbering brute and Mr. Hamilton doesn't want to be bothered with you.' He seemed rather put out but he'll have to lump it."

"How did you know I was coming here?"

"That was easy. I saw you walking along the street and guessed you were heading here." McDermott beamed. "Would you like a cup of tea?"

"No," Alasdair replied just a bit too hastily. "We don't want to disturb Voyce."

"True." McDermott showed his guest into the lounge, offered him a seat, then sat down himself.

"I'm grateful to you for seeing me again," Alasdair said as he got settled. "There are some things I'd like to ask about Robin and his friend Millie Stamford, things I should have asked before if I'd had the sense." Self-deprecation; it usually worked better than any degree of big-headedness. "Were they just friends or was there more? I suppose there was a deep amount of lasting affection?"

McDermott hid a smile. "Do you know, I thought you actors only talked like that onscreen. I suppose it must rub off in the end." Alasdair, bristling, started to frame a reply, but his host carried on blithely. "I don't think Robin ever really got on with any other woman like he got on with Millie. She didn't ever make any demands on him, for one thing. Never possessive of his attention. And she was just as disparaging of the stream of girls who ran after Robin as he was."

"If he was so disparaging of his..." Alasdair sought for the right word, "...harem, then why have one? Why bother with women if he didn't really like them?"

"Ah, I never said he didn't like them. He was the same as just about any other young man, full of life and needing to sow his wild oats. Like Voyce when he's boisterous—simply has to have some outlet. All these women he strung along were his outlet, while Millie was someone he could relax and rest with." McDermott smiled. "Millie was the only one he loved, I suppose."

"Then why didn't he just marry her?" Alasdair cast about in his brain for some sort of logic to this business. Why love somebody and then go off with girls you liked less? Sometimes there was no sense in the world. "Was she ugly or disfigured or something?" It was all he could think of and a pretty feeble bit of thinking, at that.

"Don't be daft, she was a lovely thing. It's just that," McDermott lowered his voice, even though there was no one around to overhear, "she was illegitimate and Robin's grandmother would never have let him marry someone without a decent name."

"I thought his granny had..." Alasdair just stopped himself in time. Maybe the words "turned gaga" wouldn't have been politic. He needn't have worried.

"Lost her marbles? Oh yes, but the money's all bound up in trusts. For all that Robin lived like he didn't have two pennies to rub together, that was all show—he was rolling in it. He'd wanted to 'live life like other people for a while' as he put it. But the Pierces wouldn't have let anyone without a plum in her mouth get her hands on the family silver, and they'd made sure that control outlived them."

"Ah." It was the last thing Alasdair would have thought of, although it certainly rang true. And it made sense of a couple of things. Strings of girls, all of whom were discarded, buying a suit at Waites—but could it explain the disappearance? "He must have been extremely upset when she died."

"I suspect it broke his heart. Oh," McDermott put his hands to his mouth. "I've been such an idiot. Couldn't put two and two together to save my life. You don't suppose he's taken it so hard he's jumped off a cliff or something?"

Alasdair noted that his host was still referring to Pierce in the past tense. Did he know something? Was this a clumsy attempt to bring it out nonchalantly?

"Mr. McDermott, will you be frank with me? Do you know more than you're letting on?"

"Eh?" McDermott seemed flustered. "I'm not sure what you're getting at..."

"We have good reason to believe Pierce is still alive or was a few days ago. Are you trying to tell me that you know he's dead?" No, hold on. There's another possible explanation, and a more likely one, at that. "Or are you covering up for him?"

"No!" The reply seemed just a little too forced.

Maybe sympathy would work where direct questioning hadn't. "I'm not criticising you for it. Greater camaraderie hath no man than that he lay down the absolute truth on behalf of a friend. I'd do the same for my closest pal."

McDermott sighed. "Would you? I feel such a chump about the whole thing. Not a good enough actor to keep up the charade."

"You were pretty convincing last time. I'd have thought every word you said was genuine."

"It was. Last time I didn't know what had happened to Robin. I still don't, not entirely."

"You've lost me..." If Sherlock Holmes could have made sense of this, he was a better man than Alasdair gave him credit for.

"Robin got in touch the day after you were here. Told me he was lying low—just like I said he would be—and could I cover for him if anyone came asking?"

"He told you to say he'd jumped off a cliff?"

"Not exactly. I think I rather overegged the pudding on that. He said to just put people onto the wrong track." McDermott looked pleased with himself; he must have thought he'd put on a wonderful act.

"And the right track is…?" Alasdair refused to say *No clearer as yet.*

"Don't even know myself. This all seems to be something to do with his family. Doesn't want them getting wind of where he actually is or what he's doing."

It sounded plausible, especially if the story was true about Pierce not being able to access any inheritance unless he behaved himself. "I think I get all that, but something still bothers me. Why do you keep using the past tense? It sounds as if you knew he was dead."

McDermott looked puzzled. "If you say I did, then I must have done, but I'm blessed if I know why." Either it was the real answer or McDermott was turning out to be one of the best actors Alasdair had ever played a scene with.

Chapter Eight

The taxi came off the Strand and pulled up at the front of the Savoy; Alasdair leapt out, gave the cabby a handsome tip, then looked around. It didn't take long to spot Toby. Nobody else was bouncing on the balls of their feet like a seven-year-old while standing in the opulent foyer. He clearly had a lot to report for him to look so enthusiastic. Well, that made two of them with a wealth of information to be shared. Almost a whole bottle of champagne and a plate of canapés' worth, and that took them as far as *The Strange Case of the Sherlock Holmes Quotes.*

"I never thought I'd ever meet anyone who quoted quite so freely from Conan Doyle. Most odd."

"Hold on." Alasdair wagged his finger impatiently. "I can think of another. Hampson does that exact thing, too."

"Does he? I'd never noticed. Must be that wretched Adam's apple of his bobbing up and down distracting me." Toby twirled the remains of his champagne in the glass.

"I knew there was something or other in what he said which grated. It's quotations from the books—he peppers his speech with them." He suddenly slapped the table edge, almost sending the empty canapé plate flying. "I knew he and Chesney were in league."

"Did you?"

"Yes. Well, I suspected it, anyway. Remember me saying he looked nervous when I was challenging Chesney in Johnny's office?"

"I do indeed." Toby warmed to his theme. "And that would explain how the man got my address, if he and Hampson are in cahoots in...in whatever peculiar thing it is they're doing. I'm still not clear about that."

"Tomorrow, we'll go and attack that from the other end." Alasdair nudged his friend's leg with his shoe. "Stop smirking. You've got a filthy mind, and I can see right into it."

"I'll be serious, I promise." Toby assumed his slightly wayward angel expression. "And in the interest of said seriousness, I'm going to go right now and ring Johnny."

"Why?"

"To warn him. If Hampson gets word from Chesney that we know they're up to something, he might assume we'll be able to link him as well, which could precipitate him upping sticks like Pierce did. For all you hate my friend Fisher, we should do the decent thing and warn him he might be without another secretary soon." Toby cuffed Alasdair's arm and left, returning five minutes later looking bemused.

"You look bewildered. Would another bottle of champagne help to clarify matters?" If it didn't aid thought processes, it might help them through the ordeal ahead.

"No, that would just befuddle me even further." Toby sat again, picking up his glass to twirl it meditatively. "I'll stick with this half a glass I have left."

"It'll be flat."

"I'm beyond caring." Toby looked like Fiona in one of the scenes where she had to depict uncivil treatment nobly borne.

"What is the matter?" Alasdair leaned forward, so they could talk even more discreetly.

"Nothing much, I suppose." Toby sighed. "It's just that Johnny was unusually terse. He was grateful for the warning about Hampson, delighted we'd made a bit more progress on Pierce, but not his usual loquacious self." He sighed again, a great theatrical sigh as dramatic as anything Fiona could produce. "If I didn't know better I'd have said he was trying to hurry me up and get rid of me."

"To steal your previous lines, 'Hallelujah!' Only I can't see that eventuality ever coming to pass." Alasdair frowned. "He's always a sight too eager to get his paws on you."

Toby sighed a third time. "No, let's face facts. He's probably got some bloke there he wants to play casting couches with and my presence, even over the telephone, was cramping his style."

"Have we been grabbed by the green-eyed monster?"

"No. Not me." Toby's face gave the lie to his words. "Well, maybe a bit. I mean, there was no way I was going to..." Toby lowered his voice—this might be the Savoy but you couldn't be too careful. "You know, leap into bed with him, no matter how many times he suggested it. But it was nice, in a way, to be asked." He blushed, profusely.

"And you wonder why I get jealous? Stop feeling sorry for yourself. He'll be pre-occupied with something, that's all. He won't be scurrying about, hiding the framed photo of you." No such luck.

"He never has a photo of me in his office. Has he?" Toby sounded more than a touch hopeful.

"How should I know, you egotistical little worm. And if I really believed you meant what you've just said, I'd be off like a shot. As for your friend Fisher, he's probably worried about Hampson." Alasdair rubbed his hands. "We've both smelled a rat. I bet the man's embezzled the advance takings and Johnny's running around to drum up enough cash to keep them afloat."

"Have you deduced all that from a phone call you didn't even hear?"

"Now, back to the other matter in hand, before we've used up all our play time and have to go back to work. Pierce. What on earth is he playing at?"

"Search me. If he doesn't want his family to know what he's up to, I dread to think what that might mean." Toby sipped ponderously at the remains of his champagne. "They seem to have tolerated his taking a job as a secretary, although that must have counted as being beneath him. Same with living in digs and all the fraternising with fallen women. What would it take to send them into a fit of the vapours?"

"Orgies and opium dens, do you think? Very Holmesian, if it's the latter." Alasdair sipped his champagne, too. Any more of the stuff and he wouldn't even be able to think of the word Holmesian, let alone say it. "I can't believe he'd have taken after his aunt and gone all religious."

"While I suspect you're absolutely right, I'm not sure I'd be so keen to make assumptions without proof. Sherlock wouldn't approve." Toby wagged his finger, just like Watson had done to the great man in their last film.

"Sherlock can go and stick his pipe somewhere it'll make his eyes water." Alasdair drained his glass and pushed it away.

"I'd like to see you do that thing with the pipe onscreen." Toby smiled, finishing the last of the champagne. "Anyway, we can't make any assumptions about Pierce as we simply don't know enough about him. I'm not sure even Johnny knows him as well as he thinks he does." Toby looked rueful. "Now, as you said, time's running short. What are our next jobs?"

"Following the trail of the mysterious Chesney would probably be a wild goose chase. We could put pressure on Hampson, though, and see if he'll let us know where his friend is holed up. I'll go—Johnny can't be distracted further," Alasdair said emphatically, but not soon enough.

"I think it's better that I go and see Hampson, as I was the one who had the run in with Chesney. Assuming he's not absconded to the continent" Toby had a twinkle in his eye again. "There's a better job for you."

"Why does my heart sink at the way you said that?"

"I have no idea, as I'm only going to suggest you do something you're quite familiar with. What, among your many talents are you best at?" Toby quickly raised a finger to his lips. "Shh. I'll rephrase that. Excluding the activities you can't mention in polite company, what among your many talents..."

"I suppose you refer to acting?" Alasdair raised his insured eyebrow.

"Got it in one. Now, what about taking a leaf out of old Sherlock's books, adopting some weird disguise, legging it up to Palmers Green and seeing if you can access Pierce's aunty?"

The insured eyebrow came down, almost with a thud. "Assuming I agreed to such a hare-brained scheme, how would I know where to go? There's hardly likely to be a house labelled, 'Proceed with caution, religious loonies at large.'"

"Oh, use your imagination. I'd go straight into the Post Office or some other hot bed of local gossip and start asking nosy questions. There surely can't be that many obscure sects based in the place, can there?" Toby narrowed his eyes.

"Ha-ha. Let's assume I locate the building. Let's make the even bigger assumption that they let me in. What do I ask Aunty Clarice?"

"That champagne's befuddled you. Use your brains, boy." Toby leaned over and tapped his friend's leg. "Smooth-talk your way in. It's just like scene directions. Start simple. 'Hello.' Throw in that terribly serious smile you do so well. 'I'd be obliged if I could see Miss Pierce, she's an old friend of a friend of a friend.' Look appealing at that point."

"Thank you, D. W. Griffith. I get the picture."

“Then you say, ‘I was thinking of throwing in the silver screen and want to ask Miss Pierce if this is the place to come to find peace and quiet and some meaning to my life.’ You could try wringing your hands but that might be overegging the pudding. Say you’re disillusioned with the tawdry emptiness of the cinema or some such rot. You can make up convincing-sounding twaddle; just imagine you’re taking part in improvisation.” Toby grinned.

“And if it’s as closed an order as your girlfriend says?” Alasdair shook his head. “I’ll be stuffed, then. They’ll throw me off the doorstep.”

“Oh for goodness sake, where’s your resourcefulness? Then you’d go round to the servants’ entrance and chat up a maid or even the boy who does the gardening.” Toby checked his watch. “They’re late.”

“They’re always late. Anyway, I’m not sure your great backup plan will work. Won’t the members of the order be doing the cooking and bed making?”

“Depends what sort of an institution it is. By which I mean depends how posh the members are and whether they’re prepared to sully their ladylike hands with such tasks as washing and cleaning.” Toby grinned again. “I’d put a quid on there being a below-stairs bit that’s peopled by young ladies who’ll fall for you like a ton of bricks. Just talk sweetly to them, wring out all the information you can and then run like the clappers before they can bundle you into a laundry hamper and keep you to have their wicked way with.”

“It’s the prospect of the last bit becoming reality that fills me with dread. Ah, they’re here.”

A cacophony of female giggling announced the arrival of a gaggle of four nice, posh girls, straight out of finishing school and into the “Landseer Charm and Accomplishment

Academy", all of them aspiring actresses. Toby left his chair to greet them with a radiant smile.

"Ladies." Alasdair rose, bowed and pointed to the empty chairs at their table. "Do join us. Cocktails or champagne?"

An outbreak of female giggling and debate resulted in champagne and cocktails being ordered. All talk of detecting, anonymous letters and why Johnny Fisher had been so fickle had to be put away until another time. Landseer wanted its column inches and an evening such as this–a few drinks, some more canapés, smiles, gossip and mild flirtation—was a small price to pay to keep the general public's attention directed elsewhere.

When the glasses had been emptied, the officially appointed "Out and About in Town" reporter chatted to, smiles wielded for the photographer and the last cheek kissed, the young ladies—looking less optimistic than they'd been two hours previously—had been despatched into their carriages, the status quo could be resumed.

"We've done our duty." Alasdair said out of the side of his mouth as they waved their guests off in the taxis to brave the bustling traffic of The Strand. "I hope they weren't too disappointed they didn't get the chance to wrestle one of us in the back seat."

"It's fine. They've had their pictures taken linked arm in arm with us so they're happy, they'll be all over the gossip columns so Landseer will be happy, and at least when you read the stories you'll know that you have met the girl in question this time so you'll be happy." Toby stretched his arms and shook himself. "Win all round, I'd say."

"And when some smart journalist finally puts two and two together and prints a story asking why we've not accompanied any of the many women we've been seen with down the aisle?" Alasdair shrugged. "What then?"

"You have a backup plan, of course." Toby tipped his head towards the main road and they set off to take their chances with finding a cab there. "You look at the list of women you've squired, you choose one of the ones who's now married, and preferably got a string of children. You tell the press she was the love of your life, that you were too stupid to say anything at the time and how there'll never be another girl for you. Frown when you say it—that'll work a treat in the photographs."

Alasdair kicked a stone off the pavement and into the gutter. "Isn't that just as dangerous? What if she then gets back in touch, says she'll divorce the hubby and elope with me?

"That's where the children come into the picture. You plead that you couldn't be so cruel as to spoil their lives for the sake of your own happiness and all that." Toby grinned. "People love a bit of noble suffering—don't I have to do it all the time up on the screen?"

"I assume you've already got your lady lined up for the role?"

"No, do use your head. It'd be far too obvious for both of us to play that card. I'm pleading that I suffered a terribly injury at the end of the war, when my plane came a cropper—Landseer's doctor has promised to back me up, with all the dignity and discretion he can muster." Toby smote his head with the back of his hand, one of Fiona's favourite gestures. "It means I could never be a proper husband, never make the woman I love truly happy." He pretended to stagger forlornly, so Alasdair whacked him.

“All right, Henry Irving, I get the picture.” Alasdair lifted his finger and a taxi glided towards the kerb. “Detection tomorrow morning, then a spot of lunch?”

“A late one. Can you meet me at the theatre, where I’ll be putting the thumbscrews on Hampson?” Toby opened the cab door and ushered his friend in. “I’ll stand you lunch if you can be civil to Johnny for all the time we’re there.”

“Would the sacrifice be worth it?” Alasdair waved cheerily as the cab sped off.

Chapter Nine

Next morning, Toby stopped in at Langan's en route to the Old George, following a cerebral itch which needed to be scratched. One thing they'd neglected to follow up, because it hadn't seemed that relevant at the time, was Hampson's remark about attending a meeting there and his refusal to give any clues about sort of group it was. The man didn't look like a Freemason, although there were plenty of other strange closed societies around.

He hadn't decided how to play the scene at the hotel—whether to work his way insouciantly around to the subject of who met there or ask straight out, not being entirely sure how secret this society was. He needn't have worried. Just at the opportune moment, he was called on to play the "old pals" act.

"Flight Lieutenant Bowe!" Someone who evidently held the rank of hotel manager came across the foyer with his hand outstretched. "I never seem to be here when you visit us. Do my restaurant staff look after you well?"

"Of course they do, Flight Officer Mitcham. Can't think of a single complaint." Toby shook hands enthusiastically. "My goodness, you're looking well." Exceptionally so for a man who'd had half his lower right leg blown away fewer than ten years before.

"Couldn't be better. Grace just had a little girl, this week past. Tommy's upset, of course, having had his heart set on a brother."

The domestic chit-chat carried on, with Toby happy to spend time on it. Mitcham had been a good man in the squadron, very popular, very able. Everybody had wanted him on their wing and it wouldn't hurt to have him on their side now.

"Are you here to book your wedding reception?" Mitcham beamed, maybe totting up the profits and the publicity already.

"Not yet. You'll be the first to know when one of the fillies pins me down." Toby put on his best act. "Actually, I'm here to pick your brains."

"Pick away. Although I can't guarantee the quality of product." Mitcham guided Toby into a corner of the lounge where discretion could reign. "It's not about films, is it, because I'd be hopeless. Or what about Sherlock Holmes?"

"How odd you should say that. Are you reading my mind?"

"No, I just assumed there was a connection to a club who meet here every week. The Baker Street Particulars."

Toby groaned at the name. "Would that be the crowd who lurk here on a..." he quickly worked back through the days, "Tuesday?"

"The very same, although they'd be mortified to hear themselves described as a 'crowd'." The subtle flicker in Mitcham's eye showed exactly what he thought of them

"Closed society?"

"So I believe. Membership by invitation only." A light seemed to dawn. "Are you hoping I can pull a few strings and get you one?"

"No." It was a touch too quick and too loud, although Toby was pleased to see that his old colleague hadn't noticed. "That's the last thing I'd want. It's possible some of them have taken umbrage at my Dr. Watson and are making a nuisance of themselves. You wouldn't have a list of members?"

"I'm afraid not. Anyway, even if they kept a signing in book or something similar they'd probably use assumed names."

Mitcham shook his head. "It's not discreet to speak so of one's patrons, but they're a funny lot."

Toby couldn't agree more. "You don't remember if there's one of them who looks like a weasel? Or another one with an Adam's apple as sharp as an auger?"

"I could ask the man who normally serves them their refreshments. They prefer to have just two people waiting on them—the usual secrecy nonsense. Henry happens to be here today." Mitcham signalled for one of the concierges to come over and then despatched him in search of the waiter.

Talk reverted to young Tommy and his desire to be in the RAF like his dad had been, until Henry arrived and confirmed that both a weasel and an Adam's apple were usually present at the meetings. Toby was cross he didn't have pictures of the men concerned to offer for identification purposes, just like a real detective might, although second thoughts suggested that level of preparation might just raise unnecessary suspicions. He was pretty certain he'd tracked down the right blokes and the right society.

"Henry, you wouldn't by any chance know what these chaps talk about at their meetings? I understand that you're trained to be as discreet as the day is long, but maybe you could give me a clue or two?" Toby said, smiling.

Henry looked at his boss; Mitcham nodded in approval.

"I think it's what's called a 'variation on the great game' or something like that, sir. They discuss the minutiae of Conan Doyle's stories. They were going on the other day about how it might have been possible for Watson to be injured in both the shoulder and the leg. Something about being slung over a mule." The waiter shook his head.

"Is that all they do? Have arcane discussions?"

"Bless me, sir, if that was all they did they could meet in public and not in a closed room." Henry leaned forward and all three huddled closer, conspiratorially. "They hold mock trials."

"They what?" Toby and Mitcham said at the same time.

"Hold mock trials. For people who've raised their ire. Illustrators who've depicted Holmes in a way they don't approve of. Reviewers who make uncomplimentary remarks about the books."

"And actors who portray the characters in a way they don't like?"

Henry nodded. "Actors seem to come in for particular resentment, sir."

"So what form do these mock trials take? Do they pin up a photo of the alleged miscreants and throw darts at it?" Mitcham was beginning to bridle; maybe he didn't like the thought of what was going on in his hotel, private room or not.

"Oh, nothing so rustic." Henry rolled his eyes. "They have a judge and jury, counsel for the defence and the prosecution."

"And the defendant himself? Or herself?" Toby added quickly, thinking of poor Fiona being accused over her depiction of "The Woman".

"That's the worst thing of all in my opinion, sir. They draw lots and some poor soul has to dress up as the accused and take the stand." Henry shook his head. "They seem to think it enormous fun."

Dress up? So that's why Chesney had wanted the clothes; Toby—and presumably Alasdair—must have had their name on the court roll of upcoming prosecutions. Perhaps the picture of the pair of them together was to have played a role in the charade; the mind boggled. "Thank you both, gentlemen. I think you've put my mind at rest."

"Our pleasure." Mitcham beamed, rising as his old colleague did and escorting him to the door. "Make sure you patronise us again, and not just with Mr. Hamilton. Bring your young ladies next time."

"Would you be very hurt if we didn't?" Toby waved in the direction of the hotel restaurant. "This is one of the few places in London where we get a bit of respite. Sort of a bachelors' club."

Mitcham nodded his head. "That's perfectly all right. I quite understand."

Toby sincerely hoped he didn't.

***

Alasdair couldn't believe how easy it had been to get into building which housed the Order of the Obedient Sheep. He just wasn't absolutely sure he'd be able to get out. They'd taken his "friend of a friend" story at face value and welcomed him as a potential penitent, with much sympathy, understanding and a big cup of tea. Admittedly the brew hadn't been as strong as he liked it, but the biscuits which accompanied it were exemplary—this didn't seem to be the sort of order which believed in denying the flesh too much.

He'd been shown into a light and airy office, made comfortable with his refreshments and then left while Miss Pierce was found. Alasdair leapt up as she entered the room, only to get a shock. He'd expected a thin, pious, severe-looking woman, but Clarice Pierce turned out to be large, lovely and full of life. She must have been in her fifties, but her smile was still charming.

"Mr. Hamilton." She shook her visitor's hand. "I've seen all your films. Love every one of them. We sometimes watch them here, for our weekly treat."

"Really?" Alasdair was becoming more amazed at every moment.

"Don't look so shocked. We're not hermits. We watch films and play bridge, although we wouldn't play for money. And we have wonderful barn dances. God doesn't want to stop us having fun."

"Pleased to hear it." That was the wind taken out of his sails, and all his ideas having to be realigned. "So, um, what exactly does the Order of the Obedient Sheep do? Or not do?" He narrowly avoided asking, "Is it just a walled-off social club?"

"We work, Mr. Hamilton. For a start, we provide shelter for the homeless, here." She waved her hand in the direction of the back of the building. "Many of our visitors are ex-servicemen you know. Wicked." She shook her head. "I mean the way they've been treated has been wicked, not the men themselves." Clarice Pierce let out a hearty laugh at her own joke. Alasdair remembered Toby's description of Charlotte Paddick; did Pierce like women who reminded him of his nearest and dearest? "And most of us go out several days a week—on a shift rota, we're great ones for administrative efficiency—to help at a hostel we run in Hackney."

"Oh. What do the duties there involve?" It might not have been the sort of thing Sherlock would have bothered with, but he hoped it would show appropriate interest while he got his thoughts in line.

"Ah, I see what you're thinking." If she did, it was more than Alasdair himself was managing. "The jobs involve getting your hands dirty, quite literally, so if you're serious about joining us those manicured nails are going to suffer. They won't look so nice after you've been making beds and soup."

Alasdair surreptitiously slid his hands out of view. "Why isn't this organisation..." that felt a silly choice of word, but the Order of the Obedient Sheep seemed too businesslike, sensible and efficient to be worthy of the epithet "loony sect" "why aren't you all based in Hackney, if you do so much of your work there?"

"Because we're not ascetics." Miss Pierce sounded like she was addressing a slightly backward child. "And we certainly can't serve the destitute if we're dead on our feet. We come here for a few days' rest and recuperation, then we're back on shift again."

"So it's not a closed order?"

"Not at all. We can go out and visit friends if we're off duty, or go to the theatre, or whatever we like, really. So long as we're not judging other people or throwing stones. Not literally. Or maybe literally and figuratively."

Miss Pierce started to laugh and Alasdair couldn't help but join in. If Toby ever gave him the push and Landseer thought him too old and wrinkled, he wouldn't mind coming to a place like this. Certainly a wonderfully peaceful atmosphere pervaded the whole building.

"This seems like a terribly impertinent question, but the person who told me about the order—it was a friend of Robin's—also implied that the rest of your family weren't terribly happy about you being here." Alasdair put on his best smile; if Miss Pierce liked his films, it might charm her. "I don't want to risk the approbation of my family, so...might I ask what they objected to?"

"It is a highly impertinent question, and if it were anyone else asking, I wouldn't answer it." The words might have been a touch harsh but they were ameliorated by the twinkle in Clarice Pierce's eye. "My family couldn't give two hoots about me being here— not in terms of following what I believe is my calling. It's the money. I give most of my income to the Hackney mission and have left all my worldly goods to them so they can carry on their work after my death. That's what the Pierces don't like—the goods and chattel will be leaving their grasping hands." It was the first time she'd shown any unkindness or ill-humour. Alasdair couldn't blame her under the circumstances.

"Did the Order insist that you leave your money to them?" The question came out a lot more disapproving than Alasdair had intended.

"Oh no, not at all. So if you're worried about your accumulated Landseer earnings disappearing, there's no need. Your choice. As is how long you stay here. A few days, a few months, the rest of your life. Your decision."

The light shone through the large sash window, illuminating the little motes of dust which danced like pinhead angels. Just the place for a few days of rest, if Toby became too insatiable. He shook himself, aware he'd been lulled into such a state of contentment that he'd almost forgotten the reason for his visit.

"As you've been kind enough to answer one impertinent enquiry, might I ask another? Has your nephew been to visit you recently?" He left the question at that, hoping Clarice Pierce wouldn't want to know why he was asking such a thing.

"He has. May I ask why you want to know?" The tone of Clarice Pierce's voice had altered, subtly.

Alasdair had practiced this bit of the interview over and again since he'd woken up. He took a deep breath and adopted his "worried friend of the hero" persona, the one

Toby usually had to employ. "I have a friend for whom Robin used to work. When he heard I was making this initial reconnoitre, he asked me to make polite yet discreet enquiries." As a piece of dialogue it was rubbish—stilted and unconvincing.

Clarice Pierce eyed him suspiciously. "Are you sure that your questions so far haven't all been part of a smokescreen and that you're really here to run Robin down on behalf of one of his young ladies? If you are, you can tell her that he's not like that anymore."

Alasdair thought of asking "Like what?" but the look in Clarice Pierce's eye gave him pause. Anyway, he could guess. "I can assure you I'm not, unless Johnny Fisher has turned female."

"Mr. Fisher? What a charming man." She seemed to soften again at the mention of the Lothario. "But why should he be worried? Robin's sent his resignation."

"So he told...me." Alasdair stopped the word "us" halfway out of his larynx. "But it arrived several days after your nephew failed to turn up for work. You can understand why he was worried—he even wondered if something had happened to the young man and the resignation had been faked. To throw him off the trail." It sounded such a silly theory now. Clarice Pierce certainly found it amusing.

"I think you've forgotten to leave Sherlock Holmes in the dressing room with the cape and the pipe, Mr. Hamilton. Such complicated nonsense." She rose from her chair, the interview evidently over. "Please apologise to Mr. Fisher on Robin's behalf if he's caused any trouble, but he's not to worry. All is well." With that, she left the room.

Alasdair never got to add, "How do you know about the letter?"

The young lady who'd let him in returned; he gave another little prepared speech about how he'd got a lot to consider and would go off right now and do so, then got out as quickly as he could. As he walked down the garden path to the road, something grey, purring and obnoxious started to follow him. He quickened his pace, but the wretched thing broke into a trot, winding itself about his legs and almost tripping him up. "Go away." The admonition didn't work, nor did a swift flick of his shoe.

"Can I help you?" A young man came around the side of the house, wielding a hoe. Maybe he'd whack the thing over the cat's head if he was slipped a fiver.

"If this is your cat and you can get it off me, then yes." Alasdair pointed to the offending creature. "Can you scoop him up and lock him away somewhere?"

"I'd love to, but if I get too close I'll start..." The man let out an enormous sneeze. "He's not ours, I'm afraid. He belongs to the neighbours and he's a complete toe-rag. Always winding himself around people's feet and trying to trip up the postman." He poked the cat with the end of his hoe, but it just spat and clung tighter.

"Shame we haven't got a bucket of water to tip over him, although if you keep sneezing, the little wretch will end up soaked." Alasdair thought he might start sniffling himself.

"I think he knows. When people don't like him or get a reaction to cats, he seems to make a beeline for them."

The cat looked up, offended.

The moment of distraction allowed Alasdair to disengage its claws and scoop the thing up. It immediately started to purr and look beatific. "Here, tell me where he belongs and I'll go and put him there." They fell into step, heading for the road and along to next door's gate before their paths diverged.

“Thank you.” The young man gave a mock salute then turned on his heels. Alasdair crossed the road, heading for the high street and a cab. The journey would give him a chance for a long, hard think about Pierces, male and female, and how bloody awkward they were. And why he had the awful feeling that something was staring him in the face and he’d missed it.

Chapter Ten

"Toby!" Alasdair caught sight of his friend emerging from a cab and heading for the Old George.

Toby diverted at being hailed and headed along the pavement. "You've escaped. Did they make you empty your wallet before they'd let you go?"

"They're actually not like that at all. Seemed exceedingly reasonable." Alasdair looked up at the theatre. "Any chance of delaying our interview with Johnny? I have something I want to talk over."

"Talk to me about it over an early lunch and I'm your man. I've got a lot to tell you, too, and I think I'd like you to hear it first without Hampson in earshot." They fell into step together, heading for a little restaurant just down the road where they could get their chops around a decent plate of food and talk without being overheard. By unspoken agreement, their adventures of the morning weren't referred to until they were safely ensconced at a table and some soup ordered.

"You first. You look like you're about to burst." Alasdair sipped at some mineral water; after last night's champagne, it was the best bet.

"Hampson, Chesney and their merry mates want to put us in the dock. No, not about that, dummy. At least, I don't think it is. It's about our portrayal of their heroes." Toby gave a full account of his interview at Langan's. "Grown men acting like a bunch of children."

"Oh, I don't know. It seems harmless enough and it probably distracts them from digging too deeply elsewhere." Alasdair had breathed a huge sigh of relief at just how silly the whole thing appeared. “Nuisance value, though. What do you want to do about it?”

“I’m not sure.” The arrival of the soup, with crusty, hot rolls, made the world seem a brighter place. “Still, tell me what happened with Miss Pierce.”

Alasdair related everything, the string of surprises and preconceptions dashed. “And on the way here,” he scooped up the last of his soup, “I worked out where Robin Pierce is. It’s obvious.”

“Not to me, it isn’t.” Toby rapped his soup spoon over his lover’s knuckles. “You’re being unbelievably self-satisfied. If you turn into Sherlock Holmes, I shall brain you. And run away with Fiona.”

“I’d better tell you, then.” Alasdair grinned. “I think he’s there, at the Order of the Obedient Sheep. Hiding.”

“Hiding from who?”

“Some harridan of a girl is my guess. And his aunt is covering up for him.”

“If you thought that, why didn’t you try to see him?” Toby wielded his spoon like a judge’s gavel.

“Because I’d reached King’s Cross by the time I’d had my attack of the bleeding obvious.” Alasdair pushed away his bowl, the inner man satisfied and the outer ready for action. “I think we should go back there as soon as we’ve had lunch and track him down.”

“Only if we can take proper transport. You can hail a cab while I pay.”

“Better still, I’ll get Morgan to come with the car. If we’re going to be sitting around waiting, we might as well be in something comfortable.”

***

Alasdair's Bentley had negotiated Wood Green and was heading even further north. Conversational gambits on the doings of the Baker Street Particulars had dried up and they'd reverted to discussing pirates and how the onscreen versions must be nothing like the real thing. Toby suddenly stopped bewailing his forthcoming scenes with Fiona and slapped his leg. "We've been blind. Blind as bloody bats."

"Bats aren't actually blind." Alasdair wasn't sure that was actually true, but it sounded good.

"Oh, do shut up. Robin Pierce isn't hiding."

"Then what's the silly sod doing?"

Toby grinned. "Copying Black-Hearted Fitzroy."

"As usual, you make no sense."

"Think of the screenplay. He's taken to a life of raping and pillaging and other innocent pastimes because the love of his life died before they could plight their troth. Pierce has done the same, but in the other direction. Pierce seemed to think more of Millie Stamford than any girl he'd ever known, but they couldn't be married." Toby rubbed his hands together, gleefully. "It's got all the makings of a cracking plot. You as Robin, Fiona as Millie, me as...not sure for the moment."

Alasdair ignored the blethering. "Robin becomes so upset at her death, he decides he's led a pretty poor sort of a life and resolves to make amends. At least for a while." He wasn't convinced, even if it made some sort of sense of the various strands of the case. "Would that be in character?"

Toby shrugged. "There was this bloke in our squadron, who had two brothers. One was a great womaniser, great whatever-the-equivalent-is-with-men-iser, he wasn't fussy. He drank, probably took Benzedrine, the works. The other brother got killed parachuting into Arnhem, didn't make it to the ground." He looked unusually serious. "Ronnie hadn't been able to enlist, he was rejected on medical grounds, and when his brother died, he gave up the sex and booze and went to live in at Buckfast Abbey, helping them with the grounds and their building projects. Shocked everyone who knew him. Not a word of a lie."

"I didn't think it was." Alasdair caressed his friend's hand, briefly. "So if Pierce has done the same, how do we find him?"

"I think you already might have."

Hell and damnation. Of course. "The sneezing man."

"Exactly. McDermott told you Pierce was allergic to slobbering hounds. Why not to cats?"

"I suppose it's possible." More than possible; highly likely, but Alasdair didn't want to admit that just yet.

"We're not very good detectives, are we?"

"I think we are. We appear to have solved two cases." Alasdair tried to sound more convinced than he felt.

"More by luck than by judgement." Toby tapped his friend's knee. "I bet that's what Sherlock did, too and Watson made it out to be more logical and objective than it was."

"I'm going to tattoo 'Sherlock Holmes wasn't real' onto the inside of your eyelids." Alasdair rolled his eyes. "And if you've got this all worked out, why was McDermott covering up for him?"

"Oh, Sherlock," Toby said, leaning back to avoid a clip around the ear, "haven't you worked that out yet?"

***

The light was still on in Johnny Fisher's office even though it was six o'clock in the evening. A fast-approaching opening night was evidently creating plenty of overtime.

"Looks like we've caught him." Toby was bounding up the stairs two at a time.

"If you'd let me ring ahead, then there wouldn't have been any uncertainty. And he'd have made sure Hampson stayed behind as well." Alasdair took the steps at a more leisurely pace, gradually falling behind. "Obviously the fraud hasn't been detected yet."

"It's a disgrace that telephone box was out of order. I don't know what the world's coming to." Toby stopped to wait at the top of the stairs.

"We could have found another one. We passed plenty."

"No time to lose on such things." Toby rapped at the office door and went in without waiting for an answer.

"Mr. Fisher's awfully busy..." Hampson had turned quite pale at the sight of the visitors, but his spirit soon showed signs of rallying. "Could you call back tomorrow?"

"I'm sure he'll see us." Alasdair strode towards the connecting door, as if he was about to barge through it.

"Just let him know we're here, will you?" Toby's was the voice of reason. "He'll see us." Unless the double distraction of Pierce and an impending opening night had made him even more capricious than usual.

As if to prove his unpredictability, the internal door suddenly swung open and Johnny appeared. "I thought I heard your voices. Got news for me?"

"Absolutely." Alasdair beamed. "Case solved."

"Brilliant! I knew you had it in you." Johnny slapped Toby on the shoulder then shook Alasdair's hand. "Come in and tell me all about it. Hampson, there's champagne in the cupboard—do the honours, will you?"

They were ushered into the inner sanctum, where a young man—no more than mid-twenties and ridiculously handsome—was settled onto the sofa, holding a cigarette and what appeared to be a script.

"Hugo, old man, could you give us a half an hour?" Johnny bestowed his most engaging smile, the one he usually gave Toby.

"Of course." Hugo made a slight bow towards the new arrivals, then exited stage left through the other door, the one which connected directly back to the house.

"Your new ingénue?" Alasdair asked.

"You could say that." Johnny spread his hands, smiled and changed the subject. "You have news for me?"

"We've found Robin Pierce." Toby wrinkled his nose. *Ingénue. So that's what they're calling it these days?*

"Splendid! When's he coming back to work for me?" Johnny cast a quick glance towards the outer office. "This guy's starting to get me down. He's...odd."

"We can cast some light on that, too." Alasdair glanced at Toby. "But don't get your hopes up about Pierce returning. He may not want to."

"What have I done?"

"Not everything's about you and what you have and haven't done, Johnny." Toby was being perhaps a little too harsh, but the man deserved it.

Johnny threw up his hands. "Guilty as charged, but don't shoot me for it."

Toby snorted. "Yes, well. Pierce has seen the error of his ways and decided to do something constructive with his life. More constructive than working here and attempting to seduce every woman he could get his hands on."

"Really? That's a hell of a story." Johnny turned to Alasdair, as if he'd be the more reasonable one.

"Toby reckons it would make a great screenplay," Alasdair said with a smile. "We got our first big lead when I went back to speak to the man with the dog and Toby contacted one of

Pierce's old flames." He explained their audit trail of logic and supposition right up to the point they'd sped up to Palmers Green in search of the miscreant, Toby chipping in and emphasising how brilliant Alasdair had been throughout, just in case Johnny had missed the point.

"So you went and staked Robin out? Wouldn't it have been easier to try to get a photo of him and confirm he was the man with the allergy to cats?"

"Maybe, but it wouldn't have been as much fun." Alasdair winked at Toby.

"Of course not!" Toby rubbed his hands together, recalling the thrill of the chase. "We lay in wait outside the house and when this chap emerged, we followed him. It was dead exciting, like something out of one of our films, but nobody about to shout 'cut!' just when things got interesting."

"It sounds like you've been having too much fun." Johnny smiled as well, but the usual flirtatious twinkle had definitely gone from his eye. Fickle swine.

"If you call tailing Pierce on foot all the way to Hackney and to the doors of some superior type of doss house 'fun,' then it was." Alasdair looked like he was fighting to keep his temper even.

"And what was he doing there? That's the last sort of place I'd have thought he'd be." Johnny shook his head. "Are you sure he's not lost all his money and ended up there destitute?"

"You're not following the argument, are you?" Toby, frustrated at Johnny's lack of attention, wanted to shake the man. "Pierce was helping at the soup kitchen."

"I still can't believe it. He's the last person I'd have imagined doing anything for other people. Especially anyone who might be a bit smelly or dirty." Johnny sounded like a maiden aunt in one of his popular drawing room comedies. "Are you sure it was him?"

"No doubt. I went in and asked—said I had an important message. From you. He came out straight away and asked about the theatre."

"Did he? That's good news. Shows he still thinks about us."

"I said you were concerned at his sudden absence and were trying everything you could to make sure he was all right. Not bumped on the head and pushed over a cliff." Toby still couldn't shake off the desire to punch Johnny on the nose. *This must be how Alasdair feels most of the time*. "He assured me he was fine, that he knew you'd received his letter—Aunty reported back after Alasdair's visit, I assume—so why were you bothering him while he had better things to do?"

"Better things to do?" Johnny looked like he was about to explode. "I'd been worried sick. I still don't understand why there was the delay with his resignation, if everything was above board and he really didn't want me to worry."

"I get the impression he'd had some sort of breakdown after Millie's death. I think he wrote as soon as he felt able."

"Bloody hell. What a palaver." Johnny made a fist and punched the arm of his chair. "And why did he get this McDermott to cover up for him and make it all such a big mystery?"

Toby turned to his friend. "Do you want to tell him or shall I?"

"You have the pleasure, Dr. Watson."

"Because Pierce's family would have cut him off if they'd got wind he'd followed his aunt into the place. There was a risk he'd get too fanatical and leave them his money as well."

"And you're certain he won't do that?" Johnny took a cigarette from his case.

Toby shrugged. "I don't think he knows what he wants to do. He's not burned his bridges, though. He said he wants some thinking time and that he'll understand if you don't keep the job open."

"Very magnanimous. Sorry." Johnny settled back in his seat. "That sounds ungracious, to both Pierce for his prickings of conscience, and to you two for all your efforts in tracking him down. Please forgive me being churlish; I'm feeling very tired. The upcoming opening night, you see."

Alasdair gave Toby a little sideways glance; now they could guess why the theatre manager was so weary and it wasn't anything to do with matters onstage.

Toby managed to regain his composure first. "We quite enjoyed the tracking down, really. Not that we'd necessarily leap at the chance of doing something similar in future but as a once-off..." He looked to Alasdair for confirmation.

"I'm not so sure about that. I think we've been rather good at it." Alasdair rubbed (with great care) the insured eyebrow. "I mean, we had a nice, perplexing mystery to get our minds around and we solved it in no time, even if the answer turned out to be mundane."

"I hardly think leaving behind a life of debauchery to join a monastery or whatever it is can be called mundane. And the most important thing is that we've succeeded where Johnny didn't, isn't it?" Toby cast a glance at the manager, who didn't seem to have even noticed the barb. Perhaps he'd already lost interest in the case and started fantasising about Hugo and double beds. "Anyway, we've got two mysteries and the second one isn't entirely solved yet."

"Two?" Johnny took notice again. "Oh yes, the letters and the impersonator."

“Can you call Hampson in, please?” Alasdair couldn’t help smirking; this could be fun. “We’ve got a thing or two to ask him.”

“If you wish.” Johnny raised his voice. Probably too raddled to get out of his seat, Toby thought uncharitably. “Hampson!”

A worried-looking face appeared around the door. “Yes, Mr. Fisher?”

“My colleagues have a couple of things they want to ask you if you’d be so...” Johnny didn’t get the chance to finish his sentence, the secretary turning on his heels and legging it towards the outer office door.

“Come back!” Johnny was out of his seat pretty swiftly now, followed by Toby.

“Don’t worry, he won’t get far.” Alasdair, smug, kept to his chair. “I locked the door.” He produced the key from his pocket and twirled it. They could hear the door handle being rattled furiously, then a pause before Hampson flew back into Johnny’s office, evidently en route for the door Hugo had recently gone through. Toby caught him in an expert rugby tackle and pinned his arms back.

“What on earth is this about?” Johnny asked, before the penny dropped. “Have you been writing threatening letters to my friends?”

“No, of course not.” Hampson stuck out his jaw defiantly, the Adam’s apple sharp as a razor.

“Actually, I don’t think he wrote the letters. That was his pal Chesney—the one who allegedly works for various magazines. They’re partners in crime.” Toby tightened his grip; shame he hadn’t been able to do the same to Chesney.

“We’ve done nothing illegal.” Hampson’s spirits seemed to rally.

"Not illegal, just bloody silly. They're members of a secret society." Alasdair rolled his eyes. "Don't shake your head, every word's the truth. You may not believe this, Johnny, but they're unnaturally obsessed with Sherlock Holmes and hold mock trials of people they feel have offended his immortal memory."

"It's not unnatural, it's..." The significant bit of what had been said seemed to strike Hampson. "How did you know about the trials?"

"You can't fool us. We're not just Holmes and Watson on the screen." Toby couldn't resist getting a gibe in.

Hampson wriggled, trying to turn in Toby's vice-like grip. "And that's the bloody point, isn't it? We wouldn't have minded if you'd stuck to the acting, although that's bad enough." He spun to face Alasdair, jutting his chin out even further. "Kissing Irene Adler. It's a disgrace."

"Would you have preferred me to kiss Watson?" Bloody hell, what had he done? Alasdair's anger had got the better of his common sense and the can of worms was now open.

"That would only be both distasteful and disgusting." Hampson sneered. "At least it has some basis in canon."

"Like when Holmes thinks Watson's been injured?" Toby conceded the point, although he still didn't loosen his hold.

The remark seemed to sting Hampson. "This making out that you're real detectives is taking things too far. Keep to the films and stop besmirching the image of Conan Doyle and of the great detective himself."

"I wasn't aware that we were besmirching them." Alasdair shrugged. "Johnny asked us to do him a favour and we obliged."

"But it's the way you did it. Did you hear yourselves? 'The Case of the Disappearing Secretary.' 'The Case of the

Disappearing Lothario.' Mocking the great man, as if this was no more than a game. Playing at detectives. Playing at being the detectives." Hampson looked more evangelical than any revivalist preacher. "As if either of you were capable of one-fifth of the great man's deductions. We asked you to stop but, no, no, you had to keep on with your pathetic charade. It wouldn't have been so bad if you'd just made fools of yourselves, but making Watson out an idiot and Holmes a hopeless romantic..."

Toby's urge to laugh disappeared as completely as the lothario had. Men like Hampson were too embroiled in their own interests to distinguish book from screen, or either from real life. "Oh, for goodness sake."

"I won't have you insulting my friends." Johnny narrowed his eyes. "Not while you're in my employ. I'll be onto the agency as soon as they open in the morning—you can go now and take your pay in lieu of notice."

"I wouldn't stay here, even to have the pleasure of insulting them." Hampson pulled himself out of Toby's grasp, which had loosened at last, turned as if to leave and then must have remembered the locked door. "If you'd be so kind as to let me go..."

Alasdair produced the key again, fingering it thoughtfully. "I'll consider it, but I want to make something straight. There'll be no more letters, do you understand? Tell Chesney that."

Hampson looked as if he was about to deny knowing any Chesney, caught sight of Toby making to grab him again, then thought better of it.

"If you want to hide away in a back room playing at silly arses, that's fine. Put us on trial if you like; as your pal Chesney says, it's a free country. Better men than your lot died to make it so." Toby's anger was flowing freely now, memories of colleagues burned to death in crashing planes seared on his mind. Had they sacrificed themselves for so trifling a cause? "But if I see either of you—any of you—on my doorstep, you'll regret it."

"What will you do? Take me to court?"

"Oh no, I've something better than that in mind. Alasdair and I are very popular with the press—the real press, not the sort your mate Chesney pretends to represent. They'd have a field day exposing all the secrets about the Baker Street Particulars." Toby was pleased to see Hampson blanch at his use of the name. "Not so daft, are we? We may not be your idols, but we can find out a thing or two and we know enough about the Particulars to make you a national laughing stock." He hoped the threat would sound a lot more potent than it was in reality.

Hampson looked from face to face with the air of a hunted fox, but there was no escaping these hounds. "Fine. No more letters."

"Shall I make you sign a statement to that effect?" Alasdair evidently didn't want just to have a bit part in this big scene.

"A gentleman's word is his bond." Hampson bowed. They'd have no more trouble from him, Toby was sure, even if he wasn't certain Hampson was a gentleman. "Am I free to go now?"

"You are." Alasdair made an elaborate show of unlocking the door; once Hampson had collected his things, he left with as much dignity as he could muster.

"Well done!" Toby greeted him with a huge hug as he returned. "Masterfully played. Black-Hearted Fitzroy couldn't have done better."

"Black-Hearted who?" Johnny looked beyond confused.

"We'll tell you later. Over the rest of the champagne." Toby took it on himself to charge their glasses and begin the toast. "To cases solved."

They drank. "And to cases yet to be solved?" The champagne revived Johnny enough to restore the twinkle in his eye.

"No, thank you." Toby and Alasdair made the same simultaneous reply.

"Oh come on, you could make a career..." Johnny threw up his arms to protect himself from a rain of pummelling fists, three bodies ending up in an undignified heap on the settee.

The inner door opened and Hugo's handsome young head appeared. "I say, that looks fun. Any room for one more?"

***

"Johnny must be at it with Hugo." Alasdair shook his head over his glass of white wine, as if it had played a part in deliberately misleading him. They were in a small bar off the Kings Road, celebrating their success in solving *The Case of the Disappearing Secretary* and *The Strange Affair of the Loonies at Langan's.*

"At what?" Toby was eyeing a plate of salad with alacrity.

"It. What Johnny always likes to get up to. What he tried to get up to with you under the pier at Brighton."

"Oh, it. I'm sure you're right. I'm surprised, though."

"Because you thought he was still carrying a torch for you?"

"Not just that. These last six months he was supposedly having a fling with..." Toby leaned closer, so he could whisper the name of a particularly famous actor.

"Never. He's all over the papers with women on his arm. He's..." The penny dropped. "Ah, right. Take your point." Best to change the subject. "I think I could do with a great hound like Voyce at times. Maybe McDermott would lend me him to take on set? Keep La Marsden at bay."

"There's a thought. And talking of McDermott, there's something bugging me. Why did he refer to Robin in the past tense? He said he didn't know for sure what had happened until after you'd visited that first time but was that a lie? Was it all just his subconscious, that he knew Pierce was 'dead' to his old life?" Toby finished off the last of his salad and wondered if there'd be any apple tart for pudding. This place made a wickedly good apple tart.

"Possibly, although that sounds like psychological mumbo jumbo. I suspect it's something mundane, again—living with Voyce any length of time would turn a man a bit doo-lally. Perhaps we should quiz him about it?"

"No thank you, Alasdair. I've had enough of playing detectives. I shall stick to acting and making love to you. Both of them I excel at and both of them are extremely enjoyable." Toby smiled. "Now chivvy up that apple tart or whatever sweet delights are about to appear on the table and then we can attend to the matter of what sweet delights we can indulge in for the rest of the night. I can name several."

"I bet you can. You were always very handy with ideas, Dr Watson."

"Oh do shut up, Sherlock. Or I'll hide your violin."

THE CASE OF THE UNDESIRABLE ACTOR

Overture and beginners

The girl's footsteps quickened as she entered the dark alley. The noise and safety of the busy London streets had been left behind temporarily, to be regained when she reached the end of her short cut. Her friends had told her, day on day and again not five minutes since, that she was unwise to take this route, but she was tired and desperate for home. The five minutes' walk she saved would make all the difference to her aching legs and rumbling stomach.

Too foolish to have put safety before comfort, too focussed on simply getting through the passage as quickly as possible rather than keeping alert, it seemed inevitable that the girl wouldn't notice the soft-footed figure falling into step ten yards behind her. Not until he was almost upon her, by which time it was too late to pick up the pace and escape his grasp.

"Hello, my lovely," the man rasped, one hand round her waist to pull her towards him, and the other slipping over her mouth. "What did I do to deserve you walking past my door?"

She struggled—in vain—to break the iron grip, desperate to free her mouth to scream.

"Ow! The cow bit me." The assailant flung the girl away from him.

"Sorry, Mr. Howell." She protested. "I didn't mean to."

"Oh, yes, we all believe that," he sneered. "Look at this, Robert. She's almost drawn blood."

The director, who'd left his seat at the first cry of anguish, trotted over, hands waving placatingly. "I'm sure it was just over enthusiasm at her first time being in a film with you, George. That's so, isn't it, Yvette?"

"Oh, yes, Mr. Temple. It's all so exciting." If she was acting this bit as well, the girl had a lot of potential. "I lost my head."

"Then you should get yourself back under control," George snorted. "I'm off to my dressing room. I won't be back until you can reassure me that I can get through a scene without being assaulted, Robert. If that means having to change the actress, I can wait."

"But George..."

Howell ignored the director's words. Who was the star of this film, the person who'd get the money flowing through the tills for Marquess studios? Not the production team, for a start, given that the script was ordinary, the supporting cast workmanlike at best, and only he could elevate it to something like a decent offering. Yvette wasn't going to make that much of a contribution apart from standing there looking pretty but gormless. Why did the studio insist on having such useless bints in the minor roles? How many casting couches had been lain on during Yvette's progress from the pool of extras or wherever she'd been lurking, to the role of third victim?

By the time he'd reached his dressing room, burst through the door and slammed it dramatically behind him he'd worked himself up a fair head of steam. Shame he'd had to knock the drinking on the head because this was the sort of occasion when he could have done with a stiffener.

A rap on his dressing room got answered with a curt, "Clear off!"

If that was Robert, coming to cast oil on the waters, he'd have to bide his time. If it was George's dresser, Edith, then she'd gauge his mood and be back soon with a cup of strong tea and a cheese roll. Neither of which were as good as a glass of whisky but they'd raise his spirits. Edith always knew what to do and say, which was more than could be said for most women.

He was about to go and shout for her to bring him them anyway, now he'd got those creature comforts in mind, when he noticed an envelope on the dressing table, tucked behind a pot of cold cream. Somebody must have left a note for him while he'd been on set, possibly one of his adoring fans. They had a habit of bribing stagehands—never the blessed Edith who was immune to such stratagems—to place things in his room. It couldn't hurt to read such messages, actors' egos being frail things that needed encouragement, or so he always vowed when he had a sympathetic female ear to hand. Maybe such solace was exactly what he needed now.

He slit open the envelope and pulled out the letter. The lack of the usual cloud of fragrance wasn't the only thing to make bring him up short. Here was another one.

I know what happened. We all do. Don't think you'll always get away with it.

Frozen for a moment, he read the words again, unable to believe that anybody could have found out.

Don't think you'll always get away with it.

That hadn't been in the previous notes. What the hell should he do now?

Reel One

"Hello sailor!" Toby Bowe's cheery tones came down the telephone line.

Alasdair Hamilton groaned. "I knew you were going to say that. Sir Ian's been in touch with your agent, then?"

"Of course he has. Contract's signed, sealed and delivered. I don't know why they bother to keep up the pretence of talking to our agents individually rather than saving both time and effort and nabbing us both together."

"You know exactly why they do that. More important to save scandal than save time."

What would the British cinema-going public say if it knew its favourite leading men—the pride of Sir Ian Sheringham and his studio, Landseer—continued their love scenes in the privacy of their own homes? And without the participation of Fiona Marsden, who'd been their perennial leading lady.

Hamilton, Bowe and Marsden. The British public adored the special chemistry the trio displayed on screen, one that made every scene appear real rather than acted. Although given the true situation, then Toby and Alasdair's acting skills surely surpassed those of even Olivier and Gielgud, so convincingly did they both display their adoration of Fiona on celluloid. Still, hadn't many an actor or actress being doing exactly the same thing over the years? Alasdair and Toby weren't unique in finding their own sex more attractive than the opposite one.

"Are you looking forward to lunch?" Toby asked.

Alasdair snorted. "The food, yes. Not necessarily the rest of it."

"Landseer always does put out a good nosebag. I wonder if they'll be supplying us with faux girlfriends to add to the illusion?"

"Not today, I'd guess." And thank God for that. Part of the smokescreen that helped maintain the actors' reputation was their being seen in public with beautiful young women. Rarely the same ones twice, though, because Landseer didn't want the young ladies becoming suspicious about why their charms appeared to be having no effect.

"I suppose that when Fiona's about they like her to shine like a diamond on a coal heap. No other lovelies to risk detracting attention." Toby chuckled. "They could give us plain starlets to squire on these occasions. No, belay that. They'd not let us be seen with anyone too mousey."

"I don't suppose it would go with the image. The studio powers that be think the public would expect only the most attractive women to be draped on our arms."

"Hm. I bet it's more subtle than that. A beautiful woman, and a different one each time, implies a series of flirtations. Were she homely it might suggest we'd found true love. And what would your adoring fans say if they believed you were at risk of being taken out of the marriage market permanently?"

"Less of the *adoring fans* nonsense, you cheeky bugger." Alasdair snorted. "The same would apply to you. Just as well we held those negotiations directly with Sir Ian."

At the point they'd become the hottest properties in British cinema, rather than holding out for everything in terms of film deals or size and luxuriousness of dressing room, they'd made it plain to the boss that while they'd wine and dine whichever young lady Landseer felt needed a leg up on the ladder to stardom, they would draw a line at even the suggestion of undergoing sham marriages. That way both maintained their reputation as playboys and enhanced their standing as being easy to work with and highly professional.

“And what’s all this belay rubbish you were spouting earlier?” Alasdair added.

“Got to get in character for the new role, Admiral. Splice the main brace, twelve at the grating and whatnot.”

Alasdair had been expecting this, although not at quite such an early stage of proceedings. Toby was always the same when he was getting his head round a new venture. Lots of jokes about the role and every opportunity taken for double entendres. “If I have to put up with months of remarks about masts or smut about running out the great guns, I might have to change my telephone number. Or join a monastery.”

“Spoilsport. Anyway, you could go all highbrow and call it the modern school of acting. Inhabiting the character, understanding their motivation and the like.”

“Cease and desist.” Jokes were bad enough, but this claptrap was more than a man could bear. “Don’t go all continental on me. Other people can do all that. *If I really were Admiral Pellew what would I be thinking about this orange?* stuff. I’ll stick to acting.”

Toby laughed, so heartily he almost deafened Alasdair down the line. “And that’s what we do so well. The audience wouldn’t like it if we changed our approach now.

“Heaven forbid.”

One of the reasons the three-way combination had proved such a great hit with post-war cinema goers was that many people felt they’d had their fill of harsh reality. They wanted their romances to take them out of themselves, and for those stories to be uplifting, noble, and full of people who those cinemagoers might just have been had the cards of life been dealt slightly differently. People who would never have entertained the notion that they could dance like Astaire or sing like Crosby, could imagine themselves as a Hurricane pilot as Alasdair had been in *Valour Undeterred*.

George Howell's films bucked that trend, though. They had the viewers on the edge of their seats, scared witless at times, as he terrorised his way around Victorian London or Regency Glasgow.

"Now, what about this George Howell chap they've announced for the part of Second Lieutenant Hamer?" Toby asked, reading Alasdair's thoughts as usual. "Ever met him?"

"Not that I'm aware of. Not seen any of his films, either."

"No, not quite our cup of tea." Toby cackled, but fortunately not as loudly. "Jack the Ripper hardly my idea of a leading man. I think I once saw Howell on the stage, though. A youngish Toby Belch."

"Any good?"

"Surprisingly so. Although given it was a forces' production in which seventy percent of the cast were enthusiastic but not terribly talented amateurs, it wasn't hard for him to shine."

"We'll give him the benefit of the doubt, then."

"Are there any doubts to take into consideration?"

Alasdair paused. Was he going to tell his light of love that ever since the man's name had been raised in connection with casting for the new venture, he'd had concerns? Nothing he could put his finger on, just something in the dim and distant past that rang a murky bell. Finally, he settled for a cautious, "Not sure. I have an awful feeling that I've come across him somewhere before and the association in my mind is not a positive one. More than that I can't say."

"How intriguing. Just as well you're such a good actor and won't let slip if you suddenly remember over the Brown Windsor soup at lunch that he seduced your maiden aunt."

"I won't so much as raise an eyebrow." Not even the heavily insured one. "But if I do remember I promise you'll be the first to know."

"I expect nothing less. A new film, though. Any hint of getting away on location? They surely can't film all the naval stuff in a tank at Hartshorn."

"Why not? They make the stages there pass for every other part of the world. If I had a shilling for every moment I'd spent on that site I could give up acting now." Alasdair sniffed. "There are rumours, as always. Something about a ship that'll pass for a frigate at close quarters. They'll probably have it double for all the boats in the film if I know Landseer."

"Ah yes. The camera deceives the eye. Film it on one side for the French ships and t'other for the English. Still, it'll be a nice jaunt. Just as well I've got good sea legs. And at this rate all we need is a film about the army and we'll have done all three arms of the forces."

"I'm not sure I fancy you in khaki, whereas you're alluring in blue. Let's stick to the oceans for now."

Naval heroes—they were the stuff of cinema success. Every boy wanted to be one and every woman wanted to be swept of her feet by them. Or so the executives reckoned. Errol Flynn had buckled his swash in The Sea Hawk and mutinied on the Bounty. Laurence Olivier had heroically led his band of brothers as Lord Nelson, with a saucy Vivien Leigh as Emma Hamilton. Now it was Landseer's turn to cash in on the glories of the age of sail.

Some bright spark had decided that Sir Edward Pellew would make a fantastic leading man and while Alasdair didn't quite have the thighs for the role—if some portraits of the great man were anything to go by—he had the same stamp of quiet authority. Anyway, Alasdair would look fantastic in a wet shirt. Toby would be playing Jack Nagle, a character Alexander Rattigan, their usual director, had invented as an amalgamation of all the better parts of various officers Pellew had served with. Fiona would have the part of Sir Edward's beloved wife Susan, who'd be getting a lot more on board action than she might have seen in real life and who was far more suited to La Marsden's wholesome on screen persona than a tart like Lady Hamilton would have been.

"Did you know he had a tiger, old Pellew? Or so I read somewhere. Brought it home for his wife. Or tried to bring it home and she kicked up merry hell. Do you think properties could get hold of one? I'd rather like to see Fiona tackle a tiger."

"She'd scare the pants off it. Fur off it. I can't imagine she'd stand for any nonsense. She nursed soldiers, remember? What's a tiger to that?"

"Maybe they could include a scene where she wrestles it with her bare hands."

Alasdair sniggered. "Less of that. This is supposed to be realistic, not like that dreadful pirate nonsense we did. You were probably the most gentlemanly pirate that ever sailed the oceans. And the cleanest."

Of course, he had been. Never a spot of cruelty was allowed to stain the character of whomever Toby, or indeed Alasdair was playing, and that's where George Howell would bring a real degree of novelty to the tried and trusted combination. He'd be portraying an evil-hearted—albeit historically inaccurate—villain of a junior officer. One whom Pellew would have to put in his place, several times over. There was always the added bonus of saving the audience thinking time if this particular actor played the role because they'd know that even if he started out as an apparently decent man, things would take a turn for the worse very soon. Typecasting had its advantages.

"Howell's a lucky chap. He'll have the freedom to play the nastiest of criminals. You do know that if this works, we might be stuck with him. A darker element to add variety and stop the formula getting stale."

That might be no bad thing. "Look at how successful Bogart and his chums are. People like a darker element."

"I suppose we have to move with the times if need be. And he'd be a useful addition to the yearly Holmes and Watson offering we seem to be committed to turning out. Some nasty characters in Conan Doyle." Toby sighed. "I sometimes fancy playing a villain, but Landseer would never allow it."

"Same for Fiona and me. She's allowed to make the odd error of judgment, but other than that she has to be pure as snow."

The sole exception to the formula had been when Landseer put on a theatrical version of Peter Pan to raise money for the Great Ormond Street hospital for children, when Alasdair had been cast as Captain Hook. The audience accepted that, because, in the words of a young woman Toby had overheard and gleefully quoted afterwards, "It's the stage, so it's not real, like it is in the movies."

Before Toby could recount that story for the umpteenth time, Alasdair said, "I can't stand here chatting all day. Not if I want to be on time for lunch. See you at one o-clock."

"Indeed. And later on at mine for supper?"

"Of course. With an appropriate dessert afterwards, by which I don't mean Charlotte Russe."

"I know exactly what you mean," Toby snorted. "You'll only be getting it if you behave yourself."

***

By the time lunch was over not only had Alasdair eaten his fill, he'd reinforced his view that there was something about George Howell that he didn't like, although he still couldn't put his finger on where that dislike stemmed. It wasn't just the man's oily manner with anybody female. Alasdair had also learned—and this had come as a surprise to all present apart from Sir Ian Sheringham and Alexander Rattigan—that scripts would be with the actors imminently, as shooting had to start sooner than expected. Something to do with the sailing ship which would pass for Pellew's frigate suddenly becoming available. At a more than decent price, Alasdair surmised but didn't say aloud.

Costume fittings would take place over the next few days, during which time there'd be an opening night for a stage production to which the stars had been invited and on which a three-line whip had been placed regarding attendance. The location shooting would commence in deepest darkest Dorset less than a week after that. A tight schedule and one that must be giving those in charge of organising accommodation headaches. Not a job that Alasdair envied, although he'd have his hands full with learning his lines. When he didn't have his hands full of Toby, which was a treat he couldn't get enough of.

He stopped at a kerb, waiting for a bus to pass before crossing. Easy enough not to concentrate when out and about and end up under a set of wheels.

Alasdair shuddered, experiencing what Toby would call a pricking of the thumbs. He looked about him, spotted a wooden post, and then touched it automatically, with an awful feeling that this small superstition wouldn't prove that helpful. He couldn't shake off the sense that something was about to happen in connection with the film and that the production of *Indefatigable* might prove to be less than plain sailing.

Reel Two

"Pray 'ave, pray 'ave, pray a-a-a-ve a squeeze. A squeeze, a squeeze, a squee-eeze of me oranges, me oranges, me or-or-oranges..." the soprano took a deep breath, "my Lo-ord!"

Toby groaned. Bloody modern avante bloody guard opera? You could go and stuff it. Give him a nice Gilbert and Sullivan patter song, any day, or something swish by Cole Porter, but not this load of old cobblers'. Not his idea of an enjoyable opening night, even though the Imperial Theatre was as opulent and as comfortable as any audience member could wish for.

"Remind me why we're here," he whispered into Alasdair's ear.

"Under orders to support Sir Ian." Alasdair grimaced, making his heavily insured eyebrow dance an expressive jig.

"I know that. But why this load of old drivel?"

"Surely you can't have forgotten his protégée? She's loud enough."

"Protégée? Is that what they're calling it this week?" The girl playing the lead role didn't have a bad voice, and she was pretty enough—in a Junoesque way, which was also appropriate to the part—but why on earth had she, or whoever advised her, decided to launch her career in such a dire production? *The Beheaded Lover*. Even the title made your flesh creep. How somebody could make a hash of such a cracking tale as that of Nellie Gwynne and her royal romance beggared belief, but they'd managed to, even confusing which was relevant to King Charlie.

"This should earn us plenty of credit." Toby sighed. Soon there'd be the relief of the first interval, the even greater relief of the bar and a glass of red wine, the greatest relief of their companions for the evening—Sally and Beth—going to powder their noses. At least then he and Alasdair could steal one moment of quiet pleasure.

"Not the best faux-girlfriends they've ever foisted on us." Alasdair murmured, when at last they were alone.

"More 'protégées', do you think?" Toby shrugged. "Still, if we smile for the cameras and applaud in all the right places, we'll get to go to that bucks' do we've been half promised."

Boxing, Bethnal Green, black tie and not a woman in sight. Landseer studio actors out in droves to promote the new film about a gentlemen boxer of Victorian times. Toby couldn't wait. Maybe there'd be even be pre-bout singing from some strapping tenor—it couldn't be worse than what they'd had to endure in the first few acts here.

"I've never been to a boxing match before." Alasdair seemed equally delighted at the prospect. "Will there be lots of blood?"

"Gallons, I imagine. And styptic pencils and grease and all sorts of black arts being practiced in the corners." Toby laughed. "Good, honest sport. None of your sissy rubbish." The last remark had not been just for the benefit of bystanders. Gay they might be, but effeminate they were not—which was all to the good as far as the studio was concerned.

"I'd like to see you try it." The glint in Alasdair's eyes—the same glint he'd no doubt be using as Pellew when he spied a French frigate hull down on the horizon—spoke volumes.

"You'd like to see me in shorts, dripping sweat?" Toby whispered.

Alasdair swallowed hard, concentrated on his wine glass and muttered, "Stop it!" from the corner of his mouth.

"Landseer wouldn't let me box, anyway. Too much of a risk I'd spoil my looks." Toby grinned. "That's something else George Howell doesn't have to contend with. The more battered the better. Have you seen him here, by the way?"

"He's about half a dozen rows behind us. With what appears to be a genuine girlfriend. Talking of which, here come ours."

They were spared more than a couple of minutes of chatter by the five-minute bell sounding.

"Seconds out, round two!" Toby said, brightly. "Prepared for more oranges to give us the pip, ladies?"

The girls giggled and Alasdair rolled his eyes. Business as usual. Although Toby could have sworn a certain familiar male voice breathed, "Wait till I get you on the canvas", in his ear as they sauntered back to their seats.

Once they'd settled in, Toby turned round casually, in search of their co-star. "Where did you say George is sitting?"

"A few rows back. With a charming looking young lady."

"Well, neither of them's there now. Two noticeably empty seats." Toby snorted. "Cowards. They probably think as little of this as we do, but they've not the stamina to sit it out."

"Stamina or good sense. Sir Ian will have his guts for garters." Alasdair flicked his eyebrow at Sally, who responded with giggles.

Toby gave Beth a mischievous grin. "Let's be generous and assume they're still getting their refreshments. Or perhaps George is signing a string of autographs. The Sheringham way is to sanction anything that keeps the fans happy."

"Perhaps one of them was taken ill," Sally suggested.

"Would that be a tactical illness?" Toby responded.

Sally slapped his arm. "I meant a genuine one, you old cynic."

"One man's cynic is another man's realist. Anyway, let's give hush." Toby lowered his voice. "The torture's about to recommence."

The discordant music started up, the curtain rose and once more they were transported to a version of London which appeared to be a mish-mash of every historical period from the war of the roses to the Regency. This version of the capital had never existed and Toby firmly wished that this opera never had, either.

During the second interval, they gave profuse apologies to their escorts, saying it was vitally urgent they tried to find out what had happened to their co-star. They located the major domo among the ushers and doormen, with the intention of quizzing him. Playing Holmes and Watson wasn't something that should be kept solely for the cinema.

One of the advantages to having a well-known face was that people were more likely to notice what you were up to, so if George Howell had been doing anything unusual, chances are somebody would remember. Unfortunately, that didn't apply in this case to O'Connor.

"I didn't see him, I'm afraid," the usher said. "Although I did spot his young lady leaving during the first interval, and on her own. She looked a bit upset but before I could ask if she needed any help she was through the door and off on her way."

"Can you be sure it was Mr. Howell's escort?" Toby asked. "There are so many attractive ladies here this evening I can't make out if I'm coming or going."

"Ah now." O'Connor wagged his finger. "She was wearing a striking pale green dress. My wife has something similar she wore for our thirtieth wedding anniversary; although where she got the material I wouldn't like to speculate. Probably came down with a German pilot and got hidden away until needed. Anyhow, the young lady's dress made me think of my Gertie's. I get into trouble if I don't notice such things."

Toby cuffed his shoulder. "Quite right too. Far too easy for husbands to regard what their wives wear as being of no more importance than the wallpaper."

Alasdair raised the insured eyebrow. "Ignore him. He gets a touch overexcited when he's allowed out."

O'Connor grinned. "My pleasure to help, sir. I did enjoy your last Sherlock Holmes film."

"So did we," Toby said, easing Alasdair away before either of them began grinning at the recollection of what had been an extremely frisky location shoot.

The third act of the torture commenced, building to a climax with what should have been a heart-rending tragic aria of love for a dear departed paramour. But, "My heart's bereft, my love is lost, his head has been re-mov-ed," were hardly the most profoundly moving of lyrics. The odd snigger broke out in the audience, which was a shame because the soprano was trying her best, but in the wrestling match between decent voice and the combined powers of terrible lyrics and dirge-like music, the latter were winning hands down.

When the final curtain fell, Alasdair and Toby made sure they gave the girl a huge round of applause, on the principal that every true Englishman should cheer the underdog. A good proportion of the audience followed suit, no doubt thinking that if these epitomes of style and good taste appreciated the entertainment, then maybe they should, too.

The fact that the boss would appreciate their efforts to support his latest girlfriend wouldn't hurt, either. In their position, they had to keep in everyone's favour.

As they waited for Sally and Beth to return from yet another visit to the lavatory, Toby adjusted his cufflinks and said, "So George's girlfriend left, but we simply don't know if he went with her. If he's scarpered he'll be in for a dressing down, star or no. Sir Ian believes no individual outranks the requirements of Landseer."

"We know that, but has anybody seen fit to inform George?"

"Actually, I did, at lunch, when he was having a quiet moan about how he wasn't used to having his free time organised by a studio."

"I heard something at lunch, too." Alasdair cast a quick glance over his shoulder. "Fiona said she'd heard our new co-star can be a bit hard to work with."

"Really? How did she know?"

"Hearsay, from a young actress she knows, who worked with him in his last gruesome offering. I'd like to judge him from the evidence of my own experience, but this doesn't look hopeful."

"If he's cunning he'll wander back just in time for the post-show party. The boss would be none the wiser, then."

And if Sir Ian did get wise to his new actor having missed two acts of the opera, then George would be having a black mark against his name in the book the boss kept in his brain. Sir Ian was a kind man, generous to a fault—especially where his money-spinning stars, and his protegees, were concerned—but he was renowned for bearing grudges. Except, surprising rumour had it, he didn't hold any resentment against any starlets who eschewed the offer of his casting couch, as Fiona was supposed to have, but that chivalrous allowance appeared to be the only one he made. Actors who misbehaved on set, or who didn't obey the company rules while off it, were quietly let go, with a reminder never to darken the Landseer doorstep in future.

Alasdair and Toby had kept on his good side, being so incredibly discreet—and spinning so much money—that Sir Ian smiled upon then benignly.

He wouldn't smile on George Howell, though, when he noticed the bloke's absence at the after-party.

Alexander Rattigan nabbed Toby and Alasdair as they entered the green room, where the event was being held, asking sotto voce whether they'd seen Howell, because if he didn't appear quick Sir Ian would be on the warpath.

"He's not been here since the first interval," Alasdair said. "Well break the news to the boss."

"Good man." Rattigan cuffed his shoulder. As a director, he'd built his reputation on getting the best out of ordinary material—be it script or acting personnel—and making the good into the extraordinary. Fiona always said he understood her face and ensured she never looked less than gorgeous. He understood her leading men, too, but in a subtly different way: never could a look of anything other than manly affection be discerned between them onscreen. If he had a fault, it was a reticence for confrontation, so it would prove interesting how he handled Howell on set.

When Alasdair and Toby joined Sir Ian's group to break the bad news, nobody present attempted to cover for the wayward actor, not even with a vague, "It's possible he may have received an urgent message and had to leave," as they might have done in the unlikely event of one of the other stars not appearing. Just as something had rankled with Alasdair about the newest addition to the fold, so it appeared to rankle with others.

"I know Phyllis, his young lady," Geraldine Wilson, who'd played Nellie Gwynne on stage and who was just as earthily attractive off it, said. "She and I used to be in the chorus together here. I could go to the office and see if I can ring her home, if you'd like, Sir Ian. She might be able to enlighten us."

"That's very considerate of you, my dear, but you've put in a lot of effort onstage and we couldn't impose."

"I'd be happy to do the honours," Toby offered. "When we noticed they'd both gone, earlier, and spoke to the doorman, he was worried that Phyllis may have been unwell. If Geraldine gives me the full name and address..."

"Phyllis Davis. 42 Drybrook Gardens," Geraldine said, with a winning smile. "I'm afraid I don't have her telephone number to hand."

"I'm sure the operator will oblige. Merci." Toby made a bow and legged it.

How pleasing to be first into the fray, before Alasdair was even under starter's orders. Toby enjoyed playing Watson, his usual onscreen character traits of reliability, gullibility and being over trustful fitting perfectly into the role. It was even more fun to play Holmes and Watson in real life, especially as his contribution to solving puzzles was more effective than the doctor's had proved.

The theatre manager, Whitlock, wasn't hard to run to earth and was more than happy to help, especially when Toby laid on with a trowel the story of the girl's possible illness and the leading lady's concern for her friend. The operator connected the call, and Phyllis, when she answered, sounded less than happy.

No, she hadn't the foggiest where George might have gone. As far as she was concerned if she never saw him again it would be too soon. No, she didn't want to elaborate on why that was. At which point she slammed the phone down so hard Toby's ear rang.

Now, wasn't that intriguing?

When he got back to the party, Alasdair was ensconced with Sally and Beth, so couldn't be easily cut out—to use one of the naval analogies Toby was becoming so fond of—and informed of events privately.

Sally greeted him with, "Alasdair was just telling us how much action there'll be in your new film."

"Oh yes." Toby rubbed his hands. "There's going to be a heroic scene for him. Gets to swim out to a sinking boat with a rope so that she can be hitched up and pulled safely ashore. He'll have the water soaking the manly shirt over his manly chest."

Beth rolled her eyes. "Isn't that a bit far-fetched?"

"It's the absolute historical truth. He was a right hero our Edward. Doesn't get the recognition he deserves today because old Lord Nel nabbed it all by dying at Trafalgar. I daresay that if Pellew had expired on deck rather than in his bed we'd all be more aware of him."

"Does he die in the film?" Sally looked horrified at the prospect.

"No. Alasdair's not due a death scene for another couple of films. They have to ration them out, you know, because it upsets his lady fans." Toby grinned as the famous Hamilton eyebrow shot up into its classic Alasdair's-character-is-annoyed position. He was spared being upbraided, however, by a loud cry from Geraldine—clearly still in stage mode—across the room.

"Is Phyllis all right?"

"Excuse us." Toby took Alasdair by the elbow, better to manoeuvre him to Sir Ian's group. "She appears to be. Gone home in a huff, I'd say." He gave Sir Ian a knowing look. "And George is persona non grata because he appears to be the cause of it. I assume all the other young ladies are present and accounted for?"

Geraldine scowled. "Did Phyllis think the rotter had gone off with one?"

"She didn't specify. But whatever he's done I wouldn't want to be him when next they meet."

The conversation moved on to other matters, ostensibly more socially acceptable but no less painful for Toby and Alasdair because they concerned the quality of what they'd just seen. Even their considerable acting abilities were stretched in demonstrating they'd thought the opera in any way enjoyable, despite their leading the applause which both the leading lady and their boss had noticed.

They'd hit the rather thorny topic of the libretto, when Alasdair discreetly nudged Toby and flicked the uninsured eyebrow in the direction of the door, where the theatre manager had appeared, in an evidently distressed state, trying to catch their eye.

"Sir Ian, ladies, please excuse us for a moment. This may concern George." Alasdair withdrew, Toby in his wake: once out of earshot, he murmured gleefully, "Let's go and see what's up."

"I'm right behind you." Ever since he'd first noticed George's absence Toby's mind had been turning over the possibilities for what had occurred. From the glint in Alasdair's eye, he suspected the same was true of him.

"Mr. Whitlock, did you want us?" Alasdair asked.

"Yes, although I suppose it's Sir Ian I should be talking to."

How curious. Toby nodded. "We can introduce him, if you wish."

"No, we can wait to see what you think. We have a mutual friend—Johnny Fisher—who says your discretion can be relied upon. He also says you have a connection to the police, Mr. Bowe."

"A family one, yes." Who'd be very cross if Toby was sticking his nose where it shouldn't be. "What's all this about?"

"There's been—" Whitlock ran a handkerchief across his brow, "an accident, with Mr. Howell. Although I don't see how it can have been accidental."

"Have you called the police or an ambulance?"

"Not yet, Mr. Bowe. I thought it could all turn rather awkward so I was wondering if Sir Ian and some of his friends mightn't like to take the opportunity to slip away first."

"No." Alasdair's tones would have rivalled those of Pellew himself. "If it's a police matter we should ring them straight away, and call for medical help. And all of us should stay here until they advise us as they see fit. I'll talk to Sir Ian, discreetly, and ensure that nobody leaves this room. Perhaps Mr. Bowe could be of assistance to you in the interim?"

"I'll try my best. I did first aid training in the war, and as you'll have guessed, I'm aware of some police procedure."

"He's beyond the 'elp of first aid." The manager's tones slipped several rungs down the social ladder. "Gawd, you haven't seen the state of him."

***

Whitlock hadn't exaggerated.

George Howell was far beyond the help of medical aid, with what appeared to Toby's untutored eyes to be a stab wound plumb in the left side of his chest, the blood massing on his crisp white dinner shirt. The actor was lying in an alcove off one of the corridors back of house, just around a corner from the office where Toby had made his telephone call. Most likely George had been lying there already dead while Phyllis was being contacted, although why had nobody noticed him before?

"Nobody ever comes along here," Whitlock said, his thoughts clearly going down the same lines. "I only went to investigate because..." He turned a ghastly greenish shade, as though about to decorate the carpet with his stomach contents.

"Steady on. Let's go back around the corner where we can't see him. There's nothing we can do to help the chap now, except keep gawkers away. Mr. O'Connor will have ensured the police are on their way."

They'd encountered the doorman in the corridor, Whitlock asking him to contact the authorities as a matter of urgency. And to ensure all the external doors were locked and kept locked after he'd done so.

Once they'd got safely out of sight, Toby halted. "You were saying?"

"What? Oh, yes. Nobody would usually be going to that part of the building at this time of day. Haunt of cleaners and the like. I only went to investigate because of the theatre cat. He's black and white you see, only when he came round the corner and trotted towards me I noticed that the white bits were—" Whitlock paled again.

"Yes, I get the drift." Like the old joke, black and white and red all over. "It might be an idea to see if we can locate the cat before he's had the chance to clean himself. He could be carrying vital evidence." As would the killer themselves, given how far the blood had spread, although the moggy might have had something to do with that aspect. The soiled murder weapon would be tricky to hide, especially to smuggle out of the building—why had the killer not left it there in an attempt to make it look like an unusual suicide? Although the killer could be long gone by now, those locked theatre doors having been locked too late to prevent the horse bolting.

The sound of Alasdair's voice, in conversation with Sir Ian, floated up the stairs. Toby sprang to head them off. "I'm afraid it's definitely George. Stabbed to death by the look of it. Mr. Whitlock's in a fair state about the situation."

Alasdair gave him a brief are-you-all-right glance, to which Toby nodded. He'd seen much worse during the war, and among men he'd liked better. Alasdair turned to O'Connor, who had followed them, a few steps behind. "Best take Mr. Whitlock downstairs to the green room and get a sweet tea into him if somebody will rustle one up."

"Oh, God," Sir Ian groaned, when they'd taken him to view the body. "I wouldn't wish that on my worst enemy." He eyed the corpse again, then ran his hands through what little hair still adorned his pate. "This is terrible, and not just for him. You'll think me hard-hearted, but what about the publicity? For the theatre and for the studio."

"I wouldn't worry about that." Alasdair's stern tones were evidently as clipped as he dared when addressing somebody who had such power over his career. "It's the sort of sensation that will make people flock to his last film, anyway. The man *playing* the murderer is himself murdered."

Toby nodded. A cynical viewpoint, admittedly, but probably an entirely realistic assessment of the situation.

"I'm not thinking of that, so much as..." Sir Ian appeared to be struggling for words, even though he'd have seen men killed much more brutally the best part of forty years previously. "There were plenty of Landseer people here tonight. What if one of them killed Howell? A viper in our midst."

That was a scenario that even Alasdair's finest raising of the insured eyebrow wouldn't have been expressive enough to remark upon.

Reel Three

Alasdair and Toby's romantic intentions for the rest of the night came to nothing.

They'd stayed to the bitter end of the evening, supporting Sir Ian and ensuring that distress for the other attendees at the party was kept to a minimum. Geraldine had proved invaluable in the crisis, offering to inform Phyllis of the bad news and generally preventing some of the other women present from going to pieces. They clearly bred them tough in the world of opera.

By the time the two actors had got back to Alasdair's house they'd not wanted to do more than imbibe a nightcap and flop into a pair of comfortable leather armchairs. It wasn't just a case of exhaustion—indulging in activities of a horizontal nature would have felt like an insult to the dead man.

"I have a confession to make," Toby said, as he swirled the brandy in his glass. "I've had a hankering, all evening, to do a bit of sleuthing, like we got drawn into last time. But the memory of George lying there has rather put me off. It's not a game, like locating Johnny's missing secretary."

"No. Indeed." Alasdair took a sip of scotch. "I wouldn't be surprised if they arrest Phyllis. When he interviewed us, Inspector Mayfield was adamant that the first place you looked for a killer was close to the victim. The fact she'd already left and had been in a foul mood with George was grist to his mill."

Neither of them had been impressed with this particular policeman.

"Hm." Toby stared into his glass. "I hope he isn't so blinkered as not to consider other possibilities."

"So do I." Alasdair glanced at his lover sidelong. "Perhaps you should have a little word with your father."

"Much as I hate playing the family card, I might just do that. If I think investigations are going down the wrong road. It'll be all over the newspapers so we'll be able to keep an eye on developments."

They would indeed. And how gratifying that would be. "You know I had great fun playing Sherlock Holmes, in both senses of the word. As did you. *We may well hear things* over the next few days, and while it's the police's job to look into a case of murder, were we to come across anything that was pertinent to the case it would be our duty to report it back to Mayfield."

Toby's eyes danced merrily by the fire's glow. "Does that we may well hear things bit encompass us asking pertinent questions in certain quarters? People gossip like mad when unusual events happen and they're more likely to mention things to us than to a policeman, I'd have thought. Especially with a smidgeon of encouragement."

"I'd agree with you. Although remember Holmes and Watson. It's not unknown for them to find themselves the target of the killer's wrath." This wasn't a case of a missing person, like last time. While they'd received threats then, they'd never been in the sort of danger that a madman—or woman—with a sharp blade posed.

Toby laid down his drink, to come across and perch on the arm of Alasdair's chair. "You do know that I'd rather eschew all curiosity than put either of us at risk. It would be a crying shame to have survived the war only to be killed in peacetime."

Alasdair chuckled, despite the sombre tone the conversation had taken. "Talking of which, the last time you stayed here you damn near killed me. Took me a week to recover from all that activity."

Toby rubbed his cheek. "Seeing as the time referred to was less than a week ago, that's a bare-faced lie. Not so barefaced at this time of the night, though. Your chin feels like sandpaper."

"I feel like sandpaper. Raspy all over. I need my bed, and as much sleep as I can get. I'm sorry if that scuppers your plans."

"I don't think it does. I need my sleep, too. Not least because it'll give my poor brain a chance to work through everything that's gone on." Toby caressed Alasdair's cheek once more. "We'll never be a married couple but we can play at being one. You can be me old Dutch and warm yer feet on me back."

"You sound horribly like Nellie Gwynn and her 'ave a squeeze of me oranges." Alasdair drained his drink. "And now, sleep. Before you start making terrible jokes about getting the pip."

***

The morning saw them both feeling brighter, helped by the excellent spread that Alasdair's manservant, the devoted Morgan, had laid out on the beautifully laundered white linen table cloth in an equally beautiful dining room. Tea, toast and eggs poached to perfection would set any man up for the day. Although the arrival of the morning papers, and a perusal of the headlines, soon cast a shadow on things.

"Looks like Sir Ian got what he dreaded. It's all over the front of this paper." Toby held out the Mirror to display the headline.

"If you recall, it wasn't the publicity he dreaded so much as the thought that one of us might have stabbed Howell. Now, have a gander at this one. They either went to press later or they have somebody on the inside." He opened a copy of the Express, carefully avoiding polluting the pristine cloth with the newsprint. "According to this, the police have arrested his girlfriend, by which I assume that's Phyllis although no name is given."

"Just as you predicted." Toby took the newspaper to read the story through. "This doesn't make any sense, though. It says Howell was killed around the time the third act was on but Phyllis had already gone home by then."

"Unless she came back, killed him, then returned home once more. To be ready and waiting to put on a distressed act when she was informed of his death."

"True. But she didn't sound as though she was putting on an act when I spoke to her. Nor did she sound like she was expecting a different message." Toby wrinkled his attractive nose. "I guess there's the possibility O'Connor lied about seeing her leave, the reasons for which we wot not."

"If I were Mayfield I'd be checking the dress she was wearing. There surely would have been a lot of blood."

"Ah, but how would anybody know which dress she was wearing later? Unless she was very silly she'd not have returned in an outfit as distinctive as the one O'Connor noted."

"Or she might have stayed at home once she'd got there and it was somebody else who killed him, which I think is much more likely. He wasn't exactly the most pleasant of chaps, unless first impressions deceive me." Alasdair grabbed the last slice of toast, slathering it with bramble jelly. "I can imagine he rubbed plenty of people up the wrong way."

"I'm sure all of us rub someone or other up the wrong way. We don't all end up stabbed. Not even you, for stealing the last slice."

"Morgan will make you more if you're still hungry, Mr. Hollow-legs." Alasdair cut his slice in half, offered it to his lover, had the offer politely refused, then scoffed the thing before Toby could change his mind.

The ringing of the telephone and the subsequent appearance at the door of Morgan himself, temporarily put a halt to any discussion.

"It's Sir Ian, Mr. Hamilton. Wishes to speak to you as a matter of urgency."

Toby raised an eyebrow in a gesture not quite as elegant as Alasdair could manage, but one almost its equal in expressiveness. "Stand not upon the order of your going. I, for one, am itching to hear what this is about."

"Then stand in the hallway and listen," Alasdair suggested, as he headed for the telephone and adopted his most businesslike tones. "Hello, Sir Ian. How can I help you?"

"Find me a new co-star to play the part of Second Lieutenant Hamer, for a start." The Landseer owner sounded both tired and desperate. "And then extricate Geraldine from the clutches of the police."

"I beg your pardon? I thought, according to the papers, they'd arrested Phyllis."

"Not so, old boy," Sir Ian roared. "Sorry, I'm feeling a bit worked up over this as you can imagine, although that's no excuse for deafening you. It seems Geraldine was having a fling with Howell. I had no idea."

Alasdair bet he didn't. Probably Phyllis was blissfully unaware, as well. Perhaps until just before the first interval.

"I can only begin to imagine how upset you are." Not least at all the money Sir Ian would have piled into supporting the awful opera. "Would you like me to get my agent onto seeing if anyone of the required calibre is free to take the part of Hamer? I could get Toby's man on the case, too."

"That would take a weight off my mind, given that filming is due to start so soon, and Rattigan's up to his ears in organising the practicalities. But actually, there was something else. I wasn't entirely joking when I asked you about getting Geraldine out of the cells. You've done something similar before, I believe? In the investigating line?"

"We located a missing person, yes. Murder hasn't been in our purview. Although if you believe Geraldine to be innocent we'll do all we can to help clear her name, even if I'm not entirely sure what we can achieve."

"You can talk to people, especially people in the business. They'll open up to you, more than they would to the police. And you've got an eye for spotting when somebody's acting. The police won't necessarily have that inside knowledge."

Both of those were valid points. Add them to the actors' inclination to do a bit of sleuthing and the proposal became highly attractive. "We'll try our best."

"Good man. I know I can rely on your discretion. And Toby's."

"Well I'm blowed," Toby said, once Alasdair had updated him on the half of the conversation he couldn't hear. "So she was the girlfriend they'd arrested. I wonder if Phyllis found out about his affair and that's what the row was about."

"Quite likely. Although how the police knew about Howell's affair with Geraldine when none of us did beats me."

"Phyllis probably told them." Toby, who'd been leaning against a door jamb, looking alluring, rubbed his hands gleefully. "Still, we've got exactly what we wanted. Official sanction to poke our noses in."

"Very true." In which case, they needed to start using their brains. "I don't see how Geraldine could have killed him. She was onstage for almost all the wretched production."

"In the interests of accuracy, she wasn't. Do you remember the scene in the Tower of London with the supposedly comic jailor?"

"Oh, yes. I'd tried to blot it from my mind." The start of act three had been highly derivative—the composer and librettist must have been familiar with Die Fledermaus—and also extremely unfunny. It would have given someone not appearing in it time to nip away, meet Howell and deliver the fatal injury. "Wouldn't she have been noticed flitting about, though? Especially if she returned covered in blood? That would be fine if she were playing Lady Macbeth but apart from that, it would be taking a hell of a risk."

"You know that and I know that, from experience, but I bet the police don't." Toby ran his expressive fingers across his jaw. "I wonder why they arrested her. And when and where."

"She left before us, so they must have gone around to her house, later. When whatever bit of evidence turned up to incriminate her." Alasdair shrugged. "She didn't give herself away by having hysterics when I broke the news at the party."

"Hm. I think I should go back to the theatre," Toby said. "I could say I'm looking for a scarf that Sally had last evening and reckons she's lost. I bet O'Connor or one of the others will be able to shed some light on the situation."

"Excellent." Alasdair wished he'd had that idea first, although he'd had his own brainwave, one of tsunami proportions. "I think I'm going to have a chat with Nigel Weatherly."

Nigel had been cast as one of Pellew's midshipmen, and although he was in reality a bit long in the tooth for playing a "snotty", on the screen he easily passed for a sixteen year old. He'd been playing younger than his age in many a film for Landseer over the years since his first child role.

"Nigel? Why him?"

"Because, my beautiful but oblivious love, he used to go out with Geraldine." Alasdair led the way back to the dining room. "That's why he was allowed to miss the event last night."

Toby, following in his wake in amazement, asked, "How do you get to know such things?"

"That's easy. Morgan belongs to a club for gentlemen's gentlemen. He heard it from the man who tends Nigel's father. Who is a Viscount, by the way. So he outdoes even you for rank."

Toby made an elaborate bow. "I defer to his superior breeding and to your stunning skills at fishing out tittle-tattle. Hie thee to young Nigel—should we call him 'The honourable Nigel' by the way?—and see what he can add. Offer him your manly shoulder to cry on or a beer to drown his sorrows with. All chaps together and whatnot."

Alasdair snorted. "You sound like something out of Billy Bunter. I'll give the studio a call to get Nigel's telephone number. I'll cite Sir Ian's orders so he won't be able to wangle out of seeing me. Landseer business."

"I have a feeling we'll be using that phrase quite often over the next few days." Toby leaned across to give him a kiss. "I'll ring later, with anything I've discovered. It may be late—dinner with the parents later. With any luck, father will have plenty of light to shed on the business."

"We can but hope."

Alasdair also hoped he might use his influence to get a better man onto the investigation, although that might be a wish too far.

Reel Four

London. Toby loved the place despite its imperfections, not least the smothering fogs that had a habit of descending exactly when they weren't wanted. But this morning it had on its handsomest face, the rain that had fallen in the early hours freshening the streets and gardens, and a bright sun twinkling in any drops that remained to decorate the leaves.

The unexpected beauty around him helped Toby get his thoughts in order before arriving at the Imperial Theatre. He'd not confessed this to Alasdair, but the previous night he'd been dreaming about being a witness to Howell's murder, of seeing Sir Ian himself sticking a large hat pin, adorned with a miniature of Nellie Gwynne—it was a dream, after all and therefore didn't need to be entirely logical—into the actor's chest.

He'd woken, thought, "Stuff and nonsense! Why kill one of your stars just as a film is about to go into production?" turned over and gone back to sleep. Funny to now discover that Sir Ian had a potential motive in the form of the age-old love triangle, although equally odd to think that he would be asking them to delve into matters if he were guilty. Unless he assumed they were so hopeless that they'd never get close to the truth and would simply muddy the waters for the policemen.

No, that horse wouldn't run. Sir Ian wouldn't risk exposing sixty six point six recurring per cent of his biggest constellation of stars to a charge of obstructing police business or whatever the offence was called. He would also know that Toby's father was one of the most efficient members of the metropolitan force and would either stop his son interfering if he was becoming a nuisance or snap up any unconsidered but useful trifles that Toby happened across.

Sir Ian must be genuinely concerned that a miscarriage of justice might occur, and was trying all he could to prevent it. Although a cynical man might also say that if Sir Ian helped to keep Geraldine out of the hangman's noose—or simply out of spending too long on remand—then it would likely raise his romantic standing with her. In more ways than one, knowing the boss.

Toby sniggered, and then forced his thoughts out of the gutter and onto higher matters, such as producing an effective performance for the theatre staff.

The doorman, who was in the foyer attempting to get a large notice through the doorve him a salute which Toby returned.

He eyed the board which explained in large letters that performances had been cancelled for the next few days. "Need a hand with that? It looks like it weighs a ton."

"I wouldn't say no, sir. Like shifting an elephant."

Between them, they manoeuvred the large wooden stand through the door, down the steps and onto the pavement.

"Thanks, Mr. Bowe. I'd never have managed that alone."

"My pleasure, Mr. O'Connor." They mounted the steps once more.

"Now how can I help you?"

"It's a case of a missing scarf. Rather a nice silver one. Silk or muslin I suppose—not really up on these things. Sally—Miss Chambers—was wearing it last evening. With all the unpleasantness it seems to have gone astray."

O'Connor smiled. "Would that be the young lady with you?"

"The very same." Toby suddenly remembered the doorman's sharp eye and hoped he wouldn't have noticed Sally was still wearing the scarf as she left. Hopefully she'd slipped on her coat which would cover the thing, or everyone had been too upset to notice anything so trivial. "I got a rather garbled message from my valet this morning saying that she thought she'd lost it and did I know where it was? I asked him to tell her I was dropping into town today and would make a small detour here."

"Nothing's too much bother when helping out a lady in distress. I'll go and check the lost property right away."

Toby waited in the foyer, aware of the sombre mood that hung over the place. London had seen death aplenty, right in its heart, during the darkest days of the war, but this felt different. Death striking out of place.

"It's not there, I'm afraid, sir." O'Connor's voice brought Toby out of his reverie. "We've been very careful checking through the items that turned up last night, as you can imagine. Have to give the police a full inventory, in case there's a knife or two among them." His rolled eyes eloquently expressed his opinion of the officers who'd turned up the previous evening.

"She probably left it in the cab she and Beth took home. Thank you for eliminating this option. You must be rushed off your feet what with all this awful business last night." Toby gave what he hoped was a nicely judged shudder.

"Thank you for your consideration. Not everyone's as thoughtful. Police especially." The doorman rubbed his thigh. "You'd have thought they'd show more respect to an old soldier."

"You would. Especially as you saw action in the Great War, I believe." Toby smiled, sympathetically.

"I did indeed, sir. And acted as fire warden in the one just gone. Not as glamorous as you up in your plane, but we all have to serve somehow."

"There was nothing glamorous in flying, despite what it may look like in our films." Toby patted O'Connor's shoulder. "They—by which I mean both police and theatre management—should be grateful there was somebody to hand last night who'd not panic at the sight of blood and who'd know what to do in a crisis."

That wasn't overegging the pudding. The doorman had proved himself more than capable in terms of getting things organised while the manager himself had, by small degrees, gone completely to pieces.

"Thank you, sir. It's all over the papers, though, and I suppose it will be for a week. I've even had reporters trying to ask me stuff." O'Connor looked daggers in the direction of the street, where a newspaper vendor stood next to a headline proclaiming *Screen murderer victim of brutal attack*. "No shame, some people. Just want to pry into everything."

"Indeed." Toby tried the affronted-innocent expression. "You keep on keeping mum, except if it's the police asking."

"Don't worry about that, sir. Although I'm not sure the police have got the first clue what really happened. They've arrested Miss Wilson."

"So I read. Although why they did that is beyond my comprehension."

The doorman took a quick glance over his shoulder. "I shouldn't be saying this, but seeing as you're the son of a policeman..."

Toby inclined his head, encouragingly. There had to be some advantage to his life story being spread all over the social and variety columns.

"The fact is, they found a note crumpled up in Howell's hand. It said if he didn't stop running around with everything in a skirt he'd pay for it. Seems like he has."

"Nasty. I'd have assumed the lady he was with last evening, Phyllis, would have written that."

"So would I, sir. I understand the way it was supposed to be written—all block capitals, they say—was done to disguise the writing so you could probably pin it on anyone."

"It wouldn't even have to be from a woman. There are brothers and fathers and unrequited lovers who also would want to take revenge on a lothario."

"Very true, sir, but you see," O'Connor leaned closer, "they also found the murder weapon. It was discarded along the corridor, the very route you'd take if you were heading for the dressing rooms."

Toby nodded encouragingly again, then waited. People usually liked to fill a silence.

"Do you remember that scene in the production—I saw it in rehearsal—where Nell Gwynne uses a knife to cut up an orange? They use a real blade, not a prop one. That's the knife they reckon was used to kill him and it's only Miss Wilson who uses it in the play."

Toby recalled the scene referred to. It had been an almost acceptable part of the opera. "But wouldn't that have been held in the wings along with the other props, so she can pick it up as she enters?"

"You'd have thought so, sir, but apparently she insists on keeping it in her room. It was a gift from an admirer, or so the girl in the ticket booth reckons, and she's usually right about such things. So Miss Wilson didn't want it out of her sight." O'Connor shook his head. "Nothing's more than circumstantial, but it's all looking a bit bleak for her, I'm afraid."

Toby sighed. "I fear you're right."

***

Alasdair strode down the pavement, enjoying the hint of warmth in the sun. Nowhere could beat England when her weather was behaving itself. A shame that wasn't more often.

He spotted Nigel Weatherly waiting for him and even at a distance the actor appeared to be in good spirits, hardly in need of either a good cry or drowning his woes in drink. The impression he gave as he stood on the steps of the Livingstone bar was of a man ready for a fight, with the potential opponent being the chap with whom he was in conversation. That was made plain by the line, "Going down to the police station and punching someone won't help anybody," which Alasdair overheard as he reached them.

"That sounds like excellent advice." Alasdair gave them a knowing smile.

"Don't you start, Alasdair." Nigel shook his hand. "I get enough from him. This is Cuffy Temple."

Cuffy? A public school type nickname, Alasdair guessed, rather than an aberration at the font. He thrust out his hand. "Pleased to meet you."

"Likewise. Maybe you can help talk some sense into this ass. It's about that business at the Imperial."

Alasdair nodded. "Shocking affair."

"Nigel and I made our acting debuts there as a pair of urchins. Before I realised I had no talent for acting. Makes me sad to think of the old place so besmirched." He jerked an accusatory thumb in Nigel's direction. "He wants to kick up a stink. You know they've arrested Geraldine Wilson for the murder?"

"So I hear. "

"Nigel's ex, you know," Cuffy said, earning a punch on the arm from Nigel for his pains. "What have I done now? That's the truth, isn't it? Just because she's been taken up by Ian Sheringham doesn't mean you should hide the past."

"Sir Ian." Alasdair didn't like this Cuffy chap one bit. "I thought that Geraldine was going out with Howell himself. Did I get that wrong?"

Nigel ran his hands through his hair. "Let's not discuss this out here. Cuffy, be a good chap and make yourself scarce for a while. Alasdair and I have got studio business to discuss and Sir Ian wouldn't like it if we stand gossiping like old women."

"Or start untoward rumours," Alasdair added, with relish.

"Okie dokie." Cuffy, who seemed unbothered by his dismissal, made his way off down the street, whistling.

"Fancy a drink?" Nigel asked. "I appreciate that the sun's not over the yardarm quite yet."

"Coffee for me, if this place makes a decent brew. But don't let me stop you from having a snifter. You look like you need it."

"You can say that again. This is a ghastly business."

Once they were settled in a quiet corner of the bar, Alasdair with a reasonable cup of coffee—or so the aroma led him to believe—and Nigel with a stiff whisky, they could resume conversation. "Were you there last night?"

"No. Not a big enough name to be invited." Nigel frowned. "Or maybe Sir Ian had heard about me and Geraldine, and didn't want me queering his pitch. Risking her falling for the ex again. Which presumably meant he didn't know the state of play with Howell."

"Quite." Alasdair, taking a sip of coffee, fixed the young actor with the sort of piercing gaze he'd used when playing

Sherlock Holmes. "How long is it since you and Geraldine split up?"

"About a month. And that was because she'd fallen for that rat Howell. Oh, I know I shouldn't speak ill of the dead." He raised an apologetic hand, in a gesture Alasdair was fairly certain he'd based on one Toby used in Wings of Love. "It's the truth, though. And only the truth will help now he's gone, in terms of running his real murderer to ground."

"Quite right. That's why Sir Ian has asked me to make some discreet enquiries, on behalf of Landseer."

"Discreet?" Nigel chortled. "He's good at that. I bet Howell had no idea Geraldine had her sights set higher. Mind you, I daresay Geraldine didn't know Howell was two timing her. You know, I almost pulled out of the Pellew film when I heard he was in it, but I'm afraid the moral high ground took second place to my career."

An all too common tale, if some of the rumours Alasdair had heard about the casting couch were true—and not just actresses falling prey to it, either. Terrible to be forced to make such compromises. "I too hate to speak ill of the dead—which means that's exactly what I'm going to do—but Howell didn't strike me as being particularly likeable."

"Got a bit of a reputation in the industry for being difficult to work with. Certainly for the last few films at Marquess once he'd become a star name."

"How do you get to hear all this? I thought I had my finger on the pulse but you knock me into a cocked hat."

"Ah, it's the social network of the lower ranks, as 'twere. We bit part players have to find something to do to pass the time and so we gossip about our betters." Nigel twirled his glass in his hand. "And, anyway, Cuffy's old nanny's cousin was his dresser at Marquess. Or was it his cousin's nanny. No, that can't be right. Anyway, the information came to me both ways and they agreed with each other."

"You wouldn't happen to know this dresser's name? Sir Ian is keen to do all he can to aid the police and I'd imagine Howell's dresser would know many of his secrets." The invisible nature of servants had its uses. They saw and heard things that others didn't, given that sometimes their masters and mistresses forgot they were there, or found them below notice.

"Oh, lord. Edwina? Enid? Something like that." Nigel's expression would be worth reproducing onscreen when they got to the scene where the midshipmen were struggling with their latitude and longitude calculations, so puzzled did he appear. "Look, I'm meeting Cuffy for lunch later, so I can find out the name. If you give me your number, I'll get it straight to you. With a side order of some information on where to find her. "

"Much appreciated, thank you." Alasdair lifted his cup, but the remains of his coffee had turned too cold to drink. He made his goodbyes and set off to hail a cab to take him to his costume fitting, frustrated that it took so much time to find out so little and annoyed that Sherlock Holmes seemed to have clues practically throwing themselves in his path.

***

The telephone call from Toby came as Alasdair had almost given up waiting.

"Sorry I'm late. Lots happening, of which more anon." Toby detailed his earlier conversation with O'Connor, Alasdair responding with what little he'd gleaned from Nigel.

"I suppose your father didn't have any bright ideas concerning the case?"

"Surprisingly few. We had a long conversation about what drives somebody to take another person's life. Outside a time of war, when we were all at it without a second thought, of course." Toby's loquacious manner suggested a level of insobriety well into merriment but short of incoherence. "Father reckons it's usually lust, greed and anger, if not all seven of the deadly sins."

"I don't think anybody used sloth as a motivation, but I bow to his greater experience. Still, seven deadly sins is a good place to start. Isn't that own of Howell's early films, by the way?"

"Not quite. I heard all about that from mother." Toby chuckled. "The first of Howell's Marquess studio shockers was apparently called *The Deadly Sin of Murder*. Shot him to stardom.

Alasdair slapped the hallstand triumphantly. "That's it!"

"That's what?"

"That's what's buzzing at the back of my mind like a bee bashing at a closed window. The name of the film opened the sash and let it escape."

"How picturesque. I have no idea to what you're referring, though."

"Sorry. It's the thing I said was worrying me about Howell. The thing I couldn't remember. There was a problem on the set of that film, an accident maybe, and one of the actresses was badly injured. I don't know all the details, but I do know that George Howell was present at the time and it was implied he might have been involved somehow. It clearly didn't come to anything or Landseer wouldn't have touched him with a bargepole." Like Caesar's wife, Landseer actors had to be above suspicion.

"Somebody might bear a grudge, though."

"Indeed." Alasdair's mind was going great guns now. "And here's a different thought. We know from experience that some cinemagoers get very worked up about films. Could one of them have seen *The Deadly Sin of Murder* and other similar offerings and confused the Howell they saw on screen with the one in real life? Believing he really was a personification of evil so deciding to take revenge?"

"It's possible. But in that case how could the culprit ever be run to ground? Think of the number of people who go to the pictures."

"We don't need to find out who did it. Just extricate Geraldine from the mess she's in." Much as Alasdair regretted admitting that fact, it was the truth. Once she was no longer under suspicion they'd have no valid reason for keeping involved.

"Ah. That's the lots happening I referred to earlier. They've let her go this evening."

"What?" Alasdair, overwhelmed with disappointment, slumped into the hallway chair.

"Turns out she couldn't have done it. Her dresser has been in to swear she never left her dressing room the whole evening apart from when she was onstage or waiting in the wings."

"Not even to powder her nose?"

"Well, yes, obviously, but she has her own private facility so didn't need to leave the room even to do that."

"The dresser couldn't be covering for her?" Alasdair asked, feebly, the last vestiges of a chance at playing detectives slipping out of their grasp.

"Father thinks not. Her son is a policeman, for a start, and says she's of impeccable character—not too devoted to Geraldine, either, so if there was any dirt to be dished, she'd be dishing it." Toby sounded just as disappointed. "That's not all. Her knife has turned up, tucked away in her dressing room, and no sign of its being used in the attack. As a result, Mayfield's been replaced, not an hour ago. Apparently, he refused to believe Geraldine hadn't done it. Questions have been asked in high places, as a result of which he's got the chop. Father isn't surprised—says he's never had time for the man and the results he gets are usually because the obvious suspect in a case is often the culprit. Luck rather than judgement."

"Who's taking over?"

"Matthew Firestone. Solid man. Uses his brain. Likeable with it. I can just about remember when he used to dandle me on his knee when he was a raw recruit to the force." Toby sniggered. "Father reckons Firestone refers to that fact every time my name turns up in the paper or he sees it on a film poster."

"I bet that impresses Mrs. Firestone," Alasdair snorted.

They ended the conversation with some fond words and an agreement to meet the next day, after Alasdair had been to see Edith, whose address Nigel had supplied and with whom an interview had already been agreed, and Toby had been fitted for his sailing rig.

He replaced the receiver with a sigh. Sir Ian wouldn't have further cause to sanction their involvement, so any information on the case would have to come via Toby's father or the press—the latter being more effusive yet less reliable. Taken all in all, it simply wasn't fair.

Reel Five

When the taxi dropped Alasdair off at the agreed meeting place—a genteel tea rooms just off the Old Brompton Road—the actor's spirits were still in a slump. What was the point of meeting Howell's dresser when their input to the case was probably at an end? Still, his conscience wouldn't let him cancel the encounter.

Edith, however, made a refreshing change from many of the ladies Alasdair came across. For one thing she was neither tongue-tied nor awestruck, but then she was in the business, and knew about actors and their foibles. When you had to deal with someone's dirty linen—figuratively and literally—the glamour soon wore off.

Once settled with a "nice cup of tea and a bun", which she'd chosen instead of a drink, they entered a stream of small talk about what they'd done in the war—Edith had been a nurse, like Fiona, but not at Netley—and the paths they'd trodden since. That eased the subject neatly around to her time at Marquess.

"Terrible about Mr. Howell," she said, with a hint of a sob.

"Absolutely tragic, Mrs. Daley."

"Oh, call me Edith. All my gentlemen and ladies have. I don't stand on ceremony."

"Then I insist you call me Alasdair, for the same reason." Certainly all his gentlemen had called him by that name, even if in very different and far more intimate circumstances. "They seem to think Geraldine did it, although I have my doubts."

Alasdair kept with the story as had been reported the previous day. The morning editions hadn't got wind of the actress's release and mentioning it would only beg the question of how he knew.

"Funny you should say that, because they're the exact words I used to my Clarrie. She's my daughter and a huge fan of yours, although I always tell her that Mr. Bowe's more my cup of tea. He suffers so nobly."

Alasdair just avoided snorting his own tea out through his nose. "I must remember to tell him that, next time our paths cross. What about these doubts of yours, Edith? Are they based on something you've seen or heard?"

Edith leaned slightly closer. "Well, I don't like to deal in tittle-tattle, but seeing as this is a murder case and seeing as you'd have been in the same film as him had he lived, I don't mind telling you. Mr. Howell was getting nasty letters. Two to my knowledge, but there could have been more."

"What sort of nasty letters?" The sort that had been found on his body?

Edith, fussing over her tea, flicked her eyes uneasily.

"You can tell me, in strictest confidence. I know that sometimes, doing the job you do, you can't help seeing or hearing things without meaning to."

A relieved smile lit Edith's face. "That's exactly it, sir. It was on the set of his last film at Marquess. *A Strangler's Hands*. He asked me—very curt he was which wasn't like him at all, leastways not with me—if I'd seen anyone come into his dressing room or if I'd been given a note to leave there. I said no to both. Anyway, when I was emptying his bin, which was not strictly my job but he was very fussy like that, not wanting others to pry into his effects, I noticed some crumpled up paper. I thought if I took a peep I might recognise the writing."

"Good thinking." Alasdair suppressed a smile, understanding such inquisitiveness. "And perhaps it's just as well that you did, given what's happened. What did the vile thing say?"

"I don't have the exact words, but it was something like that the writer knew a bad thing had happened and that other people did, too. And that Mr. Howell couldn't get away with it."

"No detail?"

"I'm afraid not. No details of the bad thing, or a name for who'd sent it, but then the writer wouldn't be so silly. But Mr. Howell must have known who it was. I'd seen his face when he came out of the dressing room and he was scared." She paled, recalling that day. "Really scared, not acting. He clearly had good right to be, given what's happened."

As Edith topped up both their cups, Alasdair asked, "Do the police know about these letters?"

The dresser almost dropped the strainer. Steadying her hand, she said, "They haven't seen fit to ask me about him, as yet. I suppose I should get in contact but when I look at what happened to that poor actress, I wonder if they'd arrest me instead!"

Alasdair bit back on his frustration. This woman didn't seem stupid—far from it—so why had she not gone to the police straight away with this tale of threatening notes? "I'm sure that if you took Clarrie with you they wouldn't dare pull such a stunt. And you might have invaluable information in that head of yours, if the note came from the person who killed him."

"I know, sir. I'm being silly about it. Perhaps you could have a word with them instead?"

"And have them arresting me? I wouldn't have your Carrie to protect me." Alasdair tried to laugh it off. "No, you'd tell the story better than I would. I'd imagine the police prefer information at first hand rather than hearsay." He'd once portrayed a lawyer, in his early days, and there'd been a whole palaver about whether a witness's testimony was admissible. He was sure hearsay came into things somewhere.

"Oh, all right then." Edith sipped her tea once more.

"Can I ask a personal question?"

A brief look of alarm flickered over Edith's face. "Now, Mr.—um, Alasdair—I hope you're not going to be naughty."

"Me?" He jiggled the insured eyebrow. "Far from it. I was simply wondering why Mr. Howell hadn't brought you from Landseer with him."

That had been a bow drawn at a venture, because filming had yet to start and the only information he had was an overheard conversation where one of the usual Landseer dressers was complaining that she'd rather not work with Howell as he was said to have wandering hands. It had hit the mark, though, given Edith's flushed cheeks.

"As you'll have guessed, Mr. Howell wasn't always the nicest of men. I didn't want to make a fuss, because he gave me a nice little parting gift of money, but he said that while he appreciated my service, it was time to move on. I suspect he wanted somebody younger than me. Prettier and more gullible, if you get my drift."

"I do indeed. Although have you considered that he might have found out you were aware of the letters to him and wanted to sever the connection to keep his secret safer?"

"Oh, I never even dreamed of that." She appeared genuinely shocked. "I hope he didn't think that I was likely to blab about it. I never would. Perhaps I should have, if it had meant bringing things into the open. It might have kept him safe."

"I don't follow."

"I just thought that if whatever he was accused of became common knowledge, it might have stopped his killer from taking such drastic action. Because any connection between murderer and victim would be obvious."

"Ah, yes." A good, subtle point. If nobody knew who held the grudge, nobody could point a finger. "It might have been the end of his career, though. Landseer hates scandal."

"Better the end of his career than the end of his life, surely?"

Which was another good, if far less subtle point. Still, a happier Alasdair left the tea rooms than the one who'd entered. This threat was something the police didn't yet know about, and if Toby could engineer them an interview with the knee-dandler soon, they might even be able to present it as a scoop.

***

As Toby exited the fitting room at Landseer central, he was delighted to see Sir Ian strolling along the corridor. This would suit his plans very nicely.

"Toby!" The boss shook his hand. "Thanks for all you did to help Geraldine."

"I don't think we can claim to have had much to do with it. You should be thanking her dresser."

"I will, believe me." Sir Ian lowered his voice. "And should I express my gratitude to your father for having got a better man on the case?"

Toby made his best self-deprecating gesture. "Mayfield would have been changed anyway. Firestone's a much more competent man. Would you like us to still keep our eyes and ears open, by the way?" he added insouciantly, sure that Alasdair would want to carry on the great game.

Sir Ian shrugged. "I'm not sure there's any need for that, now."

Inspiration, which had struck suddenly in the cab en route to the fitting, could be given full vent. Toby dropped into his most confidential tones. "I know what the police are like. They've got a better man on the case now but it's always possible people will want to feed him lies and stir up trouble for Landseer. They might even imply you had something to do with it."

Sir Ian's face resembled something out of a silent film, as he went through the whole rigmarole of *I hadn't thought of that* and *I did have a motive*.

"In that case, perhaps it might be wise for you to ensure that the authorities are fed the correct information."

That official sanction to carry on being nosy was good enough for Toby. Might as well make use of it straight away. "Talking of which, wasn't Howell involved in some sort of hoo-hah early in his career? When they were making *The Deadly Sin of Murder*."

"I believe so. Come along." Sir Ian led the way to his personal assistant's offices. "Ah, Brian!" He hailed as they swung through the door. "I need George Howell's file."

Two minutes later they were sitting at Sir Ian's desk with a thick pile of papers to hand, Toby slightly disconcerted by the fact that such detailed records were kept on actors. How thick must his file be?

"Ah, here we are. There was an actress hurt on the film you mentioned, but Howell was exonerated of all blame. It had been a murder scene that went awry." Sir Ian, blanching, clearly found this highly unpleasant. "He was supposed to be strangling the girl and the usual safeguards failed."

Toby nodded. In his university days he'd played someone who'd been attacked, and they'd used a standard procedure of the victim pulling the attacker's hands towards themselves while the attacker pulled them away. It looked convincing and saved harm. "Too much pressure got applied on her neck?"

"Yes. She passed out." Sir Ian consulted the file again. "She recovered, but it was the end of her career. Some lasting damage to the vocal chords. Marquess made her a generous settlement."

"In lieu of admitting responsibility? No," Toby raised his hand. "Don't feel obliged to answer that. I'll ask some questions in other places."

***

Toby, feeling very satisfied with himself at having completed his costume fitting in record time and without having to have more than one pin inserted in the material and none in his flesh, took a cab into central London, asking to be dropped off at All Souls in Langham Place. From there he could take a relaxed stroll through the side streets to Waites, his favourite tailors. He needed some new handkerchiefs and maybe a silk vest or two, and this was the best place in the entire realm to purchase them. The fact they came served with a portion of gossip (only reserved for the most favoured customers) would be a pleasant addition to an already good day

But the vest and handkerchiefs ended up having to wait, owing to Phyllis Davis appearing round a corner and almost walking into him.

"I'm so sorry. I wasn't looking where—oh!" She suddenly realised who she'd nearly barged into. "Mr. Bowe."

"Miss Davis." Toby raised his hat. "As much my fault as yours. I was in a world of my own."

Phyllis looked haggard, her face drawn and a shadow of its former attractive self, as briefly seen at the theatre. Not even a touch of powder. Toby put on his most concerned face. "You seem rather upset. Is something wrong?"

"I... I don't know, really." She passed her hand across her brow.

Toby offered her an arm. "Let's go and find you a cup of tea. You need reviving."

And he could do with some information. Could she shed some light on the note in Howell's hand or, indeed, the actress who'd been injured?

They found a convenient cafe, ordered tea and—at Toby's insistence—a cake for Phyllis, who looked like she needed a square meal or three.

"This must be an awful time for you," he said, as they waited.

"It is. Bad enough to lose your man to a murderer's knife, but then to find out you'd already lost him to another woman..." she opened her handbag, fishing out a cigarette case—one without any distinctive inscription, the sort that was so beloved of detective fiction, Toby noticed with frustration—and lighter. "Mind if I...?"

"Please do. And not for me," he said, as she offered him the case. "Gave it up during the war and felt so much better for it I didn't bother to pick up again."

"Very wise. George's uncle is a doctor. He'd advised him against it. I wish he'd advised him on his morals at the same time."

"Very true. By the by, you're not the only one who seems to have had no idea that Geraldine was involved with George. Sir Ian, our studio boss, isn't best pleased, either."

Phyllis managed a laugh. "No. We've both had one in the eye. I've always thought of her as a friend of mine—we were in the chorus together many moons ago—but this changes matters. Still, I wouldn't have wished George dead over it, and that's God's honest truth."

It appeared to be, but then Alasdair had appeared to genuinely swear undying love for Fiona onscreen. Time and again. "Is that why you quarrelled last night?"

She lit the cigarette, inhaled deeply, and then said, "Yes. He got sent a message from her and I happened to catch sight of it. I wasn't taken in by how he tried to explain the words away." She snorted. "*See you later tonight. I'll be waiting. Love and kisses*. It hardly has an innocent interpretation."

"No, indeed." And not the one found in his hand. "Did you see any other letters in his possession, then or any time else? Did he mention being in receipt of less pleasant ones?"

Phyllis shook her head. "Not that I'm aware of."

Toby now regretted the absence of tea in his cup—it would have been a useful prop and the sipping of a drink would allow him time to think. "You may not have heard, but a note was found on his body. Saying that—well, to paraphrase—"

"You don't need to paraphrase anything for me, Mr. Bowe. What did it say?"

"I don't have the exact words, but I'd heard it reported to be that if he didn't stop running around with everything in a skirt he'd pay for it."

"Oh."

"You seem surprised. As though you'd been expecting something different."

"I suppose I was. I'm not sure what, though."

The arrival of a pot of tea, and all the activity involved in dispensing, it gave Toby time for thought. Including contemplating the fact that amateur sleuthing seemed so easy in books and damned difficult in reality. Time for a different approach.

"Did George ever mention an actress who'd been hurt when he'd been filming with Marquess?

Phyllis rolled her eyes. "George mentioned several actresses at Marquess, most of whom he felt lacked any appreciable talent. One of them bit him while they were filming a scene for his last film."

"Did she?"

Phyllis stubbed out her cigarette with barely half of it gone. "It was supposed to have been an accident but I'm now wondering if his hands had wandered outside of what was required in the role."

Without comment, Toby sipped his tea. If Howell had been as unpleasant as he was painted, then why did these women go out with him? Supposedly love was blind but that didn't entirely explain it. Perhaps Howell wowed them with money or expensive gifts, or had legendary prowess as a lover. He hadn't even been particularly handsome, come to that.

At length, he said, "Why does somebody take a life? I'm being rhetorical, of course, that's not a direct question.

"It's a good one, though. That note you mentioned, the one threatening him if he didn't mend his ways, it seems awfully vague. If a brother or father was protecting their sister or daughter's virtue, wouldn't they have named the girl outright?"

"Perhaps a girl wrote it."

"Well, it wasn't me!" Phyllis seemed more amused than affronted at the suggestion, though. "I'm the sort of girl who tells somebody what I think of them to their face, and that's exactly what I did, in the first interval, after I saw that invitation to a liaison. I told him I'd had enough of his philandering. That I never wanted to see him again. I didn't..." She laid down her tea cup so she could rummage for a handkerchief. "I didn't dream my wish would come true in that way."

"None of us ever do, when we say rash things." While Toby's natural instinct was to pat her arm, he refrained: this reminded him of one of Alasdair and Fiona's love scenes and if Phyllis rebounded onto him it would be hard to explain exactly why he couldn't fall for the charms of such an attractive young lady.

"That's why I'm so upset. It's hit home today. I woke this morning and thought I'd call him to give him a chance to apologise. Then I realised I'd never talk to him again."

Toby didn't have the heart to ask anything else.

***

Toby arrived home to find a couple of messages concerning people who'd been on the telephone and wanted him to return the call. Unusually, it wasn't Alasdair's number he rang first. As a result, when he did get through to his lover, there was gleeful news to share.

"Firestone wants to see us, this evening."

Alasdair's delight filled his usually mellow tones. "That's out of the blue. Highly gratifying, though."

"Ah. That's probably my doing. I left a message to say I might have some information."

Now Alasdair sounded like a kicked puppy. "I have information too, you know."

"Don't get agitato, or I'll conveniently forget to tell you where and when we're meeting." Toby briefly shared what he'd learned before allowing Alasdair to do the same. It had clearly been a busy day. "Blimey! Two lots of threats, though. Both about the same thing, do you think?"

"Possibly. Although I don't think the present batch of two timing can go back to his days at Marquess. I rather imagine it's something else."

"The girl in the first film? Or perhaps something he did during the war? As I was sauntering home today it struck me that during the blitz things that would have been suspicious and reported to the police during peacetime could possibly have gone unnoticed then. How easy to hide a murdered body among so many dead."

"Your mate Firestone would be the man to root that out rather than us. The police have got the records—and resources—which we don't. As you well know."

Toby also knew that much of what the police found out was discovered by officers keeping their ears and eyes open, or by buying a pint for the right person in the right pub and seeing how much the alcohol loosened a tongue.

"Excuse me," Alasdair said, "Morgan's trying to attract my attention with what looks like the evening paper."

"Go to it. Might be more developments." The news of Geraldine's release had hit the afternoon editions, as Toby had seen on his travels, so Morgan must have spotted something else of note.

"Well, here's a thing." Alasdair spoke slowly, as though still taking in the story. "I have no idea if this is relevant to Howell, but it's a hell of a coincidence if not. I'm surprised they didn't try to keep it all hush-hush but perhaps Marquess studios aren't as effective in that regard as Landseer."

"You are infuriating at times. What are people trying to keep hush-hush?"

"The news about Robert Temple."

"Temple? He's the chap who directed all these horror films that Howell made his name in. *A Strangler's Hands* and *The Bodies in the Mist*. North's quite a fan—he's been telling me all about them."

Toby's valet always had an astute opinion when it came to the cinema.

"Are they any good? I know they're popular but it isn't necessarily the same thing."

Toby chuckled. "He's says they're actually quite well made, and a number of good actors and actresses made their bit-part debuts in them before they went on to better things."

"Reputation for being rather gory, though?"

Toby snorted. "Nothing in the league of Titus Andronicus, and that's cul-chah, dear boy. Anyway, what about this Temple chap? What about him, then? Don't keep me hanging here like a dog being teased with a bone."

"It's not good news. He's been rushed to hospital, dangerously ill." Alasdair sighed. "He appears to have made an attempt on his own life."

Reel Six

The meeting with Firestone had been scheduled for the Savoy, but the actors decided to rearrange it for Toby's house. The news about Robert Temple—even though neither man knew him well—had put a damper on the occasion. When Alasdair arrived, a tall, thick set man with a military bearing and a shock of salt and pepper hair was in the process of being admitted by Toby's valet.

Still holding the door open, the valet gave him a gracious nod. "Mr. Hamilton."

Alasdair returned the nod. "North. Was that Detective Superintendent Firestone?"

"It was indeed. He's with Mr. Bowe in the drawing room."

Alasdair could have guessed that, given the hearty conversation coming from that direction. He entered, was introduced, North produced refreshments and they got down to business, starting with the news about Robert Temple.

"Before I came here, I spoke to Alexander Rattigan, our director." Alasdair said. "He tells me that Temple's known for being a solid chap, good at his work. Rattigan's exact words were, 'He can make a pile of bilge quite watchable. All to do with the pacing, really, and not being over-ambitious.'"

"So well respected." Firestone nodded. "The judgment of one's peers is always to be considered."

"Do you believe this suicide attempt is linked to George Howell's death?" Toby asked.

"It's a line we have to consider at present." Firestone stared into his whisky. "His housekeeper believes he was at home last evening, possibly alone. Did your pal Rattigan have anything to say about Temple's character?"

Alasdair shrugged. "Only the sort of thing that tends to be said on these occasions. That Temple never struck him as the sort of chap given to melancholy or morbid thoughts. But many people are good at hiding their true feelings. Particularly those are who served their country," he added hastily, having strayed too close to his and Toby's great secret.

"This last war?" Firestone asked.

"The previous. Which was enough to turn many a good man a bit odd. Rattigan's words, not mine."

Alasdair had met plenty and heard of others, who'd gone out whole in mind and come back shattered.

Firestone made a note. "And is there anything on the directorial grapevine about any troubles he was having? Or indeed anything about George Howell that could have got him killed?"

"Apart from the obvious fact that he couldn't keep his trousers buttoned? I asked Rattigan both, and he said there was no more than might apply to any man."

"Thank you." Firestone took another sip of whisky. "Toby says Sir Ian asked you to keep your eyes and ears open because of his personal interest in the case, being a friend of Geraldine Wilson." The policeman raised his eyebrow—almost as eloquent as Alasdair's although presumably not insured—at the word *friend*. "While we appreciate your providing us with inside information, I hope you're not intending to get in the way of us doing our duty. Particularly in the event of Miss Wilson, or anyone else with a Landseer connection, being involved."

Toby snorted. "Heaven forbid. You know we're not that daft. Father must have told you we had some limited success in tracking down a missing person, but we're well aware we're not Holmes and Watson. We do have a sympathetic way with us, though, and it encourages folk to talk. Howell's murder has given many in our circle a hell of a shock, and when people are shocked, they want to gabble."

Firestone inclined his head in acknowledgement of a good point. "That's where the amateur has an advantage. I don't mind our turf encroached on, so long as you pass on everything relevant that gets gabbled at you. Such as...?"

Toby counted off on his fingers. "That Howell was one for the ladies, that he rubbed people up the wrong way, that he was running two girlfriends—maybe more, who knows?—at the same time."

"Ah, but we knew all that already." Firestone grinned. "It looks like the plodding coppers have nothing to learn from the well-meaning amateurs."

Alasdair bridled, despite the fact Toby had clearly taken the policeman's remark as a bit of banter. He suspected there'd be one thing the police didn't yet know, because he doubted Edith would have been to see them yet. "You're probably not in a position to say, but did you ever find out who sent the nasty letter to Howell? Not the one found on him. The others."

Firestone looked up sharply, glass halfway to his mouth. "What other letter?"

"The one that was left in his dressing room on the set of his last film. There may have been others. Hasn't his dresser been to see you?"

"If she has, then the information hasn't been passed to me." Firestone laid down his glass. "Might I use your telephone, Toby?"

"Of course. It's just on the sideboard."

They listened as he rang into Scotland Yard, piecing together from the audible half of the conversation that, as yet, no information about a note had been received. Alasdair had brought her contact details with him, which he gave to a grateful Firestone before producing a succinct account of the interview Edith had given him.

"Any idea why she was so reluctant to come and see us?"

"No. The story she gave—that she was frightened she might end up being arrested—seemed silly in the extreme and I don't think she's a silly woman."

"Hm. I think I'd better talk to her myself. Thank you." Firestone raised his glass in a silent toast.

"Talking of notes," Toby interposed, evidently wanting to get his two penn'orth in, "I spoke to Phyllis today, and when I mentioned the note which Howell had in his grasp, she seemed a bit surprised. As though she'd expected it to say something else."

"Interesting. I'd better to speak to her, as well. He was holding on to it for—I was about to say grim death, but that sounds insensitive."

"Insensitive yet accurate. It must have been tight in his grip because I didn't notice it when I saw the body. Although I don't suppose I noticed much except the blood." Toby, whose tipple that evening was brandy, took a fortifying swig. "Did you ever find the cat, by the way?"

"Cat?" Firestone almost spilled the remains of his whisky. "Am I going mad or are you?"

Toby grinned at his old friend's consternation. Another point to the tally of the amateurs. "The theatre's black and white moggy is the reason the body was discovered at the time it was. The manager told me the cat came haring round the corner of the corridor with blood on his white patches. Gave Whitlock quite a turn. I'd hate to think what the little beast had been doing, to get himself so covered in it."

Firestone glanced at the telephone. "As far as I'm aware, nobody mentioned a cat. I suppose it's hardly relevant to the case, but these little details annoy me."

"Perhaps the information got lost in transit from the previous officer who had the case." Alasdair said.

"Perhaps." Firestone knocked back the rest of his drink. "Or maybe people haven't been as frank with us as they were with you." He eased himself out of his chair. "Thanks for the hospitality, Toby. Good to meet you, Alasdair. Before I go have you any other bombshells you'd like to drop?"

"Not a bombshell as such, but another coincidence that may mean nothing."

"Go on."

"Robert Temple. Since I read the story about him in the paper, I've been trying to work out where I've heard the name, and recently at that. When I went to meet Nigel Weatherly, he was chatting to a chap called Cuffy. He whose nanny's cousin turned out to be Edith the dresser. Nigel introduced him as Cuffy Temple. Perhaps that's how she got the job at Marquess studio in the first place." Alasdair paused. "Have you a moment, Firestone? I don't want to muddy the waters with amateur theories, but I've just had a thought."

"Go on." The policeman took his seat once more.

"Nigel got cross with this Cuffy chap, when he mentioned the fact Nigel and Geraldine had been going out. That's hardly a secret, so his reaction seemed a bit off."

"I suppose he'd have the motive to kill Howell if he felt the man had stolen his girl." Firestone yawned, and then rose again. "We'll put him onto the ever-increasing list of interested parties. A list I need to sleep on before I risk jumping to the wrong conclusion."

"Good man." Toby showed him out, returning wearing a cat-with-the-cream face. "Nice chap, isn't he? Sensible."

"He'd make a good actor. Character roles. You can't read what he's really thinking."

"Excellent point." Toby poured them both another drink. "Speaking of character roles, who will they get to replace Howell? They can't write the character out without changing the whole storyline."

"Nobody springs to mind. Were I in charge, which thank the Lord I'm not, sir, I'd be looking for someone already in the cast, but none of them strike me as suitable."

"I think Nigel himself would make an extremely serviceable villain. Much easier to recast his role."

"Never, Toby. Not with a face like that. He inspires maternal emotions, so he's perfect for this someone who'll be tragically lost in a cutting out raid, or a wet-behind-the-ears Spitfire pilot, killed saving his friend on his third mission." Alasdair grinned, at the thought of the sobs in the audience and the half crowns in the cinema tills.

"But wouldn't that be the beauty of it? The unexpected? Imagine a country house mystery story. Nobody would ever guess Nigel's character was a killer with a face like that. It could only work the once, mind you, and you'd have to swear the audience to secrecy."

"True," Alasdair conceded. "But would the public accept him as such? Wouldn't they feel they'd been cheated?"

"Did people feel they were cheated when they read *The Murder of Roger Ackroyd*? No, actually, belay that. I remember you saying that wasn't playing fair."

Alasdair conceded that point, too. "What's all this *belay* stuff again?"

"Practicing for the film. You know me—always take a part seriously. What do you think of the costumes, by the way?"

"More convincing than the pirate ones. I suspect the buttons and gold braid are much brighter than they ever were in Nelson's time, but they're acceptable. I look forward to seeing you in those figure hugging breeches."

"The feeling is mutual." Toby laid down his drink, left his chair and plonked himself down in Alasdair's lap. "And so to bed?"

"I haven't brought my pyjamas."

Toby snorted. "As if you ever wear any when you're here. I've even thought of an alibi if your presence overnight is noticed. After our discussion with Firestone, you were taken ill. Talk of the murder reminded you of an incident ten years ago, when your best friend was killed in a horrible accident on the base. I refused to let you go out alone into the London dark and nobly sacrificed the evening out I had planned to nurse you. And if you're not keen on that alibi, then reverse the roles. People expect me to suffer, so let's give them the stereotype."

"You've got this well planned."

"Of course I have. Pellew's finest wouldn't have gone into action without adequate preparation." Toby gave him a kiss. "I can lend you a toothbrush and a razor if that would help persuade you."

Toby's backside squirming against Alasdair's groin was all the persuasion a man needed.

Reel Seven

Before Alasdair had finished his second cup of breakfast tea, let alone had time to leave the house, Firestone was back in touch with them. Giving the lie to his proposal of sleeping on things, he'd been in touch with his teams of officers, and with the Imperial theatre, the previous evening.

"I had a constable up half the night scouring all the original statements—such as they are—in case anything else has *gone astray* as you put it. No mention of a cat."

"Whitlock, the theatre manager, was pretty upset. Perhaps he forgot." The delights of the previous night had left Toby in a generous mood.

"Hmm. Conveniently forgot, perhaps? I spoke to Whitlock late last evening and apparently that cat wasn't seen at all yesterday. The staff there thought he'd got a fright either from the dead body itself—animals can be as squeamish as humans, they reckoned—or from all the strangers about the place."

"I'd have thought a theatre cat was used to a parade of strangers. Wouldn't bat its eye at anything."

"Maybe somebody's closed its eyes permanently. Anyway, I sent somebody I can trust to make enquiries there today, and not just about the cat. I want to know exactly who was seen where and when all that fatal evening."

"Good luck."

Toby noticed Alasdair appear at the drawing room door as he replaced the receiver. "I'll update you over a cuppa."

It only took half a cup to relate what Firestone had said, at which Alasdair had rolled his eyes and observed it was about time somebody approached this investigation logically. "For example, where was Howell between the time Phyllis flounced off and the time he was killed? O'Connor says he didn't see him leave, although he couldn't have had every door under observation. Although if Howell left, why did he then return?"

"To come to the party, as Sir Ian ordered?" Toby suggested. "The only reason he didn't actually attend being that he couldn't?"

"With the added intention of meeting Geraldine and surreptitiously organising that bit of rogering?" Alasdair grabbed the last piece of toast and began smothering it with marmalade. "Any assignation was going to have to be after the event, because there simply wasn't time in between the curtain calls and the party starting."

Toby sniggered. "Not everybody is as scrupulous in their lovemaking as you are, my dear. Howell might have only needed five minutes and a locked dressing room door. I can imagine him swanking around afterwards, right under Sir Ian's nose, treasuring his little secret."

"They d both need some brass neck to be doing that." Alasdair bit into his toast aggressively, as though it were somehow implicated in this sorry state of affairs. "Anyway, her movements are accounted for by her dresser. If Howell was about, or the dressing room door was mysteriously locked, surely she'd have mentioned it."

"How do we know she didn't? We told Firestone plenty, but he was pretty astute at not giving us much in return." Toby speared the sole remaining rasher of bacon before Alasdair could nab that, too. "I'd love to know how the police knew about Howell and Geraldine."

"My money would be on your pal Phyllis."

"I've thought of that, but I don't think the times work. Unless they were in contact with her after they came to the theatre and they heard she'd left in high dudgeon." Toby carefully took any remaining fat off the rasher before snaffling it. "I wish I knew where North gets this. It's almost pre-war quality."

"Perhaps it's better you don't know." Alasdair blew out his cheeks. "She'll have enemies, Geraldine. Any leading lady acquires one or two people who envy her status. This prop knife fascinates me. How would somebody be able to get a copy of it? Did they manage to take the thing—or a photograph of it—so an identical one could be made? Or are they one and sixpence down at Woolworth's?"

"Who knows? Perhaps whoever gave it to her exaggerated its uniqueness."

"What about this note she's supposed to have sent Howell? Surely she didn't think they'd have the chance for an assignation with both Phyllis and Sir Ian around. Why did she do it?"

"Too full of elation at how well the first night was going? Or appeared to be going?" Toby smiled guiltily at the appreciation they'd feigned. "You remember what premieres are like. A haze of well-wishing and congratulations."

"Hm." Alasdair left the table, to stand by the window overlooking the garden. "It would be a simple way of implicating Geraldine. Her weapon. A route she might have taken. A message on the body in disguised handwriting that she might just have written."

Toby went to join him, leaning casually into the strength and comfort of his back. "And who would do all that? The same person who told the police about the affair?"

"Perhaps. Which brings us back to Phyllis, again. If she and Geraldine were pals she might have visited the theatre and knew her way round. Might even have been in the chorus there."

"True, Sherlock—or should I call you Pellew, as he seems to have been as brainy and not quite as conceited."

"Alasdair will do fine." He gave Toby a squeeze of the hand. "I spoke about brass neck. Howell would have needed that in spades to be two-timing that pair without one of them becoming suspicious, if they knew each other well enough for Geraldine to have Phyllis's address. Not that I have any experience at two timing anyone, so my supposition on the degree of difficulty involved is purely theoretical."

"Did Geraldine want to get Phyllis into trouble? Could she have known something was amiss and wanted me to contact her to somehow catch her out?"

Alasdair stroked his chin, a less subtle version of his Sherlock-is-thinking gesture. "Perhaps she suspected they'd be caught in flagrante delicto, as he hadn't turned up to be doing the same with her. She might have been out for revenge."

"It's possible." Toby reluctantly moved away from his lover. The lady next door's dog had just appeared in the garden, and she was sure to follow soon. A curse on the architect of these properties who'd made the windows so large: let in light they may, but they also let in the gaze of nosey Parkers. "Is it terribly wicked to say I'd be disappointed if the murderer were one of these two ladies and if this turned out to be simply some variation on the eternal triangle—or pentagon in this case, because we seem to have more than three sides."

"Doesn't your father say that in most cases of violence, you look at the victim's nearest and dearest?"

"He does indeed, and that's what I fear. I'd been hoping for something more intriguing to get our brains around."

"Bloodthirsty little beast," Alasdair said, with great affection, "and a bloodthirsty beast I happen to agree with. I want there to be more to this than jealousy, but we mustn't let that make us blinkered."

Toby picked up a fruit knife from the table, then dropped it swiftly. "I'll never look at one of these in the same way again. That invitation to indulge in rogering that Howell received strikes an odd note with me. How did Phyllis get to see it? Howell doesn't strike me as being that lackadaisical. What if she already knew about his philandering, let her old mate Geraldine know what a rat he was, and then the pair of them were in cahoots, trying to ensnare him. Show him up in the eyes of his new studio boss, while they were at it. Only the denouement to the plan didn't happen because a third party had already got at him."

Alasdair shrugged. "That seems rather convoluted."

"Howell's love-life seems rather convoluted."

"Yes, well, some men will risk anything to get their end away." Alasdair flicked a glance at Toby, who returned a knowing grin. They'd risked everything—not least career and reputation—for the pleasures of the double bed. And they'd have done it all again, without hesitation, because this was more than just a fling. Theirs was as true a love as any they'd depicted on screen. He moved them further from the window, finding a better place to give Toby a kiss.

"Is that a signal for departure?"

"It is." Alasdair gave him another, in confirmation. "I've got lines to finish learning, and somebody I'd like to see. I have an idea."

"One you won't share with your light of love?"

"Not until I've worked out whether it's stupid. All I'll say at present is I have to see a man about a director."

And with that enigmatic statement, Alasdair gave him an unprecedented third farewell kiss and left, whistling happily.

***

Alasdair spent a good two hours and lots of mental energy, on his lines. They were straightforward enough, and fairly logical, but soon the sheer volume made his head spin. Time to take a break, let his sub-conscious process them, and instead call in a favour from an old acquaintance.

Ronnie Wade was the principal reviewer for a well-respected newspaper and a man who always gave incredibly fair summations of what he'd seen. He wouldn't praise an actor just because he was a star name, nor would he bow to studio pressure to exalt their latest venture. He'd be just as likely to give a special mention to a bit part player with three lines, all of them delivered in exemplary fashion, as he'd be to heap plaudits on the performance of the lead. The fact that he usually praised Landseer's golden trio didn't hurt, nor did his being a friend of Alasdair's from pre-Toby days. A certain amount of freedom of conversation could ensue, although probably not today. Alasdair had a clear brief in mind.

Because Ronnie didn't deal in gossip, keeping strictly to the facts as he could wheedle them out, he'd built up an astounding knowledge of what really went on during film production, rather than the official line given in the press releases. His newspaper work carried a weight of authority as a result and if there was anything noteworthy about the making of any of Howell's offerings, he'd know. And while it would have been more efficient to ring him, Alasdair wanted to make the most of the last days of freedom before filming got under way. Nothing less than lunch in a restaurant would do, and he'd be happy to pay for the treat.

As he headed out the front door, old pal contacted and lunch with him arranged, Alasdair wrested his thoughts away from Nelson's navy and into the murky world of murder. Robert Temple had tried to take his own life—was that due to guilt at having killed Howell? The director would have been well placed to leave a note, or have it left, in his star's dressing room, a note that would have deflected attention, as might the note found in the victim's hand. Temple would have been able to approach Howell without raising suspicion, and he might have borne the man a wealth of resentment for having left Marquess studios without its greatest money-making resource.

There was the tricky matter of how he'd got hold of the murder weapon, although Alasdair had a theory for that. The prop Geraldine used had been a gift from an admirer, so she said, but that didn't necessarily make it unique. What if Temple himself had been the admirer and he'd kept a copy for sentimental reasons? Although didn't it seem rather stupid, Temple—or whoever the murderer was—using such a distinctive weapon and then discarding it where it would be easily found? It would surely have been simple enough to open a window and fling it out, to be scooped up later. Or wrap it in oilcloth, slip it in a coat pocket and leave it in a dustbin the other side of London where it would have been disposed of long before the police could have located it.

The whole thing smacked of somebody choosing both knife and the location to drop it in order to point at Geraldine, either as culprit or as a heartless jilt.

Ronnie Wade's opinion of Geraldine—obtained between the soup and the fish and after the normal pleasantries and exchange of news had taken place—was a surprising one. Far from being the sort of girl who flung her affections all over the shop, she was supposed to be highly intelligent, rather easily bored, and serially monogamous.

"That doesn't accord with people saying she was going out with both Howell and Sir Ian at the same time."

Ronnie tapped the table. "I would be extremely surprised if that's the truth. I can imagine that she got rid of the small fry actor when she had bigger fish bite on her hook."

"She's certainly making her way up the ladder. Nigel Weatherly was one of the lower rungs, as well."

"For once you know something I don't." Ronnie looked impressed. "Poor Nigel. He'll be playing nineteen-year olds until he's nearly forty. I don't think he's over happy about it."

Alasdair sniffed, meaningfully. "He should start looking his age, then, if he wants older roles."

"He'd make an interesting villain, though. Creepy."

"Toby said much the same." Back to the point in hand. "I bet Howell wasn't happy to be discarded by his lady love. Not great for the ego to think there are others on a higher rung."

"I would agree. Vanity thy name is cinema actors. Perhaps he was making a nuisance of himself about it with her."

"And got himself killed in the process?" Then Geraldine would have had the best motive and if she was so intelligent, why would she have left such an obvious trail?

"It's possible he annoyed someone so much they snapped. He was the sort of man to make enemies, as you'll no doubt know if you've been playing Sherlock off screen again."

"Guilty as charged." The arrival of the sole allowed for a slight change of tack. "How did Robert Temple get on with him? You'll have heard the news about Temple, of course?"

The journalist nodded. "Are you thinking this might have something to do with Howell's death?"

"Certainly. Don't you?"

A sly grin broke over Ronnie's face. "I'm as suspicious as the next man. You might say I have a warped mind, but it did occur to me that killing your star is a great way to get publicity for the last film he made for your studios. They'll make—excuse tasteless pun—a killing at the box office."

A good point. Howell's final film had been rush released because of his studio move and had been generating excellent takings. The events of the last few days had turned out to be highly serendipitous—on his way to lunch, Alasdair had noticed more than one cinema with a queue of people waiting to see the day's first showing of *A Strangler's Hands*. "Seats will be going like hot cakes. Last chance to see him in action."

"And that would militate against any theory of Temple attempting to take his life because of money worries, reports of which there are none from the rumour machine, by the way. Word is he'd actually negotiated a deal that gave him a hefty cut of the takings. Not just for this film but all of the past ones. They'll be flooding the cinemas with re-releases so any financial problems would have to run very deep for this success not to ease them. Having said that, Temple might have been tempted to increase the value of his cut."

Alasdair considered for a moment. "I'm not sure I'd have my money on that gee-gee just yet, but I can't help feeling the murder and the attempted suicide are linked. The director kills the star—for whatever reason—and then is overcome with remorse. Is Temple the sort of man who could have committed murder?"

"I believe ninety nine per cent of men have the capability of killing somebody, were the cause just enough, in their eyes or in another's." Ronnie shrugged. "I doubt whether they all could be quite as callous as to motive."

Alasdair eyed his friend carefully before replying. "You didn't answer my question."

"Well spotted." Ronnie raised a knuckle to his brow, like a saucy sailor acknowledging an officer. "I think Temple falls into the ninety nine percent, but not into the proportion who'd kill without good reason. He's a man who could be filled with remorse, though."

So Alasdair's theory hadn't fallen at the first jump. "Did he leave a note explaining why he'd tried to kill himself?"

"Not that I've heard, although given that he's survived, and is said to be on the mend, maybe some helpful person discretely hid it away." Ronnie waved his fork. "Usually word starts to leak out, although in this instance there's nothing. I did wonder if Temple had tried to kill himself because he was ashamed of his latest offering, because it wasn't up to standard, but I've been to see it and it's jolly good."

"To my shame, I've never seen any of Howell's films. Not my cup of tea."

"You should. They're an excellent example of making a little go a long way. Perhaps too lightweight to survive without Howell's input, though, unless they can find another equally nasty and popular villain."

This might be an even better motive for the director killing his ex-star. "What If Temple realised the goose had laid its last golden egg, saw his future earnings going down the drain, and so confronted Howell at the Imperial theatre. It was one last, vain attempt to get him to stay and that confrontation went wrong."

"It's conceivable, I suppose, although here's something for you to stick in your pipe and smoke, Mr. Holmes. How did he—or anyone else without legitimate business there—get in and out of the theatre unnoticed? The place must have been heaving with the great and the good."

"Less the great and good, but plenty of people, admittedly." And that was another stumbling block. "Mind you, Howell himself seems to have been lurking around there for the best part of two acts, unseen. Perhaps Temple had arranged to meet him earlier and they stood talking in the alcove. Was Temple one of Geraldine's paramours, by the way?"

"That I don't know. He's always had an eye for the ladies, as evidenced by the fact that Mrs. Temple no longer inhabits the family home." Ronnie pushed his plate away, with a satisfied smile. "He's got a soft spot for women, too, and I don't just mean on his mattress. Quite an old-fashioned chivalrous type. Unlike Howell."

The self-satisfied expression on Ronnie's face suggested revelations were in the offing. "Tell Uncle Alasdair all."

"He was known for having a bit of a cruel streak. Manifested itself during the war, when he was a bit rough with some of the new recruits. Some people didn't like it. Others—of course—argued that he was just making men of them."

Could Howell have shown that same cruel streak with women? Or was the female angle simply a red herring and this business went back to those benighted days? That might accord more closely with the content of the threatening letters the actor had received.

"Could anyone have held a grudge against him from wartime? A relative of one of the soldiers who was maltreated? Or the soldier himself?"

"It's possible, although if every sergeant major who gave his lads a hard time was likely to find himself killed, then the police are going to be extremely busy."

They ordered dessert and coffee, conversation turning to a discreet discussion of their personal lives, couched in terms that anyone could have overheard without arising suspicion. As they reached the final dregs of their drinks, Ronnie leaned across the table, lowering his voice. "This may have nothing to do with the price of eggs, but have you heard about the actress who was hurt during Howell's first film?"

"I have indeed. Since you mentioned the cruel streak in his nature I've been wondering if that so called accident was less of a mishap than a sign of that nastier part of his personality."

"You're not alone in wondering. But the doctor said it wasn't Howell's fault, as did the actress herself. And we all know actresses would never lie in the furtherance of their career, especially if advised so." Ronnie produced a sardonic smile. "Nasty business ours, at times. Anyway, what brought it to mind was that she died, a week ago. The actress who got hurt."

This was taking coincidence too far. Three people involved with that film, all dead or hurt. "Was it related to her injuries?"

"I don't believe so. Her appendix burst, a case of severe peritonitis followed and it killed her. Even the wonder drugs couldn't stem the infection. The cause might not have mattered if someone decided to take vengeance on Howell, though. People in grief can act irrationally."

Alasdair nodded. Sherlock Holmes was mad on his logic, but sometimes the way that the ordinary man or woman in the street went about their lives bore about as much resemblance to logic as his courting Fiona onscreen bore to his life off it. “Who do you think killed Howell?”

Ronnie shrugged. “I can think of plenty of men and women who might have wished him dead. And we’ve all at some point spoken threats without meaning them. But for those desires to actually translate into murder most foul is a rare thing. I struggle to believe this was simply a matter of a discarded girlfriend. It speaks to me of somebody who could see no other way of getting what they desired, whether that was love or revenge or something else entirely.”

Which didn’t leave Alasdair much further forward at all.

Reel Eight

Toby was feeling more than satisfied about his mastery of the script. He'd been practicing words and gestures in front of the mirror and very nicely they were coming on. One or two would give Alasdair a surprise, let alone the paying public, although that was no more than the man deserved, his having been very mysterious about what he was up to.

When the phone rang, Toby expected it would be his lover, gloating over some clue he'd turned up and that expectation—of caller's identification if not of caller's self-satisfaction—was confirmed as soon as he heard the tones at the other end of the line.

"Hello. How are the lines going?"

"Spiffingly well. Yours?"

"Pretty good. I've treated myself to lunch out as a reward."

"Pfft," Toby snorted. "Lunch with somebody you could pump about Howell, I assume?"

"Naturally. Ronnie Wade. You remember him."

"The reviewer?" Toby instantly put a face to the name. They'd first met him as a pal of a pal, Jonny Stewart, who seemed to know everyone, including Superintendant Firestone. But it was highly likely that one could travel to the depths of the Arctic and find a native there who was bosom pals with one of the Stewarts; they were that sort of family. "Nice looking lad. Ran across him that evening at Sir Frederick's as I recall?"

If Alasdair's eye rolling had been audible, Toby would have been deafened by it. "As if we could ever forget."

That had been quite some bash. Another bucks' do, although not in the way that Bethnal Green boxing bouts would be. Toby and Alasdair were broad minded but Freddy's party had gone too far. When the actors had made their excuses and secured a premature exit from the event, Jonny had cadged a lift home with them, ditching the friend who'd brought him. And who'd probably never be spoken to again for getting him into such a ghastly orgy. Ronnie had taken the same opportunity to extricate himself.

"What did Ronnie have to say?" Toby listened as his lover gave an account of his lunchtime discussions, only chipping in with the odd bit of encouragement or sounding impressed. He also felt a growing delight at an impending chance of a bit of one-upmanship, suitable for practicing on actors who didn't share their latest theories with their lovers but tried them out on journalists first.

"Very interesting," Toby said when Alasdair had reached the end of the tale. "I think it would be useful to drop in and have a wee chat with Robert Temple." Before Alasdair could jump in, he added, "I'll go armed with grapes and flowers and the excuse that I'm bringing regards from those in the industry who are very concerned about him."

"You'll go in and see him? Why can't I do that? It was my idea in the first place."

"Because, dearest Alasdair, the chairwoman of your fan club isn't the matron of the hospital where Temple is at present ensconced. Mine is." Toby chuckled, revelling in the sound of stunned silence coming down the line.

"The chairwoman of your fan club? Is that who you're wining and dining with when you're not with either me or one of your false girlfriends?"

"Not necessarily. Although I've treated her to tea at the Ritz once or twice," Toby admitted, gleefully. "Bless her, she's fifty if she's a day and built like a Sherman tank, but she's possessed of a charming smile and the loveliest little hands and feet. Were I ten years older and of a different bent, I'd be chasing her round the operating theatre, I can assure you."

"And she'd be fending you off with something sharp, no doubt." Alasdair's eyebrow must have performing contortions. "Assuming this lady would really do anything for you, does that include admitting you to her domain in order to see someone at death's door?"

"He's barely that. I spoke to Miss Crouch—that's the lady concerned—earlier today, under the guise of offering tickets for the next Landseer matinee, ones that she can auction for one of her charitable causes. I may have asked after Temple's welfare as an adjunct to the conversation."

"What did your devoted slave have to say about him?"

"You'd better not call her that to her face or you'll find yourself strung up in traction for a week. And probably lose your privileges in the process." A hoary type of pun but it made Alasdair groan. "The lovely Miss Crouch told me that Temple would welcome a visit from a friendly face. She's keeping the hounds of the press at bay and generally making sure nobody annoys her charge. The reports of his condition in the newspaper have been deliberately exaggerated, I suspect."

"Hm. I suppose I should wish you good luck, but I can't help feeling you've upstaged me."

"For that, I apologise profusely. You need to start cultivating useful contacts—not just journalists—for the next time we have a mystery to stick our noses in."

Fortunately, Alasdair's response—muttered, barely audible, but probably consisting of unsavoury language—was cut off as the line fortuitously went dead. The vagaries of modern technology were welcome at times.

***

That evening, Toby had to scramble out of the door or else he'd be late, and it wouldn't do to keep Matron waiting. He'd been busy since speaking to Alasdair, spending his time primarily in contacting a few people in the business for messages to pass on to Temple. Best to have a script to work from, at least initially. He wouldn't tell the director about the conversation he'd had with Firestone, however; a Firestone who was fuming that the police had been forbidden by Miss Crouch to interview Temple, even in her presence.

"Don't you go getting out of your depth," he'd cautioned. "If he's the murderer I don't want him forewarned."

"I promise I won't. I can act, you know. I can also learn lines quickly, so whatever Robert Temple says to me I'll report back as near verbatim as I can manage. In return, can you check something for me? It might be relevant to this business. And if you could give me an answer before I set out, that might be fortuitous all round."

"Let's hear it."

"Howell's maternal uncle is a doctor. I wonder if you could find out whether he was involved as an expert in a particular case..."

Later, when Toby made his way to one of the back doors to the hospital, Miss Crouch was there to meet him. She accepted the tickets—and a box of chocolates—with great joy, then whisked him off to a small room off one of the main wards. Robert Temple, who'd clearly been warned of the visit, was sitting upright in a bed which had been made to within an inch of its starched linen life, reading a novel. The director's face was both pinched and pale.

"Mr. Bowe—Toby. Matron said you might drop in. Thank you."

"Nice to see you looking so chipper." Toby presented him with a wrapped and beribboned basket of fruit. "I suspect you'll be taking most of this home with you."

Temple produced a sardonic smile. "I'm not so sure. I think matron's keeping me here until she's absolutely certain I won't do anything silly once I'm released. She's a great cinema fan, as you know."

"And she's quite right to want to wrap you up in cotton wool. We really wouldn't want to lose you." Toby went on to relay a list of well-wishing messages, most of them genuine, from fellow industry professionals. As he reached the last of them, Temple fished out a handkerchief to blow his nose theatrically.

"You shouldn't all be so kind. I'm really not worth it."

"Nonsense," Toby said automatically, then immediately regretted it. That wasn't the way to gather information. "Why on earth should we think that?"

"Because I should have succeeded. I don't deserve to live if she's dead."

Toby thought he'd misheard. "Sorry, I'm not with you, old chap. Who's dead?"

"Alice Keyworth."

So Toby's ears hadn't deceived him. For a moment he'd thought, gallingly, Alasdair had been right and that Temple had said *I don't deserve to live if he's dead*. "Was that the young actress who recently died of appendicitis?"

"Peritonitis, yes." Temple used the handkerchief again. "You know the story?"

“Only in part. Somebody mentioned her in connection with George Howell.” That somebody—Alasdair—was going to get a jolt to his pet theory.

“Yes. It’s been shocks all round these last few weeks. Ghastly business with him, too. Although that’s not plaguing my conscience.”

“If it would help to get things off your chest, I’m told I’m not a bad listener. And Miss Crouch—matron—would wink at it, if she felt it would be of benefit.”

“Benefit?” The director shrugged. “I’ve borne this guilt for such a long time, I’m not sure if anything would help. You see, it was my fault she got hurt.”

“The accident on set?”

“Yes.” Temple appeared relieved Toby had heard of it, so he wouldn’t need to relate all the details. “The actress originally meant for the role was taken ill—appendicitis, of all the ridiculous coincidences—so we had to find a last-minute replacement. It was only a small part, one of the victims. I had no idea it would turn so nasty.”

“None of us would. Was Miss Keyworth an actress you’d used before?”

“No. She was barely an actress at all. Just starting out on her career.” Temple turned his gaze from Toby towards the window, no doubt ashamed of what he was about to say. “Howell’s dresser is—was—a woman called Edith. I always believe in helping out one’s own, and I’d got her the job at Marquess in the first place. It may have been initially because of the family connection, but I never regretted it. She and Howell clicked in a way he did with few others.”

“Is Edith your young relative’s nanny’s cousin? Or something similarly convoluted.”

Temple swung round to face Toby again. "You are well informed."

"We try to be. When it looked like Howell might be coming to Landseer, people kept their eyes and ears open in advance. You know how Sir Ian won't work with actors or actresses who have a whiff of scandal." Toby hoped the director wouldn't remember the Bowe family police connection to Howell as well as the Landseer one. Best to keep this strictly unofficial.

Temple nodded, and then turned his face to the window once more. "Alice was a sort of relative of Edith's. Daughter of her daughter's godmother, I think. That's what made it so much worse. I should have gone with an experienced actress, but we'd already lost time and I couldn't get further behind. We were a small studio in those days, with no room for manoeuvre."

"I do understand," Toby said. The industry was far from perfect, although wasn't that true of any walk of life?

"Thank you. It's such a relief to talk to somebody about this. It's such a burden to carry." Temple took a deep breath. "I should have gone through the procedure with her, made sure she knew exactly what she was doing in the murder scene, so she couldn't get hurt. Of course, it turned out she'd lied—to Edith and to me—about the little previous acting experience she'd had, so when it came to the scene itself she didn't tell us that it was uncomfortable. She just let herself be..."

"Be hurt," Toby said. "In the hands of a cruel man who didn't know—or couldn't care about—when to stop?"

This time the director turned slowly to face him, as though trying to take in what he'd said. "It wasn't Howell's fault. The doctor confirmed that. Howell was unlucky to have pressed on the wrong point. I should have made sure he'd also been told beforehand what to do. It was his first strangling scene."

"Ah, now, this doctor. The one who absolved Howell of any blame. Were you aware that was his uncle?"

"His uncle? No."

"Hardly an objective opinion, then." Toby, pleased to see the slight flicker of hope in Temple's eyes, pressed on. "Howell already had a reputation for cruelty, going back to service days. Can you be sure it was simply an accident and that he didn't lose control of himself?"

"I...I don't know." Temple, brows knitted in an evident attempt to rake through his memories, eventually replied, "There was an incident on the set of the last film he made for us. An actress bit him. I thought she was just being silly but maybe he was being too forceful with his hands again."

Toby shrugged. "We'll never know for sure, will we? But I'd say there's enough element of doubt for you to stop blaming yourself for what happened to Miss Keyworth."

Temple looked towards the window again, leaving Toby to wait patiently. His father had taught him that silence was a strong investigational tool, and that those being interviewed didn't like it, especially if they bore a guilty conscience. Toby had adapted that skill in his career, not jumping in prematurely on another person's line, and he'd use it now.

After what seemed an age and almost at the point where even Toby's patience was about to give out, the director turned back, wearing a wan but optimistic smile. "Thank you for what you've said. You've given me cause for thought."

"I'm delighted to help." Even though it appeared he'd sunk this investigational thread.

Temple held out his hand, to clasp Toby's. "I'd like to rest now, but could you do me one last favour as you go?"

"Of course."

"Please tell matron that I'm quite safe to go home, now. I have no need to be so stupid again."

And with that, the director sent Alasdair's theory down to Davy Jones's locker.

Reel Nine

While Alasdair was always delighted to see his light of love—the sun really did shine brighter when Toby was in the offing—he wasn't so happy to hear what the man had to tell him. He'd come straight from Temple's bedside, with a story to recount and a rather smug grin on his face. Alasdair settled him in the lounge with a glass of hock, and then prepared to listen.

"So," Toby said, as he came to the end of his account, "it sounds as though Temple's suicide attempt had nothing to do with remorse at Howell's death. Well, don't look so much like you've lost ten guineas. I came hotfoot from the hospital to let you know, only stopping to deliver the same information via a call box to Matthew Firestone. Least I could do, seeing as he'd found out about Howell's uncle for me."

"That was a stroke of luck."

"Luck? A stroke of genius."

Alasdair would have been happy to concede that point had his lover not continued to look so horribly self-satisfied. One could only hope that such pride would go before a fall. "So where does that leave us in terms of a theory? Back to the women scorned?"

"Women, certainly, although not necessarily scorned. I have an idea." Toby swirled his glass—a rather elegant gesture, one which Alasdair would steal for Pellew when he was dining in his great cabin. "What if Edith also found out that Howell's involvement in her friend Alice's accident had been possible covered up by his uncle? Perhaps she even had evidence of that involvement."

"That's possible, although why would she then stay with the ratbag?"

"Keeping an eye on him, of course. You want your enemies close, so you can be sure what they're up to. It would allow her to leave the threatening notes, of course. Keep him scared while you decide what to do."

Alasdair had to concede that point, too. How infuriating that he'd chased the wrong hare. "And Alice's death prompted her into action?"

"Yes, that's the ticket."

"Then she sets off and stabs him?" Alasdair shook his head, incredulously. "After a previously blameless life?"

Toby made a face. "For a start we don't know she's led a blameless life. And for another thing, she wouldn't be the first person to commit murder out of the blue. However, I think it's more complicated than that. Edith said the notes to Howell implied more than one person was making the threat. What if there's a group of people all in it together, rather like that Agatha Christie book?"

Alasdair's insured eyebrow nearly hit his hairline. "Are you abandoning playing Watson and being Hastings on the Orient Express now?"

"Don't be silly. Hastings wasn't in that story. Anyway, this case has only one stab wound so I don't literally mean a gang killed him. Just that they co-operated. Hasn't it struck you that there are lots of strange elements surrounding what happened that opening night?"

It had. Although Alasdair wasn't ready to admit that he'd been so busy trying to align them with Temple that he'd possibly become blinkered. "So who do you think was in it with her? Her Clarrie? Or was it her cousin's charge, the unfortunately named Cuffy?"

Toby leaned over to rap his knuckles. "You're being silly again. Look no further than people who were on the spot and had access to the theatre, the weapon and the victim. Phyllis. Geraldine. Perhaps O'Connor himself."

"Are you saying that Edith knew all of them already?"

"No-o, although it's possible she knew Phyllis, who could have got her old pal Geraldine on board."

"Who could have charmed the doorman?" This theory showed promise, except... "Why would they agree to be involved in murder, though? What connection could they have to the dead actress?"

"Would they need one? They're in the business; perhaps they'd feel aggrieved on behalf of a colleague." Toby shrugged. "Perhaps they just wanted to rid womankind of a potential nuisance. Some men can show streaks of violence at their most intimate moments, you know. Not the sort of thing they're likely to discuss with us, but Edith might have proved a sympathetic ear."

"This is all possible, if highly speculative, but let's run with the idea and see if we can get it to fly."

"How picturesque. We need to go kite flying—I haven't been in ages."

"Keep to the point. And talking of points," that was a link to be proud of, "why use a knife like Geraldine's if she was one of those involved? Why not use a kitchen knife, wash it and replace it in the draw?"

"It's simply a clever piece of legerdemain. She knew she'd have an alibi, and could produce her own knife, covered with nothing worse than orange flesh. As you said from the start, it looked like someone was trying to implicate an innocent person. Bluff and double bluff."

Alasdair poured them both another drink. This was getting far too much like one of Mrs. Christie's novels. "How were Phyllis and O'Connor involved? Did they do the deed?"

"I don't know who struck the blow, apart from thinking it can't be Geraldine, who seems to have an unbreakable alibi. Phyllis might have. Even if she didn't, I'm highly suspicious of her apparently having left so early. I'm so pleased we sat through the torture and at least assured ourselves of an alibi in the process. Virtue rewarded."

"Less of the virtue and more of the theory, please. What about the other note? The one Howell had on him. Who sent that?"

"Geraldine. To entice him to a tryst and thereby have him in the right place at the right time to be dispatched."

"I didn't mean that one. I was referring to the other threatening one. About not running around after anything in skirts."

"Another bit of distraction, like the replica of Geraldine's knife. Makes the real motive look like a different one." Toby rubbed his hands together. "This is meaty stuff. Back to O'Connor. He tells us that Phyllis left at the first interval—lucky for him that we asked about it but he'd have told the tale anyway, once questioned—then he finds her somewhere to hide, in a place he'd know like the back of his hand."

"I presume you're thinking that he also has something to do with the disappearance of the cat?"

"That cat's turned up again."

Alasdair took a deep breath and a large swig of wine. The smug expression disfiguring Toby's handsome face was becoming more than a man could stand. "I suppose your pal Firestone told you this?"

"He did, actually. I hate to say it, but you'd have known first if you'd not been out gallivanting with newspaper men over lunch. Our pal the policeman said he was passing here and called in to inform you, but when he rapped at the door, answer there came none." As Alasdair was temporarily speechless, Toby continued. "Apparently O'Connor found the thing this morning, lying dead as a doornail on an old bomb site that's awaiting redevelopment. About a quarter of a mile from the Imperial. He sometimes passes the place, depending on which route he takes to work, and mightn't have noticed it at all but it had started to make its presence known. Swarms of flies."

"Spare me the gruesome details." Just as well Alasdair hadn't heard about that on his way to lunch. "How had it died?"

"No idea. I suspect nobody is going to perform a post-mortem on it and hold an inquest. Firestone said he'd sent an officer to look at the thing, but it was a bit mangled. Might have been hit by a car and crawled away." Toby shuddered. "I can't see a killer carrying its carcase even a hundred yards let alone a quarter of a mile. They must have had good reason. Unless it was simply that the thing took fright because of the dead body, ran into the road and was hit, then somebody slung it onto the derelict site."

"It could be as simple as that, but I don't like coincidences, including that of the cat's corpse just turning up. What if O'Connor himself disposed of the cat and then equally conveniently 'found' it again just where he'd got rid of it of it?" Alasdair waited for Toby to make a response, but he offered nothing more than a shrug. "Although why kill the moggy in the first place? Was it carrying some clue?"

"I highly doubt it. What could it carry that couldn't be washed off or which would incriminate a particular person?" Toby's brows crinkled rather attractively as he thought this through. Alasdair resolved they must make the most of this last burst of freedom before they set off on location for the initial filming. Very little chance of effective hotel bedroom hopping when so many people would be about. But that could wait until they'd fully aired this new theory.

"Although," Toby ploughed on, "you know what cats are like. Cussed. They always make a bee line for the one person in the room who hates them. I can see a moggy finding the killer and making a nuisance, hissing at them and whatnot."

"Would that imply the killer was somebody who was habitually at the Imperial? Or else the cat threat wouldn't apply because they'd never have to see it again."

"Not necessarily. Perhaps the cat simply followed the scent of blood, then found the murderer still hiding in the building. It wouldn't leave her—or him—alone, just to be vexatious."

Alasdair wasn't convinced. "So they pick up this annoying moggy and dispatch it as they make their escape. Risking tooth and claw being applied in the process. Then carry the ghastly thing to where they can sling it away, in full view of those people milling around the London streets."

"Let's park the cat for the moment." Toby drummed the arm of his chair. "Actually, let's not. Geraldine said she knew Phyllis from when they'd appeared in the chorus together at the Imperial. So Phyllis would be well acquainted with both the cat, as per your observation, and the building."

Alasdair nodded, but he'd already discarded that trail of thought, having remembered something from his interview with Edith.

"Remember talking about how Fiona wouldn't be scared of a tiger because she'd nursed soldiers?"

Toby frowned at the sudden change of topic. "That's a big jump, from cats to tigers. I vaguely recall the conversation."

"And do you recall, vaguely or otherwise, that I mentioned Edith had done some nursing as well? She'd know where to stick a blade, and she'd probably not blink an eye at blood and gore." Alasdair sat back, triumphant, at his leap of deduction.

"An excellent point, Admiral. "

Alasdair doffed an imaginary hat. "Here's a better one. A middle-aged lady could come and go in most situations without raising any suspicions. Particularly on an opening night, with all the glamorous young things about, when she'd be beneath notice. Especially if she wore an overall and carried a bucket or broom and looked like she was on her official cleaning business. You'd remember seeing a young hoodlum with bloody hands, acting suspiciously, but would you remember the charlady?"

"Probably not. I bow once more to your deductive powers."

"That's enough bowing and scraping. I'll get dizzy." Alasdair grinned, then became serious again. "Although there is one fly in the ointment. Why did Edith volunteer all that information about the notes? And say she was afraid of being wrongly arrested. Wouldn't that rather point the finger at herself?"

"It could be a third double bluff. If Edith suspected the story about the threatening notes would come out, better that she was seen not to be hiding their existence." There was every chance that Toby was making up his answers on the spot, but he was doing it with élan. "The business about fear of arrest is possibly a stroke of genius. Oh, look what a silly woman I am, being afraid of such a thing. Did she strike you as silly, by the way?"

"Not at all. I definitely got the impression she was hiding something, though. Along with a slight sense of relief that the personal question I posed wasn't the one she was expecting."

"Maybe she thought you were going to ask about Miss Keyworth. Maybe she also thought you were no real threat. Dilettante actor with a brain like a sieve." Toby, sniggering, left his seat then draped himself elegantly on the arm of Alasdair's. "Enough for the moment. I for one am looking forward to filming getting started. It'll be good to have something to get the old teeth into apart from the Howell business."

Alasdair agreed. He, too, felt the need of turning his conscious mind off the subject and onto Sir Edward Pellew, so that the rest of his brain could mull over George Howell's death in its own good time. Tomorrow evening they'd be off on their travels, shooting due to begin imminently and probably with a reworked schedule that avoided Howell's scenes. "Is there any news on recasting Howell's role? No news of a replacement for him, last time I asked."

"Did you ask the right person?"

What bit of one-upmanship was Toby going to spring now? "And who would be the right person?"

"Alexander Rattigan. I had to ring him this morning because there was a page missing from my script and he said they were considering Nigel for the role. He'd apparently offered to do it, if that would help the studio out, even though it wasn't his usual cup of tea. They're going to give it a try." Toby twiddled with Alasdair's hair, distracting him from thinking logically. "They can promote one of the other, four-lines-in-the-whole-film midshipmen, and then get an extra upgraded to say those four lines. Simple solution and everyone happy all round."

“Apart from Howell’s devoted fans, but they’re hardly likely to want to see anyone else taking his role.”

“Landseer is supposedly adapting the script, so that the character’s truly evil nature doesn’t become apparent straight away, and thereby creating an element of surprise. That would never have worked with Howell.” Toby fiddled some more.

Alasdair shook off his lover’s hand. “Sorry to be a spoilsport, although I promise it’s only on a temporary basis. Assuming you want to take advantage of the offer of a night in bed with a matinee idol and the use of his spare toothbrush?”

“Of course. Assuming you have my cover story worked out?”

“I’m reusing the one you made up for me. That can bat back and forward between us like a ping-pong ball until actually employed.” Alasdair tipped his lover off the chair arm. “Now, behave for ten minutes. We should jot down these ideas, so we can get them sent to Firestone first thing in the morning. I’m not for a moment going to suggest that we’ve solved his case for him, just that we’ve had a few ideas that he can consider or dismiss as he feels appropriate.”

“Very well put. I believe he’s the sort of officer who doesn’t mind his subordinates sharing their thoughts.” Toby grinned. “Talking of which, you make a lovely subordinate.”

“Why can’t you behave?” Alasdair couldn’t resist a grin, though.

They went back through the theory, noting all the points in as logical an order as possible, sprinkling as much supportive fact and as little speculation as they could salt the narrative with. When it was done, checked, well blotted and sealed in an envelope, Alasdair sat back, satisfied. It may not have been his theory originally, but it was better than anything he could come up with at present.

"Will you get Morgan to drop this off at the station?" Toby asked, while resuming playing with Alasdair's hair.

"I'm in two minds. It seems cowardly to firstly send it via someone else and secondly leave it then skedaddle."

"We have every excuse. Trains to catch, films to make." Toby's fingers moved onto Alasdair's neck. "Although we could tell Landseer we'll be taking a later train than intended and will make our own way to the hotel. Mention that it's about the Howell business and Sir Ian's bound to approve. That would give us time to see the police in person."

Alasdair, more than slightly distracted by the caresses, tried to focus his wits. "There's something I'd like to do, beforehand, though. It's occurred to me that I've never seen any of Howell's films. Is there any chance that, somewhere in between me rogering you, your returning home—sated and happy, I hope—to collect your bags, telling your mate Firestone about our genius idea and setting off to the wilds, we could find a couple of hours to see *A Strangler's Hands*?"

"I'd have said time was less of an issue than getting tickets for it. They're queuing up in droves to watch the thing." Toby slid his hand inside Alasdair's collar. "You'll have to use your famous charm. Of which you have plenty."

"Smooth tongued as ever." Alasdair leaned back into the caress. "Right. As you allege Fiona said in her first speaking role, *take me to your bed and do as you wish, sultan*."

Toby hooted with laughter. "That's my joke. And, as you always remind me, she actually said *would you care to partake of a sherbet*. It's not my bed here, either, it's yours. Nor am I a sultan."

“Pedant.” Alasdair pulled his lover’s face towards his, for a proper kiss. “Will you agree to the *doing as you wish* bit, though?”

“Need you ask?”

Reel Ten

The next morning, Toby was indeed both sated and happy. Ready and able, if not willing, to face the desert of romantic opportunities in the days ahead, he launched himself at breakfast with vigour. The meal was a more hurried affair than it usually was, with so much to do in the hours ahead. He'd been tasked with scouring the paper to find an early showing of the film at a cinema where he was confident he'd be able to sweet talk the management into letting them have a seat somewhere. Alasdair, meanwhile, had telephoned to secure an appointment with Firestone that afternoon, straight after the matinee.

They shared a final kiss in the hallway—possibly the last they'd be having in a while—then headed about their individual business, only meeting again at the Regal cinema, where Toby had been promised one of the seats they kept aside for just such an emergency occasion. If they weren't royalty than at least they counted among the motion picture industry's crowned heads.

The cinema foyer was bustling with both people and excitement, most of it concerning the leading actor, rather than the film itself. If Toby heard words along the lines of, "And then he went and got himself murdered!" once, he heard them half a dozen times.

Mercifully, the house manager had promised them seats in a private viewing area, out of sight and away from the masses. Not because the actors looked down on the public—these people kept them in employment and handsomely paid employment at that—but they didn't want any fuss. They'd had the foresight to disguise their appearance, as an adjunct.

Alasdair wore large, plain glass horn rimmed spectacles that effectively hid his famous eyebrows, and a cloth cap that none of his characters would ever have sported on the screen. He resembled a slightly seedy bookmaker, while Toby had opted for a hideous coat and a homburg that Alasdair vowed made him look like a meat-flasher. He'd be not to find himself being arrested.

"I hope our Pellew effort gets as good a turn-out," Toby whispered. "Callous to say it, but it's a shame that we hadn't got some of Howell's scenes in the can before he was killed. Box office gold."

Alasdair nodded, sending the awful cap bouncing. "I wonder if his previous films were quite as mobbed."

A fortifying half pint in the bar was more conducive to both entertainment and frank discussion, rather than watching the supporting feature, which seemed cheaply made if the slight publicity was any indication. Alasdair confessed to having second thoughts about the all-in-it-together scenario, although not to the extent of cancelling their appointment with Firestone. He said he'd know by the end of the film, and refused to elaborate on that enigmatic statement. Something was going on in his brain, below the hideous hat, and Toby wasn't going to be privy to it for the time being.

When they took their seats. Toby cast a glance around before the lights went down for the main feature. Most people were still settling having—like them—slipped in during the interval. It was possible that as the film progressed Alasdair might reveal the workings of his mind and their privileged seating position would prove invaluable. Their ability to chat in the stalls would have been limited by the cacophony of "Shhh!" they'd inevitably be faced with.

"Looks rather well shot, doesn't it?" Toby hissed, five minutes into the movie.

"Temple has always had a reputation for excellent productions values on shoestring budgets," Alasdair agreed. "The key is that he keeps it simple. No trying for showy special effects."

That stratagem of the basic things done well paid dividends as the film moved through its scenes. Lots of use of clever cutting to create tension, and the hints at ghastly happenings rather than anything overt onscreen. It played cunningly on the fact that whatever the viewer imagined was going on slightly offscreen was probably worse than the reality. It was a useful way of getting things past the censor, too.

"Howell's good," Toby observed, ten minutes later. "Very good. He may have been a ratbag but he'd have made a great contribution to our film."

"He's got—had—the talent, unquestionably. And he clearly gives his fans a lot of pleasure—if you can call it pleasure when they're scared out of their seats."

That was an understatement. *A Strangler's Hands* was one of the scariest films Toby had seen in a long time; he'd only just avoided joining in the gasps and squeals from the audience.

As the film reached its shocking—and unexpected—climax, squeals had turned into full-blown screams and even Alasdair jumped in his seat. The appearance of the words *The End* on screen was greeted by a spontaneous burst of applause, one which the two actors could join in with quite sincerely. A horror film this might have been but it was miles better than the opera they'd endured.

If the applause wasn't enough, the remarks overheard on the way out confirmed the ecstatic reception the work had produced. Although it wasn't the countless compliments that attracted Toby's notice. There appeared to be a real sense of connection between the typecast actor and his fans.

"Such a shame George Howell's gone," said one young lady, hovering on the pavement with her friend. Toby grabbed Alasdair's arm, to keep him within earshot, while they ostensibly studied a notice concerning upcoming productions.

"I'd have watched every film he ever made," replied the friend. "I mean, he could have carried on until he was in his seventies, at least. These leading men are all very well with their pretty faces and insured cheekbones, but I want to see somebody really acting."

Toby, who'd suppressed a snigger at the "insured" bit, took fleeting umbrage at the implication that performers like himself were less than talented in the acting department. His annoyance was swiftly suppressed by his interest in not just what the girls were saying but by the look on Alasdair's face. Not even St. Paul on the road to Damascus could have looked so surprised and delighted.

The girls having moved off, Toby felt it was time for them to make a move, too.

"Did you hear what they said?" he hissed at Alasdair. "How insulting."

"Was it? I for one have long since given up worrying about what people think of my acting abilities."

"Liar." Toby chuckled. "Anyway, you did a great job of acting a light-on-the-road-to-Damascus moment just now."

"No acting involved. I've had an idea." Alasdair pulled off the cap and glasses, stuffing them in his coat pocket. "That's a relief. Now, let's find somewhere we can sit and chat before we see Firestone. I think we may need to change tack."

Intrigued, Toby led the way to a little square with a garden—and a convenient bench—in it. Once seated, he waited: Alasdair could never resist finding exactly the right moment to deliver a line.

"When I had lunch with Nigel Weatherly," he said eventually, "he got a bit shirty with his pal Cuffy."

"The one with the ridiculous nickname, who seems to keep popping up." Toby looked at him askance. "You're never telling me you suspect Cuffy of doing it? Harboured a secret passion for Miss Keyworth and so took revenge upon Howell for injuring her?"

"Don't be daft. That's the sort of solution you only get in poorly written mystery books. The killer's the least likely person and all that." Alasdair tipped his head back to enjoy the sunshine. How ridiculously English to be sitting in a haven of peace in a busy city, basking in the sun and discussing murder most foul.

"Enlighten me. Who do you think did it?"

Infuriatingly, Alasdair grinned and said, "I'll give you a chance to work it out first. Suffice to say I think we've been distracted by the feminine angle. By lust and jealousy and the need for revenge."

"You sound like Howell, in that film we've just seen. I think that was almost word for word what he spoke in front of the mirror. Between victims twenty-five and twenty-six."

Alasdair shuffled a few inches along the bench. "I'm just distancing myself from you in case a thunderbolt comes down. You tell such awful lies."

"Well, it was almost what he said. And I'm only twenty odd victims out." Toby inched closer again. "The bolt can get us both. Go on. We've been distracted by the feminine. Does that include the notes?"

"To an extent. I think the ones in the dressing room will turn out to have come from Edith, but those on the body were probably an attempt at diversion."

"What should we have been looking at, then?"

"Plain old-fashioned envy and the need to maintain one's livelihood."

"Not Robert Temple, surely?"

"No." Alasdair's nose wrinkled attractively. If only he were a faux girlfriend, rather than a fellow actor, then Toby could have planted a kiss on that conk. "Back to the lunch with Nigel. He got cross with Cuffy and I assumed it was for having said Geraldine was his ex-girlfriend, but in reality that was no great secret. It's exactly the sort of thing the police could easily have run to ground."

"Especially if the accessed the valets' network."

"Exactly. So it must have been about something easier to hide. Like the fact he'd appeared at the Imperial when he was just a youngster."

"Oh yes." Toby whistled, suitably impressed. "He wouldn't have been the first boy to go exploring all the ins and outs when he shouldn't have. He'd surely know his way round."

"Which would make it feasible for Nigel to sneak into the place unobtrusively and get out again. He would be familiar with Geraldine's handwriting—maybe in possession of letters he could copy the style of—so he'd be able to produce a convincing note to arrange for Howell to meet him in the theatre. It would also be feasible for Nigel to be in possession of an identical fruit knife to Geraldine's, if he was the one who gave it to her in the first place."

"And using it would get his own back on her, as well. The pointing the finger at Geraldine being a genuine thing, rather than an elaborate bluff." The notion had merit. "Although you said this was nothing to do with lust and jealousy."

"It isn't. Implicating her would have been just a nice little adjunct."

"Then for heaven's sake why did he kill—oh." Toby drummed merrily on the bench. "Oh, yes. Now I see. Shall we go and tell Firestone?"

"Of course." Alasdair jumped to his feet. "Only don't chuck away just yet that theory we wrote down yesterday. We may need a back-up to offer him should he laugh this one out of court."

Toby sighed. "True. And both theories might be a load of old codswallop. Still, we'll be away filming and by the time we're back Firestone will have got his man—or woman—and he'll either thank us profusely or we'll all pretend we never offered him any theorems in the first place."

But would Sir Ian thank them for having possibly named one of his actors as a murderer or alternatively his girlfriend as an accessory before and after the fact?

***

Matthew Firestone listened patiently to Alasdair's theory, not once giving away any hint as to whether he thought it a stroke of genius or the ravings of a madman.

The actors had, in Alasdair's opinion, been pretty clever, weaving in strands from the all-in-it-together theory into the new, Nigel-based one. If it turned out they were barking up the wrong tree, surely in that mass of information there'd be one genuine leaf Firestone could light a fire with?

"I'd like to thank you, gentlemen," the officer said as they concluded, "for not going and performing a citizen's arrest on your suspect, or by quizzing him again so he got the wind up."

"Our pleasure," Alasdair replied, unsure whether they'd just been complimented but acting as if they had.

"I suppose you'll be in at the denouement, or at least to see part of it."

Alasdair cast Toby a quick glance, puzzled at what Firestone meant.

Toby, surely with the benefit of that inside knowledge of things constabulary, seemed to have twigged. "Ah. You'll be coming down to arrest him on location?"

"Perhaps. To interview him, certainly. In the meantime, I'd like Mr. Weatherley to remain unaware he's under increased suspicion. If you can travel to filming as normal and act as though nothing has happened, I'd be most grateful."

"Of course," Toby said, with a rueful smile. "Although would it be as well to issue a general reminder to the cast about their safety? I for one will be locking my bedroom door and making sure I stick to the crowds."

Firestone grinned. "Did you really think I'd be letting you all travel off without an eye kept on you? I've already sent one of my men down there. You're all still some of my main suspects."

And, Alasdair realised with a shudder, still all potential victims. Especially those who'd stuck their noses in.

Epilogue

They were two days into filming and nobody had shown signs of homicidal tendencies, apart from the extra who'd replaced the lad who'd been promoted: he'd murdered his lines from the start. Surprisingly, Nigel had taken the boy under his wing to give him some coaching, as a result of which the lad's performance had improved. The new villain of the piece had also earned himself a debt of gratitude from the director. Could Alasdair have been wrong in his assumption that Nigel was the murderer, the man having simply and innocently made the most of the opportunity which had presented itself? Or was he guilty as hell, and revelling in his goal being achieved?

The constabulary presence—a hefty, deferential young man who wasn't just keeping an eye on proceedings but mucking in with moving scenery and the like when needed—didn't need to keep issuing reminders in terms of keeping safe. His being there was a constant, if subtle, reminder of what had happened.

Three days into filming proper, and half way through a crucial scene on board in which Nigel's character was giving the first hint of his true tendencies, Alasdair—who was making the most of a sit down and a cup of tea—noticed Firestone slip into the back of the group watching from the quay, alongside the constable. If they exchanged any words they were too softly spoken for him to overhear. Matters were clearly about to reaching a climax.

As Rattigan shouted "Cut!" reassuring his players with, "That was very good. We'll have one more take for luck," Firestone edged forward, slipping leisurely up the gangway to approach the director. For one mad moment, Alasdair thought Rattigan was about to be arrested, which would have been one in the eye for all of the theories he and Toby had come up with, but the true situation soon emerged. The policeman beckoned Nigel, who was at the wheel of the ship where he'd been being nasty to one of the snotties, and after a *who-me*? type pantomime, the actor came over. More words were exchanged, again none of them audible, even though both Alasdair and Toby—admittedly with just about everyone else on dry land—had tried subtly to inch within earshot.

It seemed to be supremely unfair that they'd miss out on the details of the denouement, which even if Firestone related them later would be cold, tasted second hand. He'd reckoned without Nigel's cunning. In an act of bravado worthy of Erroll Flynn himself, he leaped back, grabbed one of the cutlasses—genuine, not prop—that were being used to add an authentic touch to the *Indefatigable*'s deck, then swung into the rigging, brandishing the blade to keep everyone at bay.

"Don't be a fool." Firestone said calmly, while motioning for everyone bar himself and the constable to stand back. "Put down the sword and we can talk."

"I can talk very well from here. Not often I get to be centre stage." Nigel, swaying slightly on the rigging, surveyed his audience.

"He's enjoying this."

Alasdair, unaware that Toby was sidling closer, glanced round at the murmur in his ear. "I told you he wanted to be a star, not the eighth name on the credits."

"Such awful steps to take to fulfil the dream, though."

Alasdair nodded, and then jerked his head up at the mention of his name.

"Alasdair, are you deaf?" Nigel waved the weapon in his direction. "Will you listen to me for heaven's sake?"

"Of course. I've always got time for you, Nigel."

The young actor snorted. "That doesn't apply to everyone. They soon lose interest as they climb the ladder." Was that a dig at Geraldine? "It's fine for you three. The old love triangle will go on, even if you're grey at the temples. They'll say it adds poignancy to the role. Hah!" Nigel gave a dismissive gesture. "Think what it'll be like for Fiona, though. They'll replace her when she gets too long in the tooth."

Just as well Fiona was still in her dressing room, or she'd have been leaping up the sides of the ship to bash him on the conk. He'd made a good point, though.

The rant went on. "It's the same for me. At the first sign of a wrinkle that's visible onscreen I'll be chucked, unless I can carve out a different niche for myself. But nobody thinks of me as anything but the silly ass son."

"He wants his meal ticket for life," Toby breathed in Alasdair's ear, before saying loudly, "You don't know that."

Nigel snorted again, flashing the blade recklessly. "Don't you think I've tried? My agent couldn't even get me auditions for anything but the usual parts, once they heard my name. The one time he managed to sneak me in by using an assumed name, they wouldn't even listen to me."

"They refused to let you audition?"

"No. They let me read for the part, of course, but I could tell they were just being polite. Laughing inside, then they'll have ripped me to shreds afterwards."

Perhaps those in charge of casting had missed a trick. Nigel not only was showing an unheralded degree of menace, he evidently had the paranoia that seemed characteristic of many screen villains. If only he'd employed that in the right channels, he could already have been the big-name star he wanted so desperately to be.

"I asked Howell to help me. To give me some tips on playing the villain. He thought I was joking. Nobody takes me seriously."

"We're taking you seriously now, Mr. Weatherly," Firestone said. "Put down the sword and we'll be able to listen properly."

"Hah. You'll arrest me, more like. I've seen plenty of crime films and read plenty of mystery books. I bet I could give myself the caution, rather than you bothering."

"He's gone mad," Toby whispered. "I can't see how this ends without someone getting hurt."

As a synopsis of the situation that couldn't be bettered. Where Nigel had positioned himself meant he could keep everyone at arm's length, and if he was stormed he'd be able to take several body parts with him.

Firestone raised his hands. "As you wish. You're master of this ship, now, so we'll leave you to it. Ladies, gentlemen," he glanced at the film crew on board, "please will you abandon ship in a calm manner. Nobody will be hurt if we act sensibly."

Toby, as excitable as a child, was bouncing at Alasdair's side. "What's he up to?"

"Am impressive bit of seamanship, I suspect. Pellew himself couldn't have done better. The equivalent of hand to hand combat on deck."

Once the film crew were ashore, Firestone motioned for the constable to leave and then—to Alasdair's surprise—himself slipped nimbly down the plank.

"Go on, hop it, you load of cowards!" Nigel sneered, still safe in the rigging.

"Not cowards. Pragamatists. You can't sail that ship alone, and you can't live without food and drink. We won't be supplying any."

"A siege." Toby's eyes sparkled with delight. "Might be quicker if Firestone just cast him adrift. That would fettle him."

Alasdair groaned. "It would fettle the ship's owner, with it. He's having kittens already about his vessel."

The man in question was now at the superintendant's side, tugging his arm and being roundly ignored.

"I'd swim for it before I starved," Nigel said, with a sneer.

Firestone remained cool as Nelson on the *Victory*'s deck. "You're welcome to try it. See that little fishing smack just off the port bow? She saw good service at Dunkirk. The owner's always prepared to do his duty, and in this case that involves carrying several of the best local officers. Best in terms of their swimming ability, I mean. And a frogman in case you fall out of the rigging and get yourself drowned," he added, which sobered anyone present who wasn't taking this deadly seriously.

"What do you think he'll do?" Toby asked.

Alasdair couldn't get out a reply—just as well, because he didn't know what to say—as Rattigan suggested that everyone repair to the catering facility then await developments. Toby gave Alasdair a shake of the head, gestured towards Firestone, asked, "Shall we offer our help?" then sidled over to the policeman without waiting for the reply.

"What do you two want?" Nigel shouted from the rigging.

"Just a chat with an old family friend," Toby replied, pleasantly, as though addressing an old pal carrying a cricket bat rather than a man brandishing a sword. He lowered his voice, just enough that the man on the ship might catch the odd word. "What made you conclude it was him?"

"In part, concluding it wasn't Edith. You were right about her being behind the threatening notes, but she's got an alibi for when Howell was killed—she was playing rummy at her daughter's with the vicar and his sister."

Alasdair nodded. That was the sort of thing the police could ask and check up on, but he and Toby wouldn't have dared. How did these amateur sleuths not end up being thumped for their nosiness?

"Next we had a barman account for the missing time. He told us that Howell was having a stiffener or two when you were having to endure the opera. Then we tracked down the little fruit knife. Turns out it was yon Weatherly that had it made. Two of them. The assistant at the shop said he wanted one for his sweetheart as a good luck token, and one for himself."

"What are you saying about me?" Nigel yelled.

Firestone carried on, blithely. "Then his pal Cuffy, who I daresay couldn't keep a secret unless it were glued to him, says Nigel was very cut up about the gal going off with Howell. He wouldn't have been surprised at his trying to implicate her."

"To shift attention from his own motive," Alasdair agreed, then partly covered his mouth. "Let me try this. Cat. Cat. Cat." His voice rose until Nigel, straining to hear, caught something.

"What's that about that blasted cat?"

"You mean the one that came along when you stabbed Howell?" Firestone responded.

"Yes. No! Don't try to trick me, damn you!" Nigel swung the sword a bit too fiercely, lost his grip in the rigging and tumbled to the deck.

Firestone leaped up the gangway, both the constable and the actors hard on his heels. Nigel lay sprawled, left arm clutching his right, which has clearly been injured in the fall. Thank God that was his fighting hand, and the weapon had gone flying across the deck. Toby picked it up, replaced it in the rack with the other boarding arms and then quietly stood guard over them.

"Game's up, laddy," Firestone said, not unkindly. "We'll get that arm of yours seen to and then we've some questions to ask. Mr. Hamilton, is there a doctor or nurse on set?"

"I don't think so." Alasdair fought his disappointment. He was clearly going to be sent for help, and would miss out on any further developments.

"I've done some first aid," Toby chirped up, coming to the rescue. "If Alasdair can keep an eye on these weapons, I'll take a look."

Ignoring any protests from Nigel, he gave the man the once over. "Broken bone in the arm, which I can bind with my stock for the time being." He removed the item concerned and began the process of supporting the limb. "Other than that, he just seems to be winded. No evidence of a blow to the head."

Nigel sneered. "All right, Mr. Knows-everything. Just because you two play Holmes and Watson, doesn't make you as smart as they are."

"Actually, Watson always comes across as rather dim, don't you think?" Toby said, cheerfully, executing a tidy little knot in the improvised sling. "Rather like Alasdair and myself. Thick as two short gangplanks, really. But we keep our ears and eyes open."

"Yeah. Right pair of interfering busybodies." Nigel turned his attention to Alasdair. "Don't think I don't know what that cosy little lunch was about. You've been out to get me from the start."

"I'm afraid you credit us with too much intelligence," Alasdair said. "Why did you kill the cat, by the way?"

"That blasted moggy? It came strolling along, then rather than making itself scarce the bloodthirsty little beast went and got himself covered in blood. I gave it a boot up the backside, but the sodding thing followed me. I had to get out of the building before Howell was discovered." Nigel stopped, no doubt suddenly aware he'd likely just incriminated himself.

"Then it slipped out after you and kept being a nuisance? We did wonder how you'd managed to carry a dead cat through the streets of London." Alasdair put on his awed expression. "That would have been a feat requiring huge courage and guile."

"Are you saying that I'm not clever and courageous? I'd have carried three dead cats, if I'd had to, and nobody would have been the wiser."

"Mr. Weatherly I have—" whatever Firestone was about to say, most likely warning the suspect that he wasn't doing his cause any good, got cut off by Nigel himself.

"You all think I'm the soft, silly schoolboy that I've played for so long. But I'm not. I may have been too young to fight, like you lot, but where did Howell's army training get him against me? I tell you, once I'd finished him off, the cat was simple. I could have taken a brick to fifty cat's heads. Or fifty actors."

"And that really is enough!" Firestone commanded. "Mr. Hamilton, please go and arrange transport so we can take this chap to be checked over. I'll be going with him."

To that request Alasdair had no choice but to accede. Although he made a mental note that the policeman's tones had been so impressively forceful, he'd have to try and replicate them for Pellew.

"Hoi!" A shout from the quayside—in a powerful yet feminine voice—made them spin round. All except Toby, whose first aid was clearly being combined with acting as guard. Fiona, fully decked as Susan—Lady—Pellew, was making her way aboard, skirts hitched to manoeuvre the gangway. "I don't care what he's supposed to have done, he needs proper attention. Sorry, Toby, but this calls for a nurse."

"Be my guest. Air Force defers to Army." Toby rose, made a bow, and then addressed Nigel. "You'd better behave yourself. Miss Marsden nursed at Netley and she's had harder men than you to deal with."

As they waited for an ambulance to arrive, they retreated to the bottom of the gangway. All bar Fiona and the burly constable, although it would be anyone's guess who'd be more likely of that pair to prevent any attempted escape from Nigel.

"Given the circumstances," Firestone said, "I'm glad you asked about the cat and not about Howell. What made you choose that line?"

"Because he's not as daft as he makes out," Toby said, with pride. "Nigel hadn't been formally cautioned at that point, despite your efforts—let alone the fact that questioning him about the murder after his accident might have been construed by a defence counsel as being inadmissible evidence, as he wasn't in a fit state to know what he was saying. Undiagnosed concussion and all that."

Firestone nodded. "His asking it meant I didn't have to. You can all be my witnesses that I did try to stop Weatherly incriminating himself further."

"You did indeed." Alasdair glanced across to where some of the crew were still hovering, clearly uncertain about what was going on. He lowered his voice. "Will he hang?"

Firestone frowned, evidently weighing up the case. "A decent counsel would have him pleading that he's not responsible for his actions. He certainly doesn't seem to be entirely all there. Although, could he be putting it on? Would you say he's that good an actor?"

Alasdair glanced at Toby, who shrugged and replied, "Better than he's been given credit for, I'd say. But then, when was there ever a correlation between acting talent and success in the business?"

And wasn't that the crux of the whole matter?

***

Filming ended up cancelled for the day. Not only was everyone distressed by the unexpected drama, Rattigan had a role to recast yet again. Soon it was rumoured that Sir Ian was in discussion with a stage actor—a creditable Iago—who was trying to break into the cinema, but, as Toby said, that was nothing to do with them. They would film as many scenes as they could in the interim, including rescheduling some they'd planned to do indoors, although for the moment they could enjoy an afternoon off and a walk along the cliff path to a little village with a nice pub but—hopefully—neither murderers nor actors.

"Did you enjoy playing Sherlock again? In real life, I mean," Toby added.

Alasdair gave him a smile and walked a few more steps, to a stretch of path less treacherous, before replying. "Yes. Better to be in league with the police rather than always trying to get one up on them. Does your father hate the way his fictional counterparts are portrayed?"

"Yes and no. It frustrates him at times but there's an advantage to the public believing the authorities are quite so feckless. Makes the criminals reckless. That rhymes!"

Alasdair chuckled. "You're incredible. If eminently beddable. That rhymes too. Almost."

"You'll have to remember that rhyme for when we're home. No chance of anything happening here. These modern hotels. Paper thin walls." Toby paused, perching on a convenient rock to better admire the view. "This is lovely. Perhaps we should return, if we could find a place with better soundproofing."

"We could rent a cottage, with Ronnie and Jonny—they rhyme too, perhaps we should persuade them to get involved with each other–and pretend we're all down here for the fishing."

"And a break from women. The old codgers in the pub would appreciate that." Toby gave him a rueful smile. "Always acting, aren't we?"

Alasdair brushed his arm. "Except in bed. I hope you don't act there."

"I sometimes think it's the only place I don't put on a show." Toby pushed back his shoulders, stretched then began walking again, Alasdair in his wake.

If *his* bed was the only place Toby could be himself, then the world wasn't that bad.

Printed in Great Britain
by Amazon

55616196R00154